# ANGELICA

## PAINTRESS OF MINDS

# ANGELICA

## PAINTRESS OF MINDS

### A NOVEL

## MIRANDA MILLER

First published in Great Britain by Barbican Press in 2020

Registered office: 1 Ashenden Road, London E5 0DP

www.barbicanpress.com

@barbicanpress1

Cover by Rawshock Design
The Angelica Kauffman self-portrait detailed on the cover, circa 1770-75, is in the collection of the National Portrait Gallery, London

A CIP catalogue for this book is available from the British Library

ISBN: 978-1-909954-41-0

Typeset in Baskerville

Typeset by Imprint Digital Ltd

Printed and bound by CPI Group (UK) Ltd, Croydon, CR0 4YY

*For Gordon*

# PART ONE

# AUSTRIA AND ITALY

# 1

They used to say I had a talent for portraits. They. Papa, his unsuccessful painter friends and the old aristocrats, bishops and monsignori who petted me when I was a child. I look at my first self-portrait, at it and into it, until I fall backwards into Morbegno in the Valtellina, where I spent my childhood.

I stared into the only mirror in our tiny apartment, cracked and silvery. Papa and the horrid Josef shaved in it, staring at their reflected faces and chatting, while I sat quietly in a corner drawing or practising my music, hating the usurper. I was the *figlia unica* – the only and unique daughter. There was no need of any other children, and certainly not of this awkward boy who sometimes forgot he was a mere cousin and called my papa his.

When I was nine, Papa returned from Lake Constance with this sixteen-year-old lout. 'Cousin Josef will be my studio assistant now and you must stop playing with my things,' he said.

*His* things! Those paper canvas, easels, charcoal paints, crayons and brushes had been my first and only playmates. Many years later when he was dependent on me, I forced my father to admit that Josef really was his son by his first wife, whom he abandoned.

Mama made it worse. 'You have to learn to be a little lady now and stop running round in a dirty smock like a savage.

If you practise your music, we can sing together in the next concert at the conservatoire. It's time you learnt how to sew and bake. Your grandmother will help me to teach you.'

That year Oma descended from the mountains, bringing rules and dullness. From Chur in Switzerland, she carried her smelly cheeses and black clothes that stank of death. Her face was a map of poverty and suffering, places I was determined not to go to, and she and my mother conspired together to make my life as grim as theirs. There were five of us in two small rooms. My father and Josef robbed me of my studio paradise, and I was banished to light the stove, sweep the floor, darn stockings and do the work of the servant we could not afford. I felt like Cinderella with no fairy godmother to rescue me. I wept and stormed and made a great fuss, but they did not care.

'You're only a little girl,' said Papa.

'You'll never get a husband if you don't learn household duties,' said Mama.

I did have a godmother. I was named Anna Maria after her. She was no fairy, but a woman of substance who lived in Chur and sent us wine at Christmas. The Baroness de Rost. Titles make a special shape in the air when people speak them, high and arched. Such people lived in fine buildings like the Palazzo Malacrida at the end of our street, painted like a jewel box, full of people who shone and sparkled. Papa painted the ceiling in one of their salons. He told me they had roast meat for breakfast and a whole room full of musical instruments. Their six children had a vast room where they did nothing but play with toys: rocking horses, toy carriages, birds in cages, picture books, dolls who lived in their own little houses, boats, miniature castles full of lead soldiers. I hugged Lise, my only wooden doll, and thought about those children.

One wintry evening, Papa and Josef were away in Switzerland painting the walls of some rural church. After I washed the dishes I was allowed to draw as we three women sat by the stove. My mother was in a good mood; we sang together, and I forgot to sulk because music heals all wounds.

After I was sent to my bed in the corner of the room, I lay waiting for my mother and Oma to wheeze and grumble their way to sleep. When both were snoring, I put on my clothes, lit a candle in the dying embers of the stove and went into the studio. On the cold floor I sat cross legged until dawn, drawing all the animals in Noah's ark. Time melts when you give yourself entirely to paper or canvas.

I had never seen an elephant but dreamt one up as Durer invented his hippopotamus. Lovingly I drew Mr and Mrs Elephant, amiable monsters with trunks like table legs, marching into the ark. Human beings were easier to do. Mr Noah waved his arms around like the conductor of our local choir as he told the animals where to go. Mrs Noah had a shelflike bosom like my grandmother. When Mama got up to make breakfast, she found me still there and slapped me for wasting expensive paper. But when Papa saw my drawing, he said it was good.

Oma was a midwife who told disgusting stories about dead babies, screaming women and drunken nurses. 'Don't frighten the child,' said Mama.

'She will find out soon enough,' said Oma grimly in her coarse dialect.

There was often a knock at our door late at night. Oma dressed and went off into the blackness to do bloody things to women's bottoms. In church I looked around at other girls my age, feeling sure they were free to draw and play. They did not have to be household slaves. I never found out the truth, for I had no child friends. Oma told stories about her family, the de Canobias, who were once aristocrats and still had their "de" and a fancy bed carved with a coat of arms to show for it.

Mama and I were to sing together at a concert. All the best people in Morbegno would be there. It took us months to make my blue silk dress with pink bows. We borrowed the small powdered wig that covered my dark hair from the wine merchant's niece. I thought the black velvet ribbon with the gold cross my godmother sent me and my mother's borrowed earrings were the finest jewellery in the world. As always my father stood over me, telling me what would charm, impress, sell. When I painted that first self-portrait I included him, because I could not conceive of a self without him.

Mama plucked my thick eyebrows, put rouge on my cheeks and lips. 'Don't smile and show that gap in your teeth,' said she. 'Don't breathe too early in the second bar of the Buoncini aria, don't wobble on that top "c".' I clutched my music, sure that the whole town was going to laugh at me. I was close to tears when my father came in.

'Aha, a young lady,' said he with an air of relief, as if a little girl had been no use at all. He examined me, and they considered stuffing the front of my dress to make me more alluring. 'Let's show off your art as well as your music. Can you paint a portrait of yourself good enough to show them at the Bishop's palace in Como?'

So I was allowed back into his studio. The thirteen-year-old who painted that first self-portrait was already a little adult who knew that all faces must be flattered. What was I thinking as I worked? I am not pretty, but my paintbrush is a wand that can make my nose smaller, my eyes a deeper blue, my cheeks less plump. I was dressed up for that concert at the conservatory, in all my homemade and borrowed finery. Inside the rigid corset my mother said I must wear now, my body felt like a wooden oar – with which to row myself away from my provincial childhood. How difficult it was to paint that pink satin bow on the front of my dress and how terrified my eyes were whenever they stared back at me in the mirror. I held my sheets of music in front of me as if to declare, I am a young woman of many accomplishments. When Papa saw how I worked night and day to improve my painting, he said, 'Well, women can be artists.'

Mama never agreed. 'A hoyden with paint under her fingernails who stinks of turpentine. Without a dowry, who will want her?'

Then Papa began to defend me at last. 'She has talent and may yet make us proud of her.'

Mama dragged me off to help with the washing, muttering. 'Singing is respectable and may even catch a husband. But a woman who paints anything but flowers is a freak.'

'You did not always despise painters so much,' said Papa, with a smile that made Mama blush. 'Do you know, daughter, that when I was painting the ceiling of the chapel of the Prince-Bishop of Chur I heard your mother singing? Her sweet voice went straight to my heart and she climbed up my scaffolding to admire my clouds. She said they were more beautiful than real clouds.'

'Then you said you would be happy to live always in the clouds with me.' Mama sounded very silly as the two old people giggled together like halfwits. Better than the usual bitter silence between them.

Out of this first self-portrait came my first commissions, the beginning of my real life. I was baptised Anna Maria Angelica Catharina Kauffman, but Anna Maria and Marianne are dull hearthside names, so I became Angelica. My name has changed with me as I take on different identities in each language. With my father, cousins, Queen Charlotte and Goethe it had the hard "g" of "gelt guilt girl Gott"; in England my name was softened to "jelly jolly genial gee-gee". In French I sound more flirtatious – "jeune, jalousie" – avoiding the hard "g" of "guillotine". Angelique had that playful "ique" at the end, like one of the gay, menacing songs the French soldiers sang about *magnifique* and what they would like to do to girls. In Italian, my name sounds most natural to me. Angelica is the heroine of Ariosto's *Orlando Furioso*, who the English call Roland. As a girl I loved that story – the trip to the moon – I drew the hippogriff that is half eagle and half horse – wanted to be the pagan princess with my name who drives Orlando mad with passion.

With my new name I sprouted new wings of power. If I was not as good as a man, they would force me to be a woman, to make cakes and babies. Not just as good as a man but better – than Josef – better even than my father.

'Don't sign it,' Papa would say, passing off my copies of famous paintings as his own. It was not enough to paint well;

I also had to simper at the rich old men who wanted their portraits painted, allow them to pinch my cheeks – and other parts – smile smile smile which my father and Josef could not do with their long, wooden faces. When Goethe, who has very sharp eyes, saw this first self-portrait he said, 'There is a man standing behind that child with some sinister power over her.'

He was right. In the first version I painted my father looking over my shoulder as he always did. Later, as my confidence grew and his power waned, I blocked him out. There is no room for other people in a self-portrait. You might add a classical bust, as Sir Joshua often did, to remind the viewer of your greatness. But you are alone with your mirror and nobody can follow you into that painted world.

Mama was musical, but there was no music in her speaking voice, a nasal monotone full of reproach and disappointment. How she bored me and made me wish not to be like her. 'Put those dirty paints away now, Anna Maria. Come and help me with the cooking and the mending and the dusting... What do you need another book for when you have so many already?... Going out again tonight? Ah well, I have the cat for company. Those old men make too much fuss of you, child, and will scare away the young ones.'

After we moved to Como and Oma died, I did not feel like a child at all. I earned more money than Papa and Josef together; I was the one people wanted to meet. Como was the place where I tasted the keenest pleasures of my youth. I saw the rich palaces of the silk barons – rode in fine coaches – sailed in pretty boats on the dazzling lake. The old men my mother sneered at were powerful clerics who petted me and commissioned lucrative portraits. That modesty my mother preached was useless, for I saw how boldness succeeded. Monsignor Nevroni Cappuccino was delighted with the pastel portrait I did of him; he won me other commissions from rich families.

Then Papa decided we must live in Milan, so that I could see great paintings in galleries there. Women were not usually allowed to copy them, but the Bishop liked me, so he made sure I could work in all the private and public collections.

When I sat in the Pinacoteca Ambrosiana, gazing into Titian's *Adoration of the Magi*, I saw that all my attempts to paint were feeble. Here was a real scene, just as if I had wandered into the Bible and was able to spy on the miracle of His birth. I loved the little human details: the restless horse, the dog pissing against the beam. Titian's rich colours made my own look sickly. I trembled as I feared my so-called talent was all a delusion – yet Papa sold my copies for good money and Rinaldo d'Este, the Duke of Modena, commissioned a portrait of his Duchess.

Josef was sent off to mountain villages to restore obscure churches and I had Papa to myself. He became my agent and my chaperone, making sure my rich old admirers did not fondle me too much. He fixed my prices and sang my praises so that I could look demure. I painted a portrait of my parents together at that time but, in truth, they rarely were. I lost that painting years ago, but I remember how I painted them: my father stern and handsome, my mother flabby and anxious. I can hardly recall her features now, for I have no portrait of her.

Mama stayed at home while the prodigy and her proud father went to all the best houses. Coming home from some grand reception where I had said clever things, it was very provoking to be told by my mother to darn my stockings. Our lodgings in Milan were simple in comparison to the other houses I visited; my spirits plummeted as we entered the tiny hall that stank of tripe. Mama's querulous voice called out from the bedroom. 'Back at last? I suppose there were quails and rich cakes and fine wines. Don't blame me if you're up all night with indigestion, Johann. My head has been aching like the devil, but I don't matter of course. Don't bang that door! This leak is worse, Johann, you'll have to speak to the landlord in the morning.'

I had more of a head for figures than either of my parents, so I took charge of our finances. As they improved, my father took my work more seriously than his own and defended me against my mother's criticism.

'But what is to become of her?' said Mama. 'She is neither fish nor fowl, girl nor boy. Men don't like clever women. Her singing might get her a husband and we could make the best of her looks, but people will talk when they see her dressed like that.'

'She really does have talent, Cleofea,' said Papa. 'And if she is allowed to develop it freely, she may yet make our fortune. Then she will have no need of a husband.'

The first time my mother saw me dressed "like that" in Josef's clothes, she screamed. I thought it a great joke to wear his old shirt and breeches when he was away – also a convenience. I could cover them in paint or climb scaffolding to help my father without worrying about the tyranny of being ladylike. Perhaps something more? As I put on his clothes, I obliterated my half-brother Josef to become my father's *figlia(o) unica*, his unique daughter/son. I laughed and hugged my tiny mother.

'It doesn't matter. Milan is enormous. Nobody will recognise me.'

'You're not going out like that!'

'I just need to run out to buy more paper. I'll be back in a moment.'

'No!' She barred the door. 'It's monstrous – immoral – the priest will hear of it and excommunicate us. Then all your old bishops and rich merchants won't want anything to do with you, we won't be invited to any more concerts, they'll cancel all your singing engagements...' In tears, she bewailed our downfall.

I ought to have comforted her, but I was furious because I was supporting both of them by then and was used to doing as I liked. There was a scuffle at the door; I pushed past her and ran out. As I clumped down the street in Josef's boatlike shoes, I felt a surge of joy that I was out here in the world where I could do anything: paint or sing or flirt or work or talk about books.

But when I got home there was always my mother, trying to chain me to her. Like most women, she did nothing except keep house. We did share a love of music. She taught me to sing and play the harpsichord, but I had surpassed her years ago and resented her endlessly nagging me to practise. I had a good ear and could perform better than the other amateur musicians without much trouble.

When there was a concert, she became hysterical with nerves. 'Hurry up, Anna Maria, we will be late! That dress is an abomination. I can see your bosom; a young girl should not have bosoms.'

'I didn't grow them to spite you. I don't like them either.'

'That song. You must enter on the second bar. You are always late.'

'You play so slowly. I wish I had a handsome young man to accompany me.'

'Shame on you! And don't flirt or people will think you are a slut.'

'Stop squabbling.' My father, very tall in black evening clothes, looked proud to be walking to the palazzo between two elegant ladies. I noticed that most people came by carriage, that the other women wore far better clothes than us and had jewels that out-flashed the chandeliers.

When I was singing, I flew up to the painted ceiling and liquid gold poured out of my throat. To be admired and applauded was pure happiness – all my life – until just a few years ago when my voice became croaky. Even now I hum and warble in the privacy of my studio. But then, when I was young, I felt music pass through me like the wind through the trees. I thought there was nothing finer than to sing – until the next morning, when I picked up my brush to feel power quiver from my eye to my hand. It was a time of discovery and excitement – but Mama was always there, a pudding at the foot of my rainbow.

Poor Cleofea. Now, when she has been dead these fifty years, I understand her and feel guilty about my failure to love her. She loved me but wanted a proper daughter; she was terrified that what she called my "unfeminine ways" would bring disgrace on our family. Her headaches, dizziness and pains in the chest irritated me – until they suddenly became fatal. One afternoon, when she was pinning up the washing on our terrace, she collapsed. That evening she died.

# 2

My father had always seemed so proud and independent. He treated his wife as a servant. Yet without her, he could not find his gloves or prepare breakfast or remember his appointments. All those tedious household chores fell to me, leaving me no time to paint. Josef and my father demanded meals, shirts, obedience and money I could no longer earn. Three important commissions were late. My father sobbed for days and in the evening, he disappeared to the tavern. Alone with Josef, I ignored him.

'So, the little wunderkind has to darn my stockings now. I will tell our father you refuse to cook for me.'

I sat at my easel, hating him. My brush stabbed at the Bishop's nose.

'Soon we will marry you off to some nobody. You will have twelve children and forget your pretentious dreams, while I shall become a court painter somewhere in Italy or Germany. I might visit you occasionally. My poor relations.'

I bit my lip so hard I could taste blood. If I let myself shout at him I would cry, and Josef would squawk his aggressive laugh, like a crow swooping down. He threw his stockings at me and they landed in my lap, stinking of unwashed Josef. I walked over to the stove, opened the door and threw his stockings on top of the burning logs. When he advanced on me with violence in his eyes I dodged him, ran out of our apartment and went all the way to the tavern, where I pushed through the phalanx of whores and drunken sots to claim my father. He was so surprised that he came home meekly with me.

Papa finally took my side against Josef and packed him off to restore some church in the mountains. I took control of our meagre finances and would not give Papa enough to drink. I hired a woman to cook and clean and managed to finish my overdue commissions. Papa still grieved for his Cleofea. He was one of those seemingly unfeeling men whose heart held but two images: hers and mine.

After supper he sat with his head in his hands. 'Every inch of this apartment reminds me of her. A wonderful woman – a saint – Milan is a desert without her.'

I thought Milan a glorious city, but one you had to be rich to enjoy. Papa lost all his energy when he lost wife; his gloom was depleting our meagre income. I could not be my own mother father agent manager banker prodigy – so I was pleased when the letter came from Cousin Michael, commissioning us to redecorate their church in Schwarzenberg. I could remember nothing of my father's village; I had visited it only once, as a small child. In his loneliness, Papa described his Schwarzenberg as the Garden of Eden, filled with devout seraphic Kauffmans. I wondered whyever he had left this paradise.

I soon found out. The journey to Austria over the mountains was uncomfortable. There was no road to Schwarzenberg then, so we had to endure a long, bumpy cart ride in the snow. Arriving at night, I awoke from jolted sleep to see a dozen coarse faces peering at me, pointing smoky lanterns at me and commenting on my looks in their harsh dialect. So many Kauffmans. I like to tell sophisticated friends about my simple origins and often say I would like to retire to my innocent native village. Perhaps when I reach second or third childhood.

But at fifteen, scarcely out of my first, I felt like an exiled princess. We stayed with Cousin Michael in his house on a meadow, where we shared our meals with his smelly goatherds. If Kauffmans were not exactly angels, they were certainly very Catholic. Of a Sunday we had to walk for three hours through the Bregenz Woods to go to mass in the nearest church. On the other days we decorated the little wooden church where Papa had been baptised.

Up there on my wall is the portrait I painted of myself in traditional Bregenz Woods costume, the embroidered bodice and full white sleeves borrowed from a cousin. I had quite outgrown the few clothes I brought from Milan and had no money to buy new ones. I thought this costume picturesque, but the material felt rough and however many times I washed it I could not remove the stink of cheese and goats. In the portrait my face looks flat, plump, open. Was I more honest then, or only a worse painter? I sit beside my easel, clutching my maulstick like a crucifix. Indeed, it was only painting that made those months bearable.

My job was to decorate the walls of the little nave and chancel with heads of the Apostles. Having no models to sit for me, I used the heads of the villagers, all those cousins who knew my father better than I did. They stood around watching me work, making jokes about marrying me to some village oaf. I smiled, hoping they were only joking, all the while watching Papa's face in terror that he would decide to stay in this wilderness. Only in Schwarzenberg was he treated as a great painter. Every time a female beamed at him, I feared she would become my step-mother and I would be damned to a lifetime painting inn signs and portraits of goatherds. My father had no more ambition left, so I had to infect him with my own. At every opportunity I reminded him of the splendours of Como and Milan.

'But I'm getting old now. City life is so exhausting. I'm tired of flattering and boasting and calculating,' he said.

'I will work day and night to make a good life for us when we go back. They will all forget me in Milan if we stay here too long. Patrons are fickle and soon I will be too old to be a prodigy,' I said.

'People are so kind to us here.'

They were, and that is why I have remembered those Kauffmans in my will – all except my half-brother Josef, whose begging letters I ignore. I smiled back at my cousins while I schemed to return to Milan, or better still to Rome where the historical paintings I longed to do would be admired. Fortunately, Papa had a taste for good food and wine, elegant clothes and galleries.

'I need to see great paintings again, to meet people who can help me. You used to say I had talent,' I told him.

'You do. Why, when you were three years old, I taught you your letters and you turned them into exquisite illuminations.

By the time you were eight, your drawings of my plaster casts were good enough to sell.'

'Then you have a duty to promote my career as a painter. Please, Papa!' I begged. But I was very much afraid that his laziness would be stronger than his vanity and love of extravagance.

# 3

When I was young, a hundred men told me to go home to knit or sew or look after my babies – the babies I neither had nor wanted. The cleverer the man, the more subtle the artillery he employed. Fuseli used to say that women are too emotional to be great artists. When Mary Moser – who was hopelessly in love with him – abandoned flower painting to paint subjects from Ovid, Fuseli crushed her ambition. Said he: historical painting is only for men.

I was fortunate that my papa needed money and had no objection to my providing it for him, else he and my half-brother would have married me off to some lout who forbade me to do the thing I loved best. Later, I had the good sense to marry dear Zucchi, who respected my work and was content to allow me to shine – and earn. Such men are to be prized, though the world generally condemns them and calls them parasites. Two ambitions cannot flourish beneath one roof.

When I was a girl, I was torn between my love of painting and my delight in music. My father and I spent a few months at the house of the Count de Montfort, a romantic castle on a hill where I was to paint portraits of all his family. I had my own room overlooking gorges and mountain streams, delightful as the landscape in a Leonardo painting. Every night after supper I sang, accompanied by a young musician who taught music and dancing to the Count's children. Giovanni? Giuseppe? He was from Mantova – or was it Modena? He was a beautiful young man with transparent skin and spaniel eyes, who spoke excellent Italian and French. He wooed me with notes and secret meetings – then proposed to me.

'You are throwing your life away. You're a good painter but a great singer. Marry me and I will train your voice until it fills San Carlo and La Fenice. Instead of being an upper servant you will be a diva, adored in every capital in Europe.' As he spoke, another life opened out before me, like that wonderful landscape I could see from my window.

'I could not leave my father.'

'He could live with us, be your manager. We could all live in luxury. Do you know how much great singers earn?'

When I mentioned the sum to Papa later he looked impressed, though he was as unmusical as an old crow and could not tell Vivaldi from Handel.

'Have you fallen in love with this dancing master?'

I did not know if I loved him or not. As always, my ambition was more powerful than my sentimentality. I was in love with a dazzling version of Angelica who stood on an illuminated stage, applauded, bejewelled and worshipped. For a few weeks I was in turmoil. I lay awake all night trying to decide what to do – burst into tears at my easel – apologised to my sitters and pretended I was ill. I ran between my lover and the chapel, praying for strength.

The count's chaplain was a wise old priest who coaxed the story out of me. 'My child, you do indeed have a lovely voice, but have you ever been backstage at an opera house?'

'No.'

'I have, when I lived in Paris and later in Naples. I can assure you that great ugliness goes into making a beautiful opera: tears, hysteria, jealousy, cruelty, immorality. Fame attracts hatred and when those goddesses step down from the stage, they are as coarse and vicious as fishwives. You are too gentle and modest for that world.'

I took his advice. Yet whenever I am in a theatre or opera house, I feel a pull on my heartstrings as I glimpse an Angelica who might have been.

Benjamin West and I became friends in Florence where we both studied at the Accademia del Disegno. He was the first American I ever met, the only student to smile at me when I first entered the classroom, shaking with nerves. Benjamin spoke to me as one artist to another and I saw at once that he was prodigiously talented. Together we visited churches and galleries and shared our dreams of artistic success.

I was grateful because he defended me when the other students sneered at me as the only female student. I was not allowed to join men at life classes and they all scoffed at my work. I copied paintings in the Uffizi, working all day with scarcely a break, sitting beside the male students in the galleries. They all jeered at me, pinned spiteful caricatures to my easel and whispered insults. Hyena in petticoats! Blue stocking! Frumpy Austrian bitch! You're too ugly to get a man! Why don't you stick to embroidery? Don't you know there has never been a great woman artist?

When I came home in tears, my father complained to the head of the Accademia, who gave me a room in the Uffizi to myself where I could work in peace. Papa was selling my copies as originals to rich foreigners and naturally wanted me to produce as much as possible.

Only Ben was kind to me. 'In Swarthmore, where I grew up, women are respected and work as hard as any man.'

He told me he learnt to paint when the Indians taught him to prepare yellow and red pigments. Then his Quaker mother gave him a piece of indigo and made him a paintbrush out of cat hairs. Ben was my co-conspirator; I borrowed his clothes to dress as a boy – acting as his younger brother from America – in order to attend forbidden Anatomy classes. Like me, Ben had no money or education behind him, only his own ambition and determination. As we copied paintings by Titian and Correggio, we discussed ways of modernising them. We were both determined to be serious artists, to ignore capricious fashion, to paint idealistically and morally. We talked for hours as we drew each other – but there was no romance between us. He was already engaged to his Elizabeth back in Swarthmore and was too good a Quaker to betray her.

Ben and I met again in Rome, where Americans were a novelty. Ben caused a sensation when he arrived. Cardinal Albani and Winckelmann assumed he was a Red Indian – they expected him to be half naked and whooping with a tomahawk and a feathered headdress. The cognoscenti were fascinated by all his reactions and when Ben and Winckelmann went to the

Vatican to see the Apollo Belvedere, thirty carriages followed
them. When Ben exclaimed, 'My God, how like it is to a young
Mohawk warrior!' Winckelmann was delighted. He felt this
proved his own argument that the best Greek sculptures are
timeless archetypes of beauty.

All my roads then led, not to Rome, but straight to London.
The English in Rome adored art – mine in particular. They
were cultivated and the men were tall and handsome. I learnt
their language easily and found myself delightfully courted by a
circle of them. Nathaniel Dance followed me all over Italy. And
there were others...

'You are flirting shamelessly with all these young men,'
said my father. I could not believe it could be wrong to be so
happy. I took care never to be alone with any of my admirers
and did not let the concerts, dances and operas distract me
from my work.

London must be a paradise for artists, thought I, where I shall
quickly make my fortune. Ben was already there and wrote me
that he had found favour; all the beauties of Rome, Florence,
Naples, Bologna and Venice were dimmed by the allure of
London. Venice was a disappointment. Zucchi had not yet
appeared to explain it to me, and I thought it both wicked and
shabby. When we drank our hot chocolate at Florian's I pretended not to see the whores disappearing upstairs with their
customers. Canaletto's paintings flattered the city just as I was
learning to flatter my human subjects. I am staring at one of
my Canalettos now: a dream city where exquisite buildings float
in shining air.

The real Venice, in those last years of the Republic, was corrupt and heartless. Heavily mortgaged palaces rotted into stagnant canals. To use a Venetian expression, the soup had eaten up the china – the whole city was going to rack and ruin. Nobody seemed to have any money and the Venetians were idle and frivolous, their pockmarked faces concealed by white beaky masks like cruel birds. They gambled away their lives at a perpetual carnival, neglecting their wonderful art treasures. At the tables of the Ridotto, or a hundred other casinos, they lost or won fortunes in a single night playing faro, basset, piquet, biribi, primero or quinze.

Zucchi explained, 'For many Venetians, you know, gambling is a sacred ritual. They travel the world with missionary fervour. trying to set up new casinos and lotteries.'

When cheats were caught out or losers could not pay their debts, they found themselves in Piombi or "under the leads" – in prison at the Doges' Palace. As a woman who has worked hard for every penny, I despise gamblers, and so did Zucchi. There were moments when I glimpsed the Venice that I would learn to love years later when I returned with Zucchi. I adored the exotic architecture – the paintings of Veronese and Tintoretto – those moments when sunlight or sunset washed and gilded the exhausted city. But most of the time Venice wearied me. It was a *Commedia dell'Arte* play, badly acted by rakes in crooked wigs, shabby tattered brocade coats and patched shoes with holes in their silk stockings. They stayed up until dawn, flirting and gambling, and I resented the time I had to waste with them, away from my work.

Perhaps London would not have happened without Lady Wentworth. She was generous and elegant and seemed immensely rich. She knew everyone and everything – it is only now that I can see that I was her ticket out of an unhappy marriage, just as she was mine to London. Everybody called her Lady Wentworth, although she was married to John Murray, the British Resident in Venice. I think she acquired the title from her previous husband and refused to let it escape her. I was delighted when I received an invitation to her salon on the Grand Canal.

'We should not go. Murray is a scandalous fellow,' said my father.

I did not point out that the invitation was addressed to me and did not include my father, whose awkwardness was becoming a great burden to me. He refused to learn English, sulked constantly, disapproved of any activity that did not make money and interfered in my friendships.

'You cannot gallivant like this with men in public. You are twenty-four now, Anna Maria, no longer an infant prodigy. It is time you were married.'

'Why must we have this conversation every day? You know very well that marriage is slavery and would mean the end of my career as an artist.'

'If you catch a husband now, before your looks go off, you may not need to work.' I saw that he fancied himself as a pensioner in some grand mansion.

'How many times must I tell you? I don't want to be rich and do nothing. I love what I do.'

Lady Wentworth swooped as soon as we entered her brilliantly lit reception room. I had the curse, then, of seeing everything at first through my father's eyes: a vulgar woman with breasts exploding from her dress, her cheeks florid with wine and rouge. Only later was I able to see her for myself: a kind woman, no longer young, who admired my work.

'How I have longed to meet you! I adore your portraits; you paint like an angel!' she said. 'And who is this sinister *cavaliere* you have brought with you?' she added in a loud whisper that put my father in a huff for the rest of the evening.

I practised the English I had been studying. When she asked me how I liked Venice, I answered frankly, 'I feel stifled here. I can't sleep at night and during the day I can't stay awake.'

She stared at me in surprise. 'You're still very German, Miss Kauffman. One can imagine you striding through the pine forests. Most refreshing. Will you call on me tomorrow afternoon? Now come and meet my husband.'

Murray was an elephant of a man with a red sweaty greedy face. His sky-blue silk coat would have been elegant had it not been bursting at the seams. Beneath his chins his belly swelled as if he might at any moment give birth to a baby elephant. As we approached, he had an arm around two very young and pretty girls. He appeared to be bargaining with a shabby, ingratiating fellow I suspected was a *mangia marroni* – a chestnut eater or pimp. Naturally I pretended not to see this, for I was not supposed to know of such things, although I had observed many similar vignettes in Rome.

My father stood behind me, muttering his disapproval, always the skeleton at my feast. He was sixty by then, grim and inflexible. I understood that to get business from these people it was necessary to pretend to like them, but his gloomy presence inhibited my attempts to be charming.

Murray glared at his wife, removed his hand from the bosom of one of the young girls, bowed and slobbered over my hand. 'La Kauffman! Enchantée! I hope Venice pleases you?'

'It doesn't,' said Lady Wentworth. 'She is a most original and candid young lady.'

Her husband looked pained. 'You are not enjoying our city of pleasure? My dear, you must take her under your wing. I am soon to leave Venice. After twelve delightful years here I am being posted to Constantinople. We must introduce you to some amusing people.'

'I would dearly love to meet some other artists,' I replied. Murray yawned and I saw what he really felt about art.

His wife, however, had an eye. Over the next few days she took me to see the Bellini altarpieces in San Giobbe and San Zaccaria and the Tintorettos in the Scuola San Rocco. I saw that she was knowledgeable about painting.

Said I to my father, 'It will be too tiring for you to visit all these places. You had best stay here and rest.' Relieved of his disapproving presence, I felt like a child truanting from school.

I enjoyed Lady Wentworth's lively company. One rainy afternoon, we sat over a pot of tea in a coffee house near the Arsenale. 'Such a melancholy city,' said I as the rain wept into the stinking canal.

'I detest it!'

I looked at her in surprise. 'But you've lived here for years in a beautiful palace. You meet interesting people every night.'

'Bores, whoremongers and their strumpets, fops and boobies. I long to return to London.'

'O so do I! That is, I have never been there, but I like the English people I have met in Italy and believe I could be successful there.'

'You will be a sensation; I shall make sure of it.' She leaned across the table, taking my hand in her plump bejewelled one. 'You have no mother, Angelica?'

'She died when I was fifteen.'

'And too much father?'

'We've always been very close.'

'Touching in a child, but tedious in a grown woman. I have a daughter by my first marriage, but she disapproves of me.' She did not say why. 'Parents and children, husbands and wives. Murray and I have had quite enough of each other. I have no wish to go to Constantinople with him, so I've taken a house in London. Will you come with me? It will give me pleasure to introduce you to society.'

I beamed at her. 'You're like a good fairy in an old tale! You wave a wand to give me my dearest wish.'

'I've been called many things, but never a good fairy. Will you come with me?'

'My father...'

'My London house is small. There is no room for your father,' she said firmly.

When our plot was fully hatched, Lady Wentworth took me in her gondola to the modest hotel where my father and I had taken rooms. Now that I was about to leave Venice, the city's watery splendours leaked into my heart. Out came the sunshine, gilding and varnishing the rotting palaces, brightening the turds and dead cats floating in the canals. For a moment I glimpsed another Venice – the city that would enchant me years later when I saw it with my Zucchi.

In our salon I found my father. He was very grumpy and had a scarf wound around his face, his feet in a malodorous bowl of liquid. 'This city will kill me! I have my neuralgia again, my teeth ache'(he had only two remaining) 'and I'm plagued by blisters from getting lost in this vile labyrinth.'

'Poor Papa.'

'Easy to say that, but you do not care. You have new friends to gad about with.'

'To get commissions from. If I do not, who is to pay our bill here?'

For years now my father had been too frail to climb scaffolding. His eyes were too weak to do even copying and he depended entirely on me for money. Now I saw that gave me power over him.

'I hope you've earned enough to pay the quack who came just now and filled this bowl with frog spawn and mustard. Now I feel queasy on top of everything else.'

He held out his hand for money. Something about that gesture and his petulant voice decided me. 'You need our good, clean, Austrian air. Cities don't agree with you. I would love to join you in our Bregenz Woods, but Lady Wentworth has kindly offered to chaperone me to London where I hope to make my – our – fortune.'

'Chaperone you! A woman who has had heaven knows how many lovers and husbands and is now about to abscond from her latest?'

'She and Murray part amicably. Lady Wentworth will help to launch me in London society. Remember, I sent my portrait of David Garrick ahead. It has already caused a sensation. I have that letter of introduction Lord Exeter gave me to Joshua Reynolds and Nathaniel Dance has promised to help me, too.'

'What a dance you've led that poor young man. You have become quite calculating, Anna Maria.'

'My calculations will benefit us both. You need a holiday, dear Papa. I will give you money. You can stay with my aunt in Morbegno and then go to see our dear relations in the glorious Bregenz woods.' Wet, dull, a hundred miles from any significant art and too far away from me to interfere.

'I see how it is. I am to be put out to grass while you enjoy the fleshpots of London. A fine return for my years of devotion. I have been your maestro, your father, mother, agent, studio assistant. Perhaps I have given you too much freedom. But now you have no further use for me.'

As I protested, I knew it was true. My father's carping presence shackled me to his small-town mind, and I would not become truly myself until I was alone.

'When I have established myself in London, I will send for you.'

'Like a dog or a parcel. At my time of day, nobody wants me. Take care that men may want you for the wrong reasons when I am no longer here to protect you.'

'I'm quite capable of protecting myself.'

'As the glass said to the hammer. You're naïve. You trust every libertine who smiles at you. Without me to guard your reputation, you'll soon set the world a prating.'

There were many more quarrels before I set off for London in June.

# PART TWO

## LONDON

# 4

---

O
h, the joy of being untethered from my father's stiff protection! London was a *tabula rasa*. With Lady Wentworth and the people she introduced me to, I could be gay, natural, easy. I resented Nathaniel, who seemed to think he had rights over me – to think, indeed, that having escaped my father's tutelage I must be in want of another man to order me about! It was wonderful to be alone, an orphan.

Yet I can see now that in my friendships with Lady Wentworth and Joshua Reynolds, I did seek and find "parents" who could advise me. I have always chosen friends I can learn from. Who can I learn from now that I am old?

In London most artists were not kings as they were in Italy, or even gentlemen, but some kind of upper servant. As soon as I was settled in Lady Wentworth's house in Charles Street, I called on Mr Reynolds, as he then was, and admired the unique position he had carved out for himself. Despite the horrid rumours Nathaniel spread, I did not scheme to marry Reynolds, but only to study him in order to learn how to become a successful painter in London.

How I coveted his establishment in Leicester Fields. A footman in silver laced livery showed me into a grand showroom where skilled modern portraits hung alongside equally skilled forgeries of Titians, Michelangelos and Correggios. I thought I recognised the School of Thomas Jenkins, who employed an army of artists in Rome to manufacture the masterpieces Grand Tourists required. Plaster casts of classical sculptures looked down at me disdainfully.

Another footman showed me into a large painting room, where Reynolds was at work on the head of a fashionable young lady who was enthroned on a revolving chair on castors. He was a red-faced man in his forties with a soft accent that, at first, I could hardly understand. Later I learnt that the spoke the dialect of his native Devon. What with this, his deafness, and my German-Italian accent, our first conversations did not flow, but somehow we discovered we liked each other. In a smaller room I could see five young men – his pupils – hard at work copying a painting on an easel. As we talked Reynolds painted, almost dancing as he bobbed around the room chatting to me, to his aristocratic sitter and her chaperone while at the same time muttering instructions to various painting assistants and pupils.

When his sitter left, he rang a bell. 'Frances!' A very shy, homely woman stood quivering on the threshold. 'Frances, bring us some tea please.' I took her to be a servant, but later discovered she was his sister. Reynolds turned to study me with ruthless phizmonger eyes.

'I did not expect you to be so young, Miss – Fraulein – Signorina. The portrait you did of Davey Garrick preceded you to London and delighted us all.'

'I never enjoyed sittings so much,' I replied. 'He mimicked and clowned all the time. He made me laugh so much I dropped my paintbrush. That was when I made up my mind to come to London, where such amusing people congregate.'

'Ah, there is only one Davey. Of course I've known him since he was quite a boy. My dear friend Johnson was his school-master in Lichfield some thirty years back. The two of them walked to London. They took turns to ride one broken down old horse here and lived in desperate poverty. Now Johnson is very jealous of his old pupil's success. Did Davey give you his burlesque of Johnson eating?'

'He did. He is a very naughty man. All the time he sat for me he changed his expression constantly to tease me and make it more difficult to capture his face. I've seen your portrait of him, Mr Reynolds. You catch perfectly his mischief as well as his greatness. In Naples I saw his Macbeth and could hardly believe it was the same man. As you say, he is torn between tragedy and comedy. Your portrait is quite wonderful.'

My admiration was sincere. Many years later I borrowed from Reynold's painting of Garrick for my portrait of myself, hesitating between painting and music.

'Did you meet the lovely Eva? I trust she was not jealous?' said Reynolds.

'She had no reason to be.'

A man may be a rake, but a woman who flirts is universally despised. I did not tell Reynolds that Garrick had written me a note I still cherish:

*While thus you paint with ease and grace,*
*And spirit all your own,*
*Take if you please my mind and face,*
*BUT LET MY HEART ALONE.*

As soon as he had drunk his tea, Reynolds was on his feet again, waving his maulstick as he repainted the faces on several portraits that were propped on easels. 'I must go. I disturb your work,' I said.

'No, please stay. So, you want to set up as a paintress in London?'

'I would be so grateful if you could advise me. My papa has always guided me, but he could not come with me.'

At this the childless Reynolds, the least emotional of men, looked touched. 'London is expensive and painting, my dear Miss Signorina. It is a business as well as an art.' He smiled, raising his voice in one of the instructive arias he was so often to serenade me with. 'Your Pompeo Batoni in Rome, how much does he charge?'

'I believe – in English money – about twenty-five pounds for a portrait.'

'Ha! You must think in guineas, for they are more genteel. The young lady who was here just now will pay a hundred and fifty guineas for her full-length portrait. Of course, there are artists who are fools with money – like poor old Hogarth, who lived over there on the other side of the square and died penniless last year. His work is far too sentimental for my taste. It is not the heart nor the eye, but the mind which the painter of genius wishes to address…'

Sitting in the window of his magnificent painting room, listening to his splendid phrases, I felt that the life I had always wanted was at last within my reach.

'If you must imitate other artists, choose only the very best. You saw my Old Masters as you came in?' I did not tell him they were very new masters. 'I steal from them. I try to discover their secrets. You must do the same. I suppose you will get a husband? I hear Dance is infatuated with you.'

'I have no plans to marry.'

'Good. An artist married is an artist ruined.'

That first intoxicating week in London, I also met up with Benjamin West and his bride, Elizabeth.

'I hear they call you the American Raphael!' I clasped Ben's hand and gave my other hand to Elizabeth when they called on me at Charles Street. They were a handsome young couple, tall and slender, their clear eyes shining through the foggy morning.

'Now you're in London there are so many people I want you to meet,' said Ben. 'Does Nathaniel Dance still follow you everywhere? Has your father really allowed you to come here all alone?'

'I'm not alone. Lady Wentworth is immensely kind. We live here *en famille*.'

It was true. She gave me a large painting room at the top of her house and boasted of my talent to everyone. I already had several portrait commissions, although I could not persuade my patrons to pay for the grand historical and allegorical works that I, like Ben, longed to paint. Anxious as always about money, I worked all day in the murky light, often needing expensive candles even in the morning. In London people said it was a glorious day if you could see the sun through the smoke.

Lady Wentworth chaperoned me in the evenings. I sang whenever she asked me to and smiled at the fashionable people she introduced me to. I felt a little like her performing monkey – but also like the petted daughter I had never been. My parents were too poor to spoil me. My own mother never showed her affection for me and after she died, I became my father's support. It was very agreeable to be called darling and poppet – to be bought elegant clothes and geegaws – to be told I was clever and pretty. Lady Wentworth, having separated from her husband, feared to be thought a woman of slight character, and I could not parade myself alone as a young, unmarried foreign woman. Together we were respectable, and we could negotiate the dangerous shoals of society. The season was over; it ended with the King's birthday – The Birthday – on June the fourth. Yet there were still hundreds of salons and concerts that first summer in London.

Late at night we returned home through the crush of carriages. I was exhausted, having risen at six to start work, but I enjoyed that last intimate half-hour when we sat in Lady Wentworth's little drawing room over a tray of tea.

'Here it is! Our chatter broth.' She yawned and sank into the cushions on her sofa while I sat on the chair opposite to pour our tea. The green and yellow stripes of her sofa – my turquoise silk dress and her purple one – the peacock clothes of the men we met that night, handsome in their lace, diamond buckles and powdered wigs – how brilliant the world was before the French drained it of colour!

'The Duke was very attentive to you, my dear. Do you like him?' Lady Wentworth asked me.

'I thought him a titled ape.'

She laughed. 'You are very scornful. Do you really not care for men?'

'O yes, but as friends.'

'Not as husbands?'

'Women marry because they can't support themselves. I, however, mean to work hard all my life and earn a fortune.'

'Then, if you do marry someday, take care to hang onto your own money. Murray had far too much of mine.'

'I think I would know a fortune hunter,' I said.

'But your handsome devoted Nathaniel Dance cannot win you?'

'He's too young. I like to learn from people. From you – from Reynolds.'

'Ah, so Reynolds holds the key to your heart?' she asked.

'Not my heart, but my head. He knows so much.'

'He is twenty years older than you and a bachelor. There have been rumours. I heard he was infatuated with Kitty Fisher a few years back.'

'Who is she?'

'Why, the famous courtesan. He painted her portrait and appeared to be enslaved.'

'I go to his house to learn.'

'But you go there almost every day, *carissima*. People will gossip.'

'May I not choose my own friends?'

'Certainly, my poppet, but guard your reputation well. Those things don't disgrace men that ruin us poor women.'

Nearly forty years later, I smile to remember Lady Wentworth's sensible advice and look up at the portrait Reynolds did of me then. I am very young, holding a blank sheet of paper and a quill as if he is about deliver one of his lectures to me and I am to take notes. Next to it on the wall of my studio is my portrait of him.

When Reynolds sat for me, soon after my arrival in London, he arranged every detail to make it quite clear that this was the portrait of a great artist. The bust of Michelangelo seemed to be whispering to him: 'Mr Reynolds, welcome to Elysium, come take your place amongst the gods.' I smoothed away his smallpox scars and his disfigured upper lip. Books and papers were carefully placed to stress that he possessed intellect as well as genius and, behind him, an empty canvas awaited the muses. *Le grand gout* did not yet exist in England, but we artists were to create it, and so our portraits had to be grand and heroic.

The smell of wine was always on his breath – the snuff he took constantly – the wax and bitumen he mixed with his pigment. I copied Reynolds in many things, but not in that, fortunately, for the bitumen never dried in the damp London air. Years later, his paintings cracked and the colours fled. He gave me so much valuable advice: use as few colours as possible, do not crouch to the great… I can still hear his affable Devonshire accent. He was a Gentleman Artist and I wanted him to teach me how to be a Lady Artist. Reynolds, who was earning six thousand a year, set my prices at twenty guineas for a head and up to sixty guineas for a full-length life-size portrait. Generously, he praised my work to everyone and introduced me to rich women who commissioned portraits from me. I painted them in mythological poses out of my favourite stories from Homer and Ovid, always flattering them.

'You throw yourself at that fat old man!' Nathaniel hissed one morning, bursting into Lady Wentworth's morning room just as we finished breakfast. She withdrew discreetly, raising an eyebrow and shaking her head as if to say, 'I warned you.'

Nathaniel made me feel tired and cold. In Rome his adoration had been pleasing. I did not contradict him when he said we were to be married in London, for I wanted very much to go there. Now I felt like a horse that had bolted and feared being captive again. My father's reproachful letters, Nathaniel's accusations – Reynolds was the only man who allowed me to grow and become myself.

'My mother was almost hysterical with rage when she woke that Sunday to find you gone, on the coach to London, without a word of thanks,' Nathaniel continued. 'She says you are the rudest baggage she ever met, and the most conceited. Even so, I am willing to marry you.'

'You are too good for me.'

'Certainly. I have showered you with favours, but you give nothing in return. Without me, you would not have met Garrick or Lady Wentworth. But now you find Reynolds can be more useful than me, so you drop me like a piece of horse shit. People say you visit him at all hours.'

'That's not true! I'm never alone with him, if that's what you think. There are always servants – assistants – sitters.'

'Are you in love with him?'

'No.' That word confounded me. It made men and women foolish, humiliated them, led to hot, groping shame, to the slavery of marriage and the degradation of childbirth. I did, of course, "love" many things: art, music, my work – my papa, at a safe distance. But to be in love – to fall into that morass of sticky, messy, hysterical feelings – was clearly a mistake. Women in operas did it and look what happened to them.

'You look at me with disgust. You were friendly enough in Rome, when I introduced you to people and encouraged your ambition.'

'Friendship. Yes, Nathaniel, I can give you that.' I smiled and held out my hands. When he advanced with more rage than love in his face, I backed towards the window.

'You say that, but you do not trust me.' He flung himself into a chair, put his hands over his face and sobbed noisily into the debris of marmalade and coffee pots.

I think Lady Wentworth was hovering outside the door, for she entered just then. saying brusquely, 'Come, whimsyhead, have you forgotten that we have an appointment with the milliner?' We did not, but her fib served to get rid of Nathaniel.

My intimacy with Reynolds never threatened me. He introduced me to his friends, who were always interesting. Most of them were writers, not painters. I enjoyed conversation with Goldsmith and Burke but Johnson, who Reynolds said had formed his mind, always made me uncomfortable. 'Portrait painting is a most improper pursuit for women,' he told me. 'It is indelicate to stare into men's faces.'

I stared into his in some amazement. He was about sixty, enormously fat with a monumental Roman nose, prominent flubbery lips, and scars all over his face. His wig was far too small for his head, singed on one side because – I later discovered – he had used a candle to read by and held it too close. He had lost the use of one eye, and the other peered back at me disapprovingly. As he drank his fifth cup of tea he dribbled, and when he picked up a piece of cake, the veins in his forehead bulged as he sweated profusely. Remembering Garrick's naughty mimicry of Johnson eating, I stifled a giggle. Johnson had been Davey Garrick's schoolmaster, and to me he always seemed to be one still, lecturing and haranguing. 'The ideal woman moves in the domestic sphere and does not stare at men!' he said.

Reynolds defended me. 'Miss Angel has lived in Italy, Samuel, where manners are not the same as ours.'

'I have never been to Italy, but I have heard that it is the seat of lewd and lascivious behavior, where every lady has her *cicisbeo*, who attends on her in all public places, sits in her box at the playhouse and attends her in her coach. And the husband never thinks it necessary to be jealous.'

'There are as many respectable women in Rome as in London, Dr Johnson,' I said.

'Indeed? Let us hope that you live up to your name.'

'It's not her real name, Samuel, but my pet name for her,' explained Reynolds. 'She paints like an angel and moves in a higher sphere than the rest of us.'

'A paintress, being irrational like all women, cannot possibly aspire to the heights of history painting, but may, perhaps, succeed as a portrait painter.'

'I have every intention of succeeding as a history and as an allegorical painter as well,' I insisted.

'Indeed? I had rather see the portrait of a dog I know than all the allegorical paintings they can show me in the world,' said Johnson, bowing sarcastically and turning away. He was a widower and I wondered if his wife had died of mortification. 'Ah, there is my dear little Fanny! Such a modest little person, bursting with artistic talent.' He walked off with a lurching spasm, as if he was battling with chains, and proceeded to make a great fuss of Reynolds's shy sister.

Later that afternoon Reynolds said, 'My dear, I find your candour delightful, but if you want to get on in London, it might be wise to cultivate a little decorum.'

He then handed me two books: Fanny Burney's *Evelina* and Congreve's play, *Love for Love*. Because I wanted passionately to get on in London, I went straight home to devour them both.

As guides to conduct, they puzzled me greatly. I thought Evelina herself was absurdly prudish, but I admired Miss Burney's novel and later illustrated it. Miss Prue, the naïve country girl in Congreve's comedy, gave me further lessons in hypocrisy. "Pooh, pox, you must not say yes already; I shan't care a farthing for you then in a twinkling.... All well-bred persons lie. Besides you are a woman, you must never speak what you think; your words must contradict your thoughts; but your actions may contradict your words. So, when I ask you, if you can love me, you must say no, but you must love me too.... If I ask you to kiss me, you must be angry but you must not refuse me."

My dearest wish was to learn enough decorum to succeed in London society and to accompany Reynolds on his nightly excursions, but it seemed that these two were not compatible. Along with Johnson, Burke, Goldsmith and other writers, he attended a Literary Club that met at the Turk's Head in Gerrard Street. Artists congregated at Old Slaughter's coffee house in St Martin's Lane. I imagined myself shining in such company and waited for the invitation that never came.

I confided in Lady Wentworth who said, 'My dear, women are less free here than in Rome or Paris. English men prefer wine and gaming to us. They dislike women who are both polite and artistic – they mock them when they are alone together.'

'Yet Reynolds's friends are themselves artists and writers. Dr Johnson does not like me, I know, but Fuseli is very friendly.'

'Fuseli is not a gentleman. You must confine yourself to polite society. Don't shock people by outlandish behavior, else you will lose all your patrons.'

Lady Wentworth and I attended a couple of Elizabeth Vesey's Tuesday evening assemblies of the famous Bluestockings in Clarges Street. Our hostess was the daughter of a bishop and the wife of a Member of Parliament who (said gossip) betrayed her dreadfully. Elizabeth Vesey moved among us graciously with her ear trumpet. Her friends called her Sylph because she was so slender, and the conversation was witty and learned. At the end of the evening Johnson, Reynolds and other members of their Literary Club dropped in after their dinner at Turk's Head. I suspected that their drunken dinners were more amusing than our sedate *conversazioni*, but I heeded Lady Wentworth's advice.

# 5

---

Lady Wentworth remained my friend and oracle, although I soon had to move out of her little house. It was not enough to have a painting room; I needed a showroom as well to display my work. I found a suite of rooms in Suffolk Street for two guineas a week, with my food and servant costing another guinea. Anxiously I did my sums.

'You've been so kind to me,' I told Lady Wentworth. 'Without you, perhaps, I would never have left Italy. I might have died without seeing Paris and the wonderful colours of Rubens.'

'You exaggerate, child,' she replied. 'You are prodigiously talented. You will conquer the world.'

It was exciting to live alone for the first time in my life. When I woke up in the middle of the night, my head buzzed with conversations from the day before. Then I remembered the unfinished portraits jostling for my attention. Instead of worrying that I might disturb others, I was free to go down to my painting room to work until dusk – to eat when I was hungry or not at all. My rooms were small, but they were mine. Mine also were the decisions about who to meet, who to trust, which commissions and invitations to accept, and how much to charge. So, I began to be Londonised.

After Papa died, I found that he'd kept all my letters. I have them in front of me now. It was delicious to boast about my success – but to keep him away by warning him that London was scandalously expensive. "We would have to have a servant and a maid – decorum demands it. I am now known by every-one here, and in the public eye.... I have finished some portraits, which are snapped up by everyone. Mr Reynolds is excessively pleased with them.... The Queen was delivered of a child only two days ago; as soon as she is better I shall be presented to her.... the Duchess of Ancaster visited me and saw my work two days ago; she is one of the principal ladies-in-waiting at court..."

I did not keep Papa's letters, but I remember how much they irritated me by their endless petulant complaints about his health and his demands to know when he could come to join me. London was a brilliant stage; I wanted to perform there alone, without any grumpy old Pantaloon lurking behind me.

Ben West, who was a great favourite with the royal family, offered to present me to Queen Charlotte. Said Lady Wentworth, 'I've heard that she is very stupid and disagreeable. But, still, a queen is a queen.'

She advised me as to my clothes and etiquette at court and lent me some jewels. I spent a fortune on the right clothes: a blue silk gown with a side hoop petticoat and a yellow silk mantua. I practised my curtseys and worried about how I should address Queen Charlotte. Nervously, I submitted to the hairdresser who came to me early that morning. I had not enough of my own hair to look tall, as the fashion was, so he extended me with great rolls of horsehair and greasy pomatum. By the time I was suitably tortured, I felt as if a dozen birds had nested on my head and I could hardly move in my stiff-backed gown.

Shaking, I arrived at the palace in a hired coach, expecting an ordeal of formality and coldness. To my astonishment, the great Queen was a tiny creature, three years younger than myself and very relieved to be able to speak German to me. She spoke of her admiration for women who wrote or painted – for Fanny Burney and the painter Mary Moser. I was delighted when she begged me to paint her portrait.

When she sat for me, I came to know the Queen better. She had been taught music by Johann Christian Bach and painting by Gainsborough and was passionately interested in all the arts. When I told her that I sang and played, she invited me to take part in their family concerts. I liked her for her kindness and honesty.

'English people do not like me much, because I am not pretty,' she confided in me.

Indeed, she was not. She had a dumpy figure and a colourless face with small eyes, wide nostrils and full lips. She was quite plain until she spoke, and then her face became animated by intelligence and charm. I chose to paint her allegorically, as a goddess about to awaken the sleeping fine arts in England. The beautiful golden cupid boy she was about to touch was her eldest son, Prince George.

Well, times change and so do people. My friend Cornelia writes me from London that Queen Charlotte is old and snappish now. Perhaps her sweet nature has been soured by her husband's illness and the debaucheries of the "Prince of Whales" – a fat, middle-aged cupid, whose selfishness is said to be at the root of his father's madness. I well remember how she despised frivolity and immorality.

As a painter I felt I was making great progress, but as a woman I did not know who I was. The marriage question would not go away. A suitable husband needed to be immensely rich, famous and devoted – yet unconventional enough to allow me to continue to paint and sell my work. I never forgot Lady Wentworth's advice and was quite determined to hang on to my own money. Joshua, as I called him by then, was both rich and famous, but was not in want of a wife. As I came to know his household better, I silently observed that his sister Fanny detested Giuseppe Marchi, his studio assistant.

Joshua found Giuseppe in the Piazza di Spagna as a fifteen-year-old urchin and brought him back to London, where they lived together for forty years. Once, when I called on Joshua very early in the morning, I saw the two of them emerge from the same bedchamber. Joshua was fond of painting link-boys, who had a certain reputation for offering gentlemen more than torches at night. Gossip? I let the unfounded rumours about Joshua and myself flap around our heads like silly gulls while I flirted with the younger sons of aristocratic families, who would not dream of marrying a foreign Catholic.

Although I treasured my newfound freedom, I feared to lose my lady patrons if the faintest whiff of scandal assaulted their delicate nostrils. A husband was like the label on a bottle of medicine: without it the contents were suspect, but with it came reassurance and wholesome guidance. Romance – love – passion – all that seemed shallow, a game played by men and women who had no proper occupation.

Then I was invited to a concert at the house of Dr Burney, Fanny's papa. Most English people despised music; they called an oratorio a "roaratorio" and an opera an "uproar". When I complained of this to Lady Wentworth, she smiled condescendingly and explained, 'But, my dear, nobody fashionable actually listens to music.'

As soon as I entered Dr Burney's drawing room, I knew I had found an oasis where people loved music as much as I did and took it as seriously as it must be taken. That evening I sang an aria from Handel's *Acis and Galatea* and played some tunes from Johann Christian Bach's *Adriano in Siria* – with passion, knowing that my audience had ears instead of cauliflowers in their heads. When I finished, a handsome young man clapped rapturously and begged to be introduced to me.

'I have longed to meet you, Miss Kauffman. I adore your wonderful paintings. May I visit your studio? Now I find you are a nightingale as well as a genius.'

Count Frederick de Horn was all pink and gold and lapis lazuli, a "Dresden figurine of a fairy prince", as Lady Wentworth remarked acidly when she met him later. Like many Swedes, he was an excellent linguist, slipping between English, German and French as easily as I did. That evening he did not leave my side.

After the concert he insisted on partnering me in every dance. He was the most graceful dancer I have ever seen – I can still see him after all these years. Out of the cobwebs of my mind he leaps, bows, smiles into my eyes, waves his elegant hands and gazes into my soul.

There were also less spiritual attractions. He mentioned his vast estates in Sweden – his military honours – his picture collection to which he longed to add my paintings. I noticed he wore a large golden cross and spoke humbly of his audience with the Pope. When we left Dr Burney's, the Count insisted on taking me to my lodgings in Suffolk Street in a splendid carriage attended by footmen in green livery.

'I am staying at Claridge's, but my suite is rather poky. Next time I come to London I will take a house. May I call on you tomorrow and be permitted to choose a few paintings to ship back to Sweden? Perhaps a dozen to start with?'

'My showroom is very small, for I have not been in London long. I can show you only a few portraits I am working on.'

'No matter. We have spoken of historical and allegorical painting. Your talent is wasted on mere society portraits. I would like to commission a series of large works. Perhaps stories from Ovid or Homer? Or both?'

After he kissed my hand and left me at my door, I ran upstairs to the window of my tiny showroom to watch his elegant carriage leave. He was standing there still, his hand on his heart as he stared intensely up at my window. Our eyes met – I felt a whirl-wind in my soul. That night I lay awake for hours on clouds of fairy dreams. The music – his beautiful face and manners – the passion in his deep blue eyes! Estates, a title, a fortune at my disposal.

# 6

---

Poppycock. Young women are taught to revere such tosh, to place all their hope in it. I, however, had spent my youth murdering such hopes. I was determined to work and succeed, to make money, to avoid the shoals of matrimony and motherhood. Yet some corner of my soul must have longed for the old stories – for poetry romance and happy ever after. Forty years on, I weep at my humiliation.

What if I had not gone to Dr Burney's that evening? Or if I had played and sang, but ignored the tailor's dummy with his marzipan castle? There were so many admirers then, including Nathaniel, who truly loved me... but no, I could never have married Nathaniel.

Horn was so handsome and I was so young, alone in a city I did not really understand, with my father – who had always told me how to behave – far away. Yet I did not feel young, but rather like an old maid – much courted, but never by the right man. I did not want to marry another artist. I wanted a fortune – a title – adoration. No young English aristocrat would consider marriage to a woman who was a foreigner, a commoner and a Catholic. Was I really such a *calculatrice*? Joshua used to say that only a true painter can only be married to his art. *Her* art? Although I never doubted that I was a true painter, there was a void at the heart of my life – one the Count de Horn seemed perfectly designed to fill.

After that first meeting at Dr Burney's, he visited me every day. His enthusiasm for my painting – for my self – was irresistible. I did not resist. Very soon we spent hours alone together. My heart went pit-a-pat when the maid announced him. There were long conversations – longer silences.

Between our meetings he sent flowers and billets-doux. I could not sleep for thinking about him. All day long I talked to him in my head, wishing I was holding his elegant hand instead of a piece of charcoal or a paintbrush. Work, which had once been everything, no longer satisfied me.

I am becoming indiscreet, scribbling on about myself like this. Yet these memories are still so alive, I cannot contain them in my head. I might die tomorrow, and these notebooks may fall into the wrong hands – destroy the good character I have struggled all my life to preserve. Well, I will write what I must. In England, at this time of year, they make gigantic bonfires and burn a Catholic – an effigy, but very lifelike. Hating us as they do, they dance around our auto-da-fé. Children whoop, set off fireworks and roast chestnuts in our ashes. Such a bonfire must I make of my letters, papers, memories and thoughts. But not yet.

I knew that Horn was welcomed in all the best houses in London and I could not stop my imagination from following him there. How many ambitious mamas and beautiful young ladies with dowries must have been in pursuit? He was young, handsome, clever, rich, titled – a catch, as the English say. A catch is also a song – or a fish – in their slippery language. I wanted to sing duets with him forever – to swim in the warm pool of his adulation.

One afternoon he came early when Lady Wentworth and Mary Moser were with me. They left at once, with meaningful smirks and glances. I smelled gossip brewing, but did not give a fig.

'You are more than usually beautiful today, Angelica,' said Horn. 'What are you working on? Ah, how magnificent! How I long to see my house in Stockholm filled with your paintings. If only you could accompany them.'

'What do you mean?'

He actually went down on one knee. 'Will you do me the honour of being the Countess de Horn? I am not a genius like you, but I can offer you a lifetime of love and great estates. I will share half my vast fortune with you. Is it enough?'

It was. But Lady Wentworth had always said one should not accept a first proposal of marriage too eagerly. So I was silent, gazing down at his golden skin and his clear blue eyes, which were staring up at me so frankly.

'I wish I could offer you the famous de Horn diamonds and emeralds now, but they are in the bank in Stockholm,' he continued. 'Of course, we don't have to live there. Would you prefer London or Paris?'

'O Frederick – I need to think. Please get up.'

As I raised him from his knees, we became intertwined. He kissed my hands, then my mouth. We lay on the couch together, whispering, caressing, forgetting time.

Then it was dark – our clothes were in disarray – there was sticky blood between my legs. I thought my monthly visitor had arrived and felt ashamed. He was so clean; his breath was sweet, and the thick blond hair beneath his wig was perfumed with rose water.

'May I stay the night?' he whispered.

My maid – neighbours – patrons. They would all be scandalised and would abandon me! I had not quite lost my senses. 'No. Go now. When you come tomorrow afternoon, I will give you my answer.'

That night, my castles in the air grew foundations and wings. I am going to be a rich Countess with a beautiful Catholic husband who loves and encourages my work, thought I. Never again will I have to accept dull portrait commissions; I can devote the rest of my life to religious and historical painting.

The next afternoon, as soon as he entered my room, I stammered my acceptance. Such raptures and kisses! I instructed my maid to tell any other callers I was not at home and willingly entered into the paradise he offered me.

'My sweet Angelica! The only angel that has come down these thousand years.'

'When shall we be married, Frederick?'

'As soon as I can arrange it. Leave everything to me. When the happy knot is tied, I believe I will be the happiest man in the world.'

'Shall we announce our engagement at once?'

'Perhaps not. You see, my family might object – they are snobs and philistines. I think it might be best if we marry in secret.'

'How romantic!' So there were families in paradise. I thought guiltily of my own father, who would have to be informed. Tomorrow. Today there were only embraces and promises.

These memories are still so vivid after forty years. I can feel his warm touch – his long, manicured fingers stroking my hair, playing my body like a harpsichord. I gave myself to him wholeheartedly – for we were engaged, soon to be married. We would spend the rest of our lives together. After he left at midnight, I could not sleep for excitement.

At six, there was a hammering at the door. My maid rushed down in her nightgown to open it. Frederick rushed in, covered with the slush and dirt of the February streets.

'Frederick! Where is your carriage?'

'I must not be seen in public. My enemies have pursued me to London.'

'What enemies?'

'Did I not tell you? I am being persecuted, accused of treason against the King of Sweden. I thought I was safe here in London, but I've just heard that my government means to extradite me and force me back to Stockholm.'

'Treason?' In England, I knew, the punishment for treason was to be cut up and quartered alive. I felt sick, but told myself to be strong for him.

'I must leave my suite at Claridge's. If I am discovered, the Swedish ambassador will clap me in irons and send me back. To be executed.'

'O Frederick! To think of your dear handsome head being parted from your perfect body!' I burst into passionate tears.

He held me in his arms until I was calm enough to speak. My tears soaked his pink brocade waistcoat and as he spoke, I felt the reverberation of his rich baritone voice. 'You can save me, Angelica, if you really love me.'

'I do!' sobbed I.

'Then we must be married at once. I will be under the protection of the English crown and my enemies will be unable to
destroy me.'

'Of course – I would do anything for you!'

'My Valkyrie! My noble girl!'

'Then, when we are married, we will be able to visit your
estates and castles and get those jewels out of the bank, won't
we?'

'Of course. It's all a terrible misunderstanding.'

'You do still want to commission all those paintings from
Horace and Ovid?'

'They will be my most treasured possessions. I shall hang
them in the entrance hall of my mansion in Stockholm, next to
my Rembrandts and Caravaggios. Or perhaps in the library of
my castle in Uppsala.'

'But where are you living now, dearest?'

'I hate to ask this of you – a gentleman should never ask a
lady for money –'

'How much do you need?'

'A hundred pounds would secure me new lodgings. For some
reason, the banker's draft I am expecting from Stockholm has
not arrived at my bank.'

He watched as I went to the safe in the corner of my studio
to get the money. I have never trusted banks and like to have
cash in the house.

We were married a week later in a Catholic ceremony at
the chapel in the Austrian Embassy. It was the day before
St Valentine's Day. The secrecy I had at first thought so romantic

made me feel nervous and lonely. In England it is illegal for a priest to marry a Catholic couple – he may be executed, and the couple may be imprisoned. So, like criminals, we scurried across the snowy courtyard to the chapel. I was heavily veiled and Frederick's wedding clothes were the same blue silk suit he had been wearing for weeks. There was no wedding feast or journey – no friends to wish us well. After the dismal ceremony, we parted.

That night, Frederick visited me in secret and left at dawn. From my window I watched him creep away, looking over his shoulder fearfully as if expecting to be attacked or arrested.

I thought of what he had said about the protection of the English crown and decided to confide in Queen Charlotte. Yes, I thought – there were flashes of intelligence during those stupid months. I never stopped working, very conscious that I needed every penny I could earn, as my aristocratic bridegroom had somehow mislaid his fortune.

How kind she was. I requested a private audience with the Queen in a small room in St James's Palace. After I explained my situation, the Queen gave me a long thoughtful look, stammering and blushing.

'Are you happy, dear Angelica?' she asked, in her direct German way.

'O yes, your Majesty. He's a wonderful man, so handsome and intelligent.' My eyes were full of tears of happiness – or something.

'The Count de Horn, you say? Well. I do not like all this secrecy, my dear. The marriage between two wonderful people should be publicly celebrated.'

'Is it true that now we are married, Frederick will be under your protection? And so his enemies cannot persecute him anymore?'

'Of what do these enemies accuse him?'

'I don't really understand, Your Majesty. Of treason, I think.'

'So! I would like to meet him. Please bring your new husband to be presented at Court next Friday.'

When I rushed home with this good news, Frederick was not pleased. 'I can't possibly go to Court.'

'But why not? It's such an honour to be invited.'

'As if I need honours! In Stockholm, the King calls me his best friend.'

'Really? Then why doesn't he help you now?'

'I told you, because of a foolish misunderstanding. I must wait for my friend to arrive in England. He will explain everything.'

'What is your friend's name?'

'The Count – the Duke of Malmo. You ask too many questions, Angelica.'

'But what shall I tell the Queen?'

'Tell her whatever you think best. My little wife. My little genius. Put down that paintbrush.' Then he gagged me with kisses and banished all thought, as we resumed our delightful love games.

# 7

---

At the end of March, I asked, 'When does your friend arrive?'

'What friend?'

'The Duke of Malmo.'

'O, he wrote me from Paris that he will not come to London after all.'

'Then let us go to Court without him. Please, Frederick, I must not offend the Queen, for my career depends on her patronage.'

'You think too much of your career. You are the Countess de Horn now.'

'Shall I write to the Queen to ask if you can be presented to her next week?'

'No! That's quite impossible. I have no suitable clothes to wear.'

'I will buy you new clothes, my darling. You can wear all your decorations and medals – you'll be the handsomest man at Court, and I shall be so proud of you.'

'I could not possibly accept. You have given me quite enough.'

This was true. My safe was almost emptied of the money I had worked so hard for. As we could not live together openly, he had to maintain a separate establishment in Covent

Garden. Naturally he needed servants – a maid, a cook and a valet. I kept only a maid, but he was accustomed to armies of flunkies. Proudly, he told me that he had never dressed himself or drawn his own bath. I asked if I could visit his new apartments.

'I'm afraid they might follow you there.'

'Who?'

'My enemies, of course. The secret agents who pursue me. No, my darling, we must preserve the utmost secrecy.'

The letter to my father was never written. Each morning at first light, my husband disappeared to his enigmatic other life. Now it seems extraordinary that I did not question this. But at the time I was lulled – stupefied? – by the joys of our lovemaking. All day long I painted, and when my friends visited me, I did not mention my marriage. I will tell them when the time is ripe, thought I. But Frederick's affairs grew more and more complicated. As the light faded, he returned to me – a creature of the night – suspicious and in much fidget.

'Who did you see today?'

'Joshua called and Lady T came to sit for her portrait.'

'Reynolds is a great gossipmonger. Did you speak of me?'

'No, Frederick, I never do. Did you ask your bank what became of the money the Duke sent you?'

'Always money. How mercenary you are,' he said. Then we shared a simple meal. The wine calmed him down and he smiled at last. O the dear charming man, thought I, as his candid blue eyes gazed into mine and he led me to our marriage bed.

The next few months were bewildering. I could not eat or sleep – even now I tremble to remember that time. My father suddenly wrote to say that he and his niece, Rosa, were on their way to London. Rosa was to keep house for us, and he would manage my affairs again.

That summer they arrived. To see him again was to become his infant – pupil – daughter. Frederick entered without warning and shook my father's hand vigorously. 'Delighted to meet you. May I call you Father?'

'I am not a priest,' said my father coldly.

'Your daughter has not told you of our marriage?'

Papa looked at me with horror, Frederick with rage. Had the window been open, I would have jumped out of it.

My father called me a nincompoop and a slut, while Frederick sulked and pouted. My house in Golden Square, that had once seemed so big, was far too small for the four of us. No more nights of sweet dalliance. In came the bill for those we had rashly enjoyed: a few months later, my cousin Rosa whispered that I was with child

'How can you know this when I do not?'

'Your belly is swollen, and you vomit every morning.'

At this news, my father insisted that his grandchild must not be born a bastard. 'A secret marriage is no marriage at all.' And so that autumn, Frederick and I were married again, in a Protestant ceremony at St James's Piccadilly. A funereal wedding – gloomy faces – doubts gathering like vultures.

Then came a note from the Queen, asking to speak to me privately. I rushed to the palace to meet her in an anteroom. She was looking very sad.

'My dear, I have bad news. The Count de Horn has been at Court.'

I was bewildered. 'My husband, Your Majesty?'

She sighed. 'No, Angelica. When I congratulated him on his marriage to you, he looked amazed. Then he told me of a German manservant who stole money, jewels, papers and clothes from him a few months ago. I am afraid your husband is an imposter – an adventurer. O, how I wish I did not have to tell you this!' I curtseyed, backed away and fled from the palace.

That morning, I could not bear to return to Golden Square. Unable to walk more than a few paces in my cumbersome court dress, I begged to have a chair called and told the men to carry me through the streets of London for an hour.

'Where to, my lady?'

'Anywhere.'

They opened the top of the sedan chair to make room for my wig. Inside, I drew the curtains to avoid curious eyes and allowed myself to be blinded by tears of shame and humiliation. It was a little hour of privacy, when I needed not to worry about my reputation – father – husband. Alone in my expensive silk lined box, I sobbed.

Lifting a corner of the curtain, I saw that we were crossing a bridge. I wondered if the river below was deep enough to drown us – me and my baby, who would not be the heir to the Count de Horn, but the baseborn child of a scoundrel and a fool.

Shivering and wet from the dirty snow that fell like my frozen dreams, I returned at last to Golden Square. My father and Rosa were not a bit surprised. I alone had been stupid enough to believe in Frederick. When he came that night, the three of us confronted him with his lies. And instead of denial or apology, Frederick bellowed that he would blow his brains out.

'Then please do so in the street, not on our good carpets,' said my father, opening the front door for him.

But Frederick stayed and became a tyrant. For a week after that dreadful scene, I was ill with a fever and influenza. I lay abed, hoping to die. Downstairs I could hear shouting and raving – I sensed the misery that seeped through doors and walls into my room. Kind Rosa nursed me; she brought me soup and made me eat. She told me that when my friends visited me, Frederick stood at the front door, abusing them and ordering them to leave.

I felt like a marionette that had been dropped and abandoned. Who, then, controlled my strings? The answer boomed in my empty room. As always, my prayers strengthened me and I saw that only my own discipline and hard work could mend my broken life.

One cold morning, I slipped downstairs to my studio and started to paint again. At my easel – belonging to myself again – I could bear to listen to the violent tantrums in the next room.

That last scene with Frederick distresses me still. My father and Rosa were out. I was still in my bedchamber when in burst Frederick, with such rage in his azure eyes that I whipped under the bedclothes.

'I must speak to you alone while that old fool is out of the way.'

O stubborn heart! It beat for him still and was up at my mouth as I hid from his musical voice. Even in anger he is handsome – seductive. I must not look, thought I.

'Look at me, damn you!' He pulled away the covers and gripped my shoulder through my nightgown. I stared at him in terror, half expecting him to produce a blunderbuss, to blow out my brains and his own. There was such violence in his voice as he roared on. 'You are my wife, you little hypocrite. Now you think me a rascal, but a few months ago you used all the arts of your sex to captivate me. You are a flirtatious old maid, desperate for a husband – a rich one. 'Tis only my want of money makes me repulsive to you now.'

If only he *was* repulsive. My soul tossed up and down. I was silent – a cowardly rabbit in the paws of a wolf. He did not paw me, but if he had, I know I might not have been able to resist.

'I am handsome and clever. Why shouldn't I have what my father has?'

'Is the Count de Horn your father?' I spoke at last.

'Titles, money, accidents of birth! They are all you care about. Five minutes to make a bastard and a lifetime to degrade and insult him. Now you call me a fraud and a liar – but everybody lies! They all pretend to be richer, better, kinder than they are. They all bow to stupid ugly men who are fatpurses, while I, who can speak and dress and dance to perfection, am become a bugbear.'

'The world is as it is, Frederick. You cannot steal another man's name and masquerade as what you are not.'

'Why not?'

'Because –' I struggled to remember. 'Because servants belong to one class and masters to another.'

'I care not a fart for your classes. Nature has made me an aristocrat. I read and studied so hard to improve myself.'

'But it is all a sham.'

'You sneer at me, but you yourself were not born a lady. In the beginning, that was why I liked you – I saw that you were born to working folk and rose through your own merits. Why should I not do the same?'

Before I had to answer this thorny question, my father returned and Frederick fled. Many years after that dreadful scene, I went to see *Figaro* and *Don Giovanni* at the opera. I wept while all around me laughed, recognising my charlatan of a husband in Figaro and Leporello. How often are servants cleverer than their masters.

Deeply shaken, I tried to avoid both my husband and my father. At every opportunity, Papa reproached me. 'You ungrateful baggage! After all my care and teaching, to fall for his tricks and lies. He's a fortune hunter, a flunkey, a fop who takes snuff every few words, a dancing master who dresses in frills and furbelows and stares at himself in the mirror for hours! He may ruin us yet. We may come to the workhouse!'

Whenever Frederick and my father met there was an explosion. My husband demanded all my money. Papa said our marriage could not be valid if Frederick had lied about being a Count. In misery, I folded my hands over my guilty belly and listened to their harsh voices. One day, Frederick threatened to beat my father – then shouted that he would take the phial of poison he always carried with him. Hearing this, I rushed into the next room to stand in the doorway. Frederick grasped my arm, his fingers leaving bruises on the flesh he used to kiss.

'Angelica, you must come abroad with me.'

'I can't. I must finish these commissions, or there will be no money for any of us.'

'Then give me enough money to leave England.'

'How dare you speak to my daughter like that!' Papa roared.

'She is my wife and her property is mine. Get out of my house, you stupid old man!' shouted Frederick, threatening to beat my father with the stick he carried.

'Frederick – no – I can't bear this. We must separate.'

At this he rushed to my safe – I had foolishly told him the combination number to dial – seized all my remaining money and ran out of the house.

For days we had no news of him. I did not know if I was heartbroken or relieved. 'He has murdered your reputation, and leaves you with his brat,' said my father.

Then along came a lawyer with a greasy wig and weasel face. 'Madame, my client – your husband – demands your presence and all your possessions.'

'What is your client's name? How can you represent a man who has no name?' Papa demanded.

The lawyer ignored my father. 'If those terms are unacceptable to you, my client is willing to agree to a formal separation and compensation of five hundred pounds.'

'Compensation for what?' roared my father. 'For being loving and gullible and trusting?'

We had to haggle, as if my marriage was a broken-down old nag at a horse fair. The price went down to four hundred, then to three hundred – I was not worth much. Every day my belly grew bigger and my self-possession dwindled. Then the letters began to arrive. Many of my friends had heard rumours of my troubles and wrote to assure me of their affection and respect for me. Yet, all around me, I heard London snigger.

A letter came from a Frau Brandt, informing me that she had married my husband in Hildesheim when he was a lieutenant in the army of Frederick the Great and had five children by him. The anonymous letters were the worst: Frederick, said one, was the by-blow of the current Count de Horn and Cristina Brant, one of his maids; another note, printed in capital letters, warned me that my husband meant to kidnap me. He had hired cut-throats and prepared a carriage and horses for flight to the coast, where a boat was to take me, bound and gagged, to France. For weeks I did not dare to leave the house. Other letters informed me of other Fredericks with other names – my husband had as many incarnations as Zeus.

In February, almost exactly a year after our first wedding, I was granted a divorce on the grounds of bigamy. My father insisted that my marriage had never been consummated and I was a virgin. I kept quiet. I knew that bigamy was a capital offence and could not wish death on a man I had loved so recently. I did not pursue Frederick. But I knew I would never trust a man again.

My father used to tell me an old German folk tale, *Rumpelstiltskin*, about a girl who spun straw into gold. She needed a mysterious little man to help her – I, however, earned gold all by myself. Then, in order to keep her child, she had to guess the name of the little man. But I? I lost my child and did not even know the name of my man. I never saw him again.

# 8

Marriage! It is marriage itself which is the snare for women, though men say we ensnare them. A good marriage – how are we to believe in any other desirable future for ourselves? Says Lady Wentworth, 'But of course you must marry. It's better to be married to a dog or a horse than not to marry at all. But preferably, my charmer, to Sir Dog or Lord Horse.'

Spinster, old maid, on the shelf, dowdy, frumpy, withered – I know from my dear, brave friend Cornelia how cruelly the world speaks of unmarried women. Once, she told me, a gentleman at one of my *conversazioni* here in Rome snubbed her, then stared at her back and said, 'I don't know what the devil a woman who can't get a husband lives for over thirty, for she is only in other folks' way.' A woman who breaks the conventions is despised. Yet one or two have beauty and courage enough to defy the world – Emma Hamilton is such a woman, and Kitty Fisher was another. Joshua was just as obsessed with Kitty as Romney was later with Emma; he painted Kitty again and again.

When first I visited Joshua's studio, I saw his unfinished portrait of a pale young woman with a lovely oval face, playing with a parrot that sat on her finger. Her lips were slightly parted as if she was flirting tenderly with the bird. 'Who is that, Mr Reynolds?'

'My darling Kitty.'

'Your darling?' Perhaps in those early days I had some hope – soon lost – of conquering that chilly heart.

'She has many darlings. You must be the only woman in London who does not know who Kitty Fisher is.'

When I returned home, Lady Wentworth enlightened me with a smirk. 'I have observed her progress for years. Such harlots are amusing although, of course, they can never be received in polite society.'

She showed me pamphlets and cuttings from newspapers that I read avidly, viz. 'Apology for the Conduct of K- F-r' – a newspaper article in a broadsheet with the title *The Hundred Pound Miss* – claiming that Kitty had eaten a bank-note for a thousand guineas on a slice of bread and butter.

There were admiring descriptions of her sumptuous clothes and diamonds. Kitty was the "Darling of the Age" and the "Admiration of Every Eye". There was a rhyme I did not understand: "Lucy Locket lost her pocket / Kitty Fisher found it / Not a penny was there in it / Only ribbon 'round it."

When Lady Wentworth whispered its meaning to me, I gasped with shock. There was also a newspaper advertisement – I have it here – for a painting by Joshua: Kitty Fisher as Cleopatra. It showed her dissolving a pearl in wine after a wager with her Anthony. I was shocked to see that my revered maestro was criticised by the impudent Grub Street hack, who wrote that Joshua was "as injurious to the true principles of painting as a fine prostitute to the establishment of morals".

My nemesis Nathaniel Hone, who was to cause me such distress a few years later, also painted Kitty with a kitten (kitty), trying to catch a goldfish in a bowl (fisher). Reflected in the bowl are the faces of a crowd of people looking through a window. I became as fascinated by Kitty as all the rest of the town. When I begged Lady Wentworth to let me keep her little collection, she laughingly agreed. 'It is part of your education, my dear.' I have them still. They will be the first things to be thrown onto my bonfire – no, first will be Horn's love letters.

This young woman, the same age as me and also from a poor background, achieved fame and fortune by selling her body. Later, in 1767, the famous Kitty married a Member of Parliament. And just a few months later – even as my own life fell apart – hers ended. It was the talk of the town that she was buried in her finest ball gown. She lived her brief life in public – those paintings of her were reproduced a thousand times.

One afternoon I called on Joshua to find him red eyed and grief stricken. My own spirits were very low – my body shattered – we sat together in silence like two wounded soldiers.

Now, when they are all dead, I wonder, did the wicked spirit of that beautiful girl possess me during those months? I had no mother or sister to advise me and could not confide in Lady Wentworth, knowing her to be a great gossipmonger. Alone in London – woefully ignorant yet convinced I knew the world – I was flattered by the success that had come to me. Duped, tricked, deceived – yet for those few months, how happy and free I felt! Horn was a siren. Why are they always represented as female? A man may also lure his victims onto the rocks and wreck their frail boats.

Queen Charlotte, knowing all, forgave me. I think of her when I hear people rant about the despotism of kings and queens. Her disapproval would have murdered my hopes in London, but instead she helped me onto the safe raft of the new Royal Academy. The Queen has always been a great champion of talented ladies; even now she protects my clever, penniless Cornelia (who complains, however, that the court is very gloomy and dull). In those days the Queen was young and determined that "the men", as she called them, should not have it all their own way. I think she liked Mary Moser and me because we were about her age and spoke German with her, and also because she admired our work.

As for Joshua, I wonder if he would have chosen me to join his Academy if the Queen had not insisted. He liked to keep his life in separate compartments. He loved the demi-monde; in the morning he painted courtesans and mistresses, paid beggars to pose as angels and link-boys to play Cupid. He took Venus's head from his servant's sixteen-year-old daughter – her body from a beggar woman with her infant naked on her lap – his Iphigenia was modelled on a raddled courtesan. 'I must always have nature before my eyes,' said he with a pinch of snuff.

In the afternoon he painted his aristocratic patrons, who would not wish to be confronted with a beggar, however pretty. I used to visit him in the late afternoon when the light was fading and my eyes were so tired that I could not continue with my own painting. How much I learnt from watching him. He usually did a face in about four hours, then his pupils and drapery masters did the rest. When he was late with a commission, he allowed me to contribute, viz. 'Miss Angel can finish that wing,' or 'Angelica, make the fingers a little more genteel, will you?' His studio was a manufactory – a very successful one.

I envied his income and respected his industry but was never quite sure which compartment I belonged to.

It was a kind of patriotic dream, that Academy. Joshua longed to be taken seriously, to be more than a phizmonger. For years he and the other artists muttered in the coffee houses and taverns (from which I was excluded) that they were regarded as tradesmen, not gentlemen. They formed clubs – quarrelled and jostled for power – just like the artists I have known here in Rome.

One evening I was invited to supper in the splendid dining room at Joshua's house in Leicester Fields. William Chambers was there, boasting of his travels in China and Paris and Italy, along with George Moser, Mary's papa. He was Swiss, the manager of the St Martin's Lane Academy. Moser was not exactly an artist, but he knew a great deal about art and made beautiful gold trinket boxes, cane heads, watchcases and enamel necklaces, which his daughter showed me. That evening the food was simple: beef and dumplings sent in from a local cookshop with a great deal of claret. The conversation, however, was extremely complicated. My English was not so good then and I may have missed some of it. Mary and I were still good friends; we occasionally lapsed into comfortable German together as the men's conspiracy raged over us. Joshua, at his most pompous, proposed several grandiose toasts: 'To Protestant Great Britain's rebirth as the noble republic of Ancient Rome!'

'To the death of British philistinism!'

'To our native *Accademia*!'

We all drank heartily as our mood grew even more exalted. Chambers, who had been the King's drawing master, was confident that the royal family would support our new enterprise.

'We don't want any riff-raff,' cried Joshua. 'Membership must mean something, like a patent of nobility.'

'We must be arbiters of taste,' proclaimed Chambers, rising unsteadily to his feet to propose this as a toast.

'We must be international. Should we exclude artists who have not studied in Rome?' Moser glowed with happiness as if his hour had struck.

That started a passionate argument. Joshua fetched paper and pens and they drafted a constitution.

The next morning, when I woke with a headache and could not start work at dawn as usual, I did not know if that conversation was any more than a tipsy fantasia. But the idea spread like the measles and there were many other meetings I was not invited to.

Forty of us were to be elected – how that "us" poured balm onto my lacerated soul. My spurned lover, Nathaniel Dance, was to be among the chosen. I tried to avoid him, for I knew his love had turned to bitter anger. There were many squabbles – yet somehow Joshua held us together in his vision of a company of artists who would, he said, wipe away the stigma all foreign critics threw upon his nation – that they had no genius for historical painting.

In our splendid new Academy, students were to copy the old masters, learning to draw and paint from living models. This training would be free, paid for out of the profits from exhibitions. The King himself was to be our patron – painting was to be respectable at last. We painters and sculptors revenged ourselves by excluding engravers and artisans.

We were all summoned to St James's Palace for a ceremony to establish the Royal Academy of Arts. I wore the excruciatingly uncomfortable court outfit I had made when I was first presented to Queen Charlotte. Nervous, proud, fizzing with ambition, I stood in the dark, ancient palace, looking around at the assembled faces. Many of us were not English – without foreigners there would be no art or music worth mentioning in London. The King beamed at Ben West and glared at Joshua, who he never liked. The Queen was also present and was most gracious to Mary and me, who she regarded as her protégées.

That day as I left the palace, I felt safe in liberal England. After only two years in London I had friends – patrons – a fine house in Golden Square. Papa had been very surly with me since he had arrived in England to discover my disastrous marriage, but now he began to smile on me again.

There was a song we sang to inaugurate our new Academy. All sitting together at a long table, smiling, linking arms, swaying and drinking, we toasted our glorious future:

*'A new Augustan age appears,*
*The time, not distant far, shall come,*
*When England's tasteful youth no more*
*Shall wander to Italia's classic shore;*
*No more to foreign climes shall roam;*
*In search for models better found at home...'*

Yes, that was when Joshua began to change. To me he was always kind, but he began to take on the grand manner he advocated in painting. In conversation you felt that he was wearing a toga, like Cicero, instead of his stained and faded working clothes. When the King offered him the (unpaid) presidency of the new Academy, he at first refused – which mightily offended the royal family.

Then Joshua went running to Burke and Johnson for advice. He confided in me that he was afraid of taking on a vast amount of paperwork and tedious responsibility in return for far less money than he already earned. The King had to offer him a knighthood before he would accept. Many of his old friends felt betrayed. None of us – no artists at all – were invited to the intimate dinner he gave to celebrate his knighthood. Burke was there of course, and Johnson, who (Joshua told me proudly) forsook his usual dish of tea and actually drank a glass of wine to the health of Sir Joshua. People called him "Sir Josh-u-ay" to sneer at his Devonshire accent.

# 9

Now that we were a *Royal* Academy, we needed a palace to be royal in. Old Somerset House was a gift from the King, who had so many houses. We paid no rent – but then, who would have paid to live there? It did not feel a bit palatial, more like Sleeping Beauty's castle – a forlorn memory of dilapidated splendor, where cobwebs, mice and dust mocked our delusions of fame. Protector Somerset built it as a monument to his greatness – and was executed before he could live in it. Inigo Jones remodelled it for Queen Henrietta Maria, who lost her throne when her husband lost his head. Later it belonged to Queen Catherine of Braganza, who had the misfortune to be married to a rake. I loved to sit alone in the dark chapel where those two Catholic queens used to worship, inhaling the sweet decay of stale incense and exiled faith.

The Great Fire stayed away from the oldest part of the palace, as if afraid to disturb its melancholy spell. I wandered through those vast, crumbling rooms full of hideous old furniture. There was an audience chamber with a throne fit only for a ghost and a long-deserted gallery where courtiers once paraded their finery and tittled their tattle. The room our students used as a library was hung with decayed old tapestries – all was tattered silk, faded crimson velvet curtains, rats, spiders and dust. Once,

I surprised a moth-eaten old lady who was creeping out of her grace-and-favour apartment. We both screamed, not sure which of us was the phantom. I loved to walk in the beautiful formal gardens on the river.

Chambers demolished that old palace – yet I can still see it there behind the rational glory of his modern brainchild. Well, I have always liked ruins, and now I am become one. Strange that when I think of London, as I so often do, it is Chambers's most un-London-like courtyard that comes first to mind. I walk in spirit beside the terrace overlooking the Thames – so much more energetic than our Tiber – to watch the ships. Then I cross the great courtyard and gaze up at his fine building, which looks as if it belongs in Paris. My imagination improves the weather, washes away the fog, and gives me a clean, bright summer's morning, the cold stone warmed by sunlight. I walk on younger, stronger legs towards the Strand, where our Academy rooms are, where I was commissioned to paint the ceiling in the Council Chamber.

Proudly, I made my subject a woman painter carrying out the four tasks of her profession: my Invention showed a woman with wings on her head, looking up to heaven; my Composition was also a female, struggling with a chessboard and compasses; my Design sketched the Apollo Belvedere; my Colour was a girl with a pet chameleon, who reached up to the rainbow. Are they still there, I wonder, or have they been painted out? Fashion moves on and each generation despises the art of those who came before them.

Zoffany painted a life class at our new Academy. Mary and I looked down wistfully from the wall like ancestors. We were present only in our portraits, for it would not have been decent (we were told) for us to attend. The men were all there, of course, squabbling and joking and swaggering as they do in all their clubs. They did not want a woman there unless she was naked or a servant.

To my fury, they refused to allow me to draw from the life – then complained that the people in my paintings had no bones. Fear of scandal made a coward of me. I clung to my safe little island – to my house in Golden Square, where my household was smoothly run by my sweet cousin Rosa and where my father grimly chaperoned me. As I approached thirty, I hoped they would no longer call me a coquette.

The English love to be shocked. Chambers's new Somerset House opened with a great fanfare – the newspapers called it "the finest public building in London", but the public were determined to be scandalised. One hack begged Joshua, "though neither a father nor a husband yourself," to remove the plaster casts of naked men. He said they were "the terror of every decent woman who enters the Antique Room." A plaster cast of the Venus de Medici was considered equally unseemly. Antique nude male sculptures were described as a "temple to Priapus" and plaster fig leaves had to be added. In Italy, educated people see only beauty. But in England they look at art through a veil of prudery.

I knew that one breath of scandal would destroy me. So I buried myself in work, particularly my history paintings for dear Theresa Parker at Saltram. Hector, Andromache, Ulysses – these were noble subjects, a welcome relief from the endless portraits the English wanted from me. Joshua taught me to work fast and the money rolled in. He used to say, 'An historical painter paints man in general; a portrait painter a particular man, and consequently a defective model.'

Said Chambers, laughing, 'Soon I shall need to build a hospital for all the impoverished young painters who follow your advice, Joshua, and try to get a living from historical painting.'

As very few patrons wanted our historical or religious paintings, we decided to give them away for free. Said Joshua, 'A noble painting outlives the painter.' Naturally, we were all desperate to be remembered by posterity, so we offered to paint large works for St Paul's Cathedral, hoping to start a fashion for churches in England to have altar pictures as they do in France and Italy.

For a few months this project entranced me. A portrait hangs in a private drawing room and then, when the subject dies, is banished to the attic. But a large painting in a great cathedral! Thousands gaze at it. It might outlive the century – might even be admired in three hundred years. I thought of all the churches I had visited in Italy, to stand before some candlelit masterpiece. We artists met to talk with great excitement of our ambition – of our enormous paintings which would share the values and virtues of the Old Masters and have a public purpose...

A foolish dream, from which we soon awoke.

Said the Bishop of London, 'It will be thought to be the introduction of popery.' That word all British bulldogs growl at. Our poor paintings never left our studios. Then that brute Hone made his own cruel satire out of our frustration. Nathaniel Hone was one of the founder members of our Academy. I thought him amiable enough then, but he must have secretly hated me. Tears of humiliation still choke me when I think of it. O the past – how alive it is!

'Have you seen Hone's painting, Angelica? Everyone's talking about it,' said Nathaniel Dance with a provoking snigger, when I meet him in the courtyard of our new Academy one morning. He had not spoken to me for over a year. He means to do me harm, thought I, and wondered how I ever could have considered him for a husband.

In *The Pictorial Conjuror Displaying the Whole Art of Optical Deception*, Hone mocked both Joshua and me. How I wish I could forget his horrid painting, but it burns behind my eyes like acid. He mocked Joshua's ear trumpet, his habit of adding dignity to his portraits by inserting motifs and postures from the old masters, his elegant new clothes. Even worse, there was a little girl who resembled my self-portrait as Hope standing at the conjuror's knee, looking up at him adoringly. Naked nymphs cavorted in front of St Paul's, waving palettes and paintbrushes while a naked female with long, dark hair, wearing only high boots, brandished a paintbrush as if it were a sword.

Of course Joshua and I were furious at the vile suggestion that he plagiarised from the old masters and that we had an improper relationship. Hone tried to apologise; he called on me, but I refused to admit him. Joshua and I made sure his horrid painting was rejected by the Academy's committee. We thought that was the last of it – for if the public did not see his lies, they could not harm us.

But no! The scoundrel defied us. Hone showed his scurrilous Conjuror in a room he hired in St Martin's Lane, opposite Slaughter's coffee house, the haunt of every artist in London. I knew they were all laughing at me. A woman who paints or writes or distinguishes herself in any way will always be hated, called an Amazon, insulted. Only marriage puts an end to gossip.

Peter Pindar's beastly poem enraged me: "Angelica my plaudits gains,/ Her Art so sweetly canvas stains,/ Her Dames, so gracious, give me such delight / But, were she married to such gentle Males / As figure in her painted tales / I fear she'd find a stupid wedding night."

# 10

---

This is not romantic – but the truth is, I cannot remember when first I met Antonio Zucchi. He was a friend of my father's, trusted and familiar, and was often at our house in Golden Square. We knew the same people and art was our sun; we circled around it like hardworking planets.

The first time I ever remember being alone with him was one wet afternoon at Kenwood. I had to deliver my painting of Tasso's story, *Rinaldo and Armida*, to Lord Mansfield. I took a cab from Soho to Highgate, where the elegant, newly rebuilt house shone white against its green setting. When I opened the door of the cab, luscious scents of damp earth and grass apologised for the weeping grey sky.

Said the butler, 'His Lordship is still in London. Shall I show you into the library, Madam?' I was an honorary madam by then, with no intention of earning the title.

Zucchi was in that beautiful room, one of the harmonious masterworks of his maestro Adam. He was perched up a ladder painting the ceiling and strewn all around on the floor were the charming little paintings he had done to ornament the ceiling. We met as old friends, as fellow tradesmen, come to offer our skills in the great house. I was pleased to see him, glad that I had come myself instead of sending an assistant with my painting.

I liked Lord Mansfield; he was a brilliant lawyer who said the most comical things imaginable with the gravest face. Also, of course, I hoped to get more commissions from him.

Zucchi came down from his ladder and we slipped easily into Italian. When the butler brought a tea tray, we sat comfortably in front of the fire to talk.

'I think the English build these wonderful houses because it's always raining outside. So they have to look inwards – at paintings and books,' I said.

'Yes, these great houses are masterpieces – but cold ones, with no sun to warm them. Let me see your painting.'

When I unwrapped it for him, he looked at it with just the right balance of admiration and criticism. 'Fortunate Rinaldo! To be abducted to a magic island by a beautiful nymph.'

'Better that than to have to fight in a stupid crusade. Do you think she looks like a woman in love?'

'What does a woman in love look like?'

'I have no wish to remember.'

'Your women have always more life in them than your men,' he said. He showed me the paintings he had done in oil on paper that were to be fixed to the ceiling. 'This is an Epithalamium, a wedding poem.' He leaned a little too close to me.

'Charming!' I moved away.

'Don't you think a wedding between true minds, as Shakespeare puts it, is a wonderful thing?'

'No,' said I. 'Trickery and lies.' Bigamy.

'I'm sorry, I've been tactless. Look your last on my paintings, for once they are up there on the ceiling, nobody will ever really look at them again.'

'Yes, I often worry about the fate of my children when they are swallowed into the maws of these magnificent houses.'

'One day they will be spat out and sent to the attic. But you have had such stupendous success that perhaps your children will be allowed to stay in the drawing rooms. I hope so.'

He looked sincere as he said this, and I smiled at his generosity. He did not begrudge my achievement like most men I knew, who felt a woman had no right to earn more money than they did. I had always thought of him as an old man – as my father's friend – yet he climbed easily up and down the ladder. How old was he, then? Forty something? Once that seemed so old, but now it loomed just ahead of me like a carriage lamp in a fog.

'Congratulations, Antonio. My father says you are to be an Associate of our Royal Academy.'

'Yes, I'm to be permitted to join Mount Olympus as a junior god. I know what Chambers says about my work.'

'Kind friends always repeat these things.'

'He says that my little paintings are like desserts on a plate. "Bad copies of indifferent antiques."' His eyes flashed and I saw that he had pride in his work, as an artist should.

Then we amused ourselves abusing Chambers, whose pontifications had offended us both. We laughed and sipped tea, and for half an hour I felt I lived at Kenwood – a fine lady in a great mansion. In another room, one of the young ladies was practising the harpsichord. Thought I, I could play far better than her when I was nine years old, yet how much easier her life will be than mine. This girl I will never see, with her elegant clothes and clumsy hands that have never worked at anything harder than embroidery – joined now by a thin, flat, wobbling voice. Soon a dowry will buy her a titled husband, and she will go to live in another beautiful house stuffed with paintings sculptures, servants, children, dogs...

'I don't really envy these people,' said I, hoping my words would kill my thoughts.

'Why should you envy anybody? You are a muse, a Minerva. You are La Kauffman!' Zucchi always knew how to handle me.

'How kind of you both to bring your treasures to my humble house,' said a voice. Lord Mansfield, like his house, was not a bit humble as he strode across the room towards us.

We stood up, flustered, worried that he had been there for some time listening to us – to upper servants gossiping. His long, clever face beamed on us as he brought the great world into his library, the politics and affairs of state that paid for our art and books. The shrewd old lawyer admired our work.

Then he said a curious thing. 'I see that you two are twin souls. It shines out of your work and your faces.'

After that meeting at Kenwood, Zucchi and I became closer. Not in that hysterical, thoughtless way – I hoped I was finished with all that – but like two parallel streams that roll across a landscape, separated but aware of each other, before at last they tumble together into the ocean.

Those London years brought me fame, money and satisfaction. I was fêted – invited everywhere – my work was engraved all over Europe. It was turned into china by Worcester, Derby, Sevres and Meissen; the new technique of transfer printing meant that work signed with my name, but not actually painted by me, could appear on commodes, vases, teapots, coffee pots and fans. It pleased me that people who were as poor as I once was could "own" me as well as the royal family. They all sat for their portraits – even the King himself.

Music, as well as art, enriched my life. Most evenings I played or sang at private parties. Zucchi was often at our house in Golden Square. My father and I would dine with him *en famille* when our work was at last finished. It was comfortable to sit together as we ate the food sent in from one of the Italian restaurants in Soho. We three chatted, laughed at English customs, and tore at the reputations of rival artists. It pleased me that Zucchi always treated me with respect. I came to need his warm, brown eyes gazing at me – his admiration of my work – his patience.

Most of the time I did not allow myself to think of my marriage. Yet when I woke in the middle of the night it was there, an incubus I could never awake from. Somewhere in the world my husband was alive, under yet another name, cheating yet another woman.

I was courted because I was rich and famous and enjoyed the company of men. Now that I was a connoisseur of hopeless love, I was kind, I hope, to the men I rejected. In each of them, behind his smiling countenance, I saw a gaoler. Thought I: this one really loves me for my money – that one will never permit me to paint once I have accepted him – this fellow will be jealous if I outshine him. My peculiar status, neither married nor unmarried, was a kind of freedom, because I could not legally marry.

Women in general mourn their departed youth, but I was happy to become too old to bear the children I did not want and to trade a few wrinkles for celebrity and independence. Yet

I was not quite independent. In public my father was my self-less assistant and manager, but when we were alone together, he turned back into my strict papa.

'So, you want to die an old maid?'

'I shall not marry again, if that's what you mean.'

'We have yet to rid ourselves of your first disastrous choice. I've had another letter about the Papal annulment.'

'No! I can't bear to talk about it again. I have to work. I must finish that painting for Saltram.' I turned to leave the room, but my father gripped my arm.

'That dreadful man is still your husband.'

'I paid him off. What more can I do?'

'You should get rid of him once and for all. We have to swear that the marriage was never consummated.'

'We must lie to the Holy Father?'

'A mere formality. Then when you are free again – these things take years, unfortunately – you must marry a good man who will look after you when I am gone. Someone who will take over your money affairs – you have no head for business – but not rob you. Someone who will respect your talent and be proud of your achievements.'

'O yes? Where am I to find this paragon?'

'He is under your nose, you silly girl. Antonio Zucchi would marry you tomorrow.'

At first, I laughed at this idea. Other men were younger, better looking, more exciting. Yet Zucchi was always there, a rock of calm affection in a seething ocean of malice. I felt this most strongly when Nathaniel Hone painted his spiteful Conjuror. He mocked my friendship with Joshua and tried to humiliate me. In my imagination I was a heroine, an (almost) virgin queen of the arts, pure and noble, far above the petty, flirtations and domesticity of ordinary women. But Hone's attack on me forced me to realise that the Angelica in my head had no existence beyond it. Out there in the cruel London tittle-tattlery, one breath of scandal would destroy everything I had worked for. My patrons would abandon me, and my work would become unsellable. Even more than scandal, I feared being laughed at. A woman alone is always considered ridiculous.

Then, after I had been in London thirteen years and expected to stay there always, change came very fast. The Papal annulment was at last granted, and we heard that my fraudulent husband was dead. Zucchi again asked me to marry him. I accepted him gladly but insisted on drawing up a marriage contract. Here it is! A document worth a thousand love letters. I shall not throw this onto my bonfire. "And to enable her to enjoy the dividends thereof exclusive of the said Antonio Zucchi, her intended husband, who is not to intermeddle therewith; nor is any part thereof to be subject to his debts…" Yes, a fine start to a sensible marriage.

I shut my eyes and return to a perfect morning in London. Just after our Academy moved to the elegant new Somerset House that Chambers built, I went there to supervise the installation of my allegorical paintings for the ceiling of the Council Chamber. My vsions of Invention, Composition, Design and Colour – it delighted me to think they would be seen forever by the greatest painters in England. Zucchi was beside me, helping me, a reliable husband to shield me against slander and scandal. After all my declarations that I would never marry again, I found that I loved being married to him.

I wandered off alone through the beautiful new rooms. Chambers was a cold man, but an inspired architect. As I looked down on his glorious courtyard, a rare sun washed the dirty London air, as if the neo-classical building were a timeless magnet that attracted the weather of ancient Greece and Rome. The stones were gilded and the windows glittered. Excited as a child at the seashore, I ran downstairs into the beguiling courtyard, crossed it and passed through to the great terrace beyond. Beneath me the river shone; a hundred boats sailed and beat their oars to the heart of the great city. I was part of all this splendour, my reputation as an artist assured, my dignity restored.

Richard Samuel included me among his *Nine Living Muses of Great Britain,* and his painting was shown at our Academy exhibition. There sat I in front of the temple of Apollo in the glittering company of talented clever women I admired. As Zucchi said, we were all distinguished by our brains and by the way we earned our living by them – except the Queen of the Blue Stockings, Elizabeth Montagu, who was a great society hostess and had no need of money.

The scholar Elizabeth Carter stood beside me. 'I suppose that must be you, Angelica, as you are sitting at your easel. Samuel should have asked us to sit for him; perhaps he was frightened of us. I cannot find myself there at all. Where is my sharp nose and thin mouth? Our faces are quite identical, and we are all as frilled and furbelowed as angels on a cloud.'

'That must be Elizabeth Sheridan, playing the lyre. I suppose Samuel means to get on and advance his career by flattering us all.'

'Stuff and nonsense!'

But I *was* flattered. I returned many times to gaze at that painting. At last I belonged in London and dared to feel safe. How foolish.

# 11

─────────────

Lord Gordon was the populist head of the Protestant Association. He made outrageous claims, such as that there were twenty thousand Jesuits hiding in tunnels under the River Thames, waiting for orders from Rome to rise up and attack London. Naturally the mob – always eager to hate foreigners – believed him. When Parliament passed a bill to reduce discrimination against Catholics, Lord Gordon stirred up a rabble to hunt us down like rats.

Joshua knew there was trouble brewing but decided to defy the mob by holding a party at his house in Leicester Fields. All was gay and delightful – until we heard violent shouts and huzzahs outside. Rushing to the windows, we saw a crowd of villains breaking into the house of Joshua's neighbour, Sir George Savile, who had introduced the Catholic Relief bill. Vile fellows they were, dirty and ragged, armed with axes, clubs and iron bars. I knew Savile – he was the kindest of men. We feared for his life as we watched them sack his house. They broke his windows and piled up all his furniture in the middle of the square. Then they forced Sir George's servant to bring a candle to set light to it. The bonfire they would like to toss me on, thought I, hiding behind the philosophical bulk of Johnson and Joshua. Joshua, who often amused himself by going to public executions, prided himself on being imperturbable, a marble statue representing classical virtues.

In the carriage going home that night, Zucchi and I were not so calm. We saw that most of the houses had a candle burning in the window – a kind of insurance policy against the rage of the mob – and blue ribbons hanging out as evidence of their staunch Protestantism.

'Wake up, daughter! The mob is coming for us!' My father hammered with his fists on our bedroom door early the next morning. I was shocked by the fear in his voice.

'Hide the crucifixes and your mother's rosary. Quick, girl! Cover up that religious painting on your easel!'

Our maid, a young Irish girl called Bridie who was also a Catholic, came back from market with a knot of blue ribbons pinned to her bonnet.

'O Madam, don't go out today! Last night there was looting and burning all over London. Bernie the fishmonger says the mob broke into Newgate, smashed the gates, set all the prisoners free and set fire to the prison. There's houses and shops boarded up all along Old Compton Street. I was able to find this bit of fish and some turnips and a stale loaf of bread, and then a gang of low, dirty fellows waving axes grabbed me. They said they'd slash me to pieces if I didn't wear Lord Gordon's blue cockade. O please don't make me go out again! I shall be murdered for certain sure.'

Bridie was a sensible girl, not given to hysterics. I sat her down with a dish of tea and secured the shutters on all our windows. I could see "No Popery" chalked in huge letters on the front door of a neighbouring house and a large sign that read "This House True Protestant" affixed to the ground floor window of another house in our square.

That was the last I saw of the outside world for days. We could not even go out to buy a newspaper and nobody visited us. Suddenly we were outcasts – figures of hate – ashamed of the one thing we could not change, the very religion we were born into. Even I could not work under such conditions. Papa already had a weak heart; he lay prostrated on the sofa in the drawing room and demanded querulously, 'Well? Have they broken into our house yet? Is the revolution come to Golden Square?'

Bridie and I were busy in the kitchen, trying to turn our meagre food into meals for four people. Living as we did in the middle of Soho, surrounded by shops, we had never thought to lay in supplies. Now we were reduced to eating gruel for breakfast and mousetrap cheese for dinner. My Zucchi remained calm and did not complain. There was no traffic in the streets.

An ominous silence was broken by a roar like a thousand hungry lions. The roar retreated – then came nearer. Zucchi and I looked at each other and held hands. We wondered how it would feel to be torn to pieces.

That evening we knelt to pray.

'But what are we praying for?' asked Zucchi in his practical way.

'That God may preserve us,' said I.

''Tis God has got us into this pickle.'

'SSSH!'

Then Bridie and I prayed, and I felt stronger. My father remained on his sofa with his eyes shut, hands folded like an effigy. Tears came to my eyes as I thought: the worry of all this will kill him.

We had to sit out the long, June night. We dared not light a candle in case the mob saw it and attacked our house. Bridie set up her bed in the kitchen and my father drifted in and out of the sleep of old age. Zucchi could sleep through an earthquake, but I was ever a light sleeper. All the energy I usually poured into my work fizzed and crackled as I strode around our dark house. At any minute now, the mob would come to burn down our house – my work – the money I'd saved – the furniture and clothes I'd worked so hard for. We would be left standing in the street in our nightclothes – no, for surely the mob would toss us onto their bonfire.

Shadows, creaks, snores, distant screams, shouts, huzzahs, a dog barking. Creeping to a window, I opened the shutters an inch to peer out. Somewhere over there I could see a fire glow like blood against the night sky – then another – yet another. All London was burning and we, as Catholics and foreigners, were to feed the flames.

After three days we had no crumb of food left in the house, so Bridie ventured out into the streets again, wearing a blue cockade and a "No Popery" sign pinned to her bonnet. As soon as she left the house I felt ashamed of my cowardice for letting her go alone and sat trembling on the sofa, listening to Papa's prophecies of doom.

'We shall lose everything! They will burn down Somerset House and all your work. Then they'll come to get us here, drag us from our beds, loot and burn everything we have. We should have stayed in Rome, where everybody is a Catholic – or with our kinsfolk in the Bregenz Woods where such things do not happen. O why did you force me to come to London?'

I wanted to slap him and point out that I had supported him in comfort for many years and that it was he who insisted on following me to London. But I bit my tongue, for he was old and ill. Even Zucchi was pale. He squeezed my hand and whispered, 'We will escape from these barbarians. Then, with talent and hard work, we shall make a new life for ourselves.'

The hours when Bridie was gone were very long. Then, at last, we heard her voice, heaved away all the furniture we had barricaded against the front door and embraced her. She brought an odd selection of maggoty beef, mouldy potatoes, stale bread and wild stories.

'Sweet Jesus, the things I've heard! They say the mob sacked a distillery on Holborn Hill that's owned by a Catholic fellow. The streets ran with spirits and the low brutes drank it from the gutters. I had to hammer on the doors of the shops to let me in, for the poor wretches expect the villains here at any minute, looting and burning. No carriage is safe in the streets. There are windows smashed – they've attacked the Bank of England and burned down the Sardinian Chapel. Are them Sardines not Eyeties like you, Mr Zucchi?'

That night was the most terrifying of all. At sunset we heard a pattering of feet outside – it became a rumble – then a storm of shouting and drunken singing and screams. 'Burn the Papists!' 'That's their bloody devil-worshipping house!'

We were quite sure they had come for us. The four of us sat huddled together in my drawing room in silence. There was the sound of smashing wood and glass – crazed laughter – sparks appeared in the cracks between the shutters. We crept upstairs, thinking to flee across the roofs rather than be roasted alive. But Papa could hardly climb the stairs, let alone go mountaineering across the rooftops. I knelt on the top stair and prayed while my father quivered beside me.

Zucchi lifted the skylight to look out. Said I, clasping his feet, 'No! They'll see your head silhouetted and shoot – they may have firearms. O my darling, don't leave me!'

'They are not outside our house but swarming all over Count Haslang's house and chapel. I can see their torches – listen!'

We heard screams, drunken laughter and song. 'When they've destroyed everything there, they will come here. O why did you ever make me live in this savage country?' wailed my father.

All night we waited for them. Papa fainted with terror and had to be carried to his bed. We others stayed at the top of the house, ready to flee when the mob broke in. I gathered the few belongings I would be able to carry over the rooftops – some money, jewellery, and a small painting that I could sell.

If we did not break our necks, perhaps we could start a new life somewhere else.

'We'll leave London, go to Venice,' I whispered to Zucchi.

Towards dawn we heard pistol shots.Zucchi peered out again and reported, 'The soldiers have come at last! They are arresting the villains who are too drunk to resist. I think we are safe now.'

But I never felt safe again in London. All the years of success, kindness and politesse were wiped out by those days of fear. We began to make our preparations to leave for Italy.

Eventually we pieced together the events of that terrible week. My clever friend, Lord Mansfield, was a victim of the mob. They smashed the windows of his coach and destroyed his house in Bloomsbury because he had recently passed lenient judgment on a Catholic priest. Then they forced Lady Mansfield to come out of her house, bringing her jewels and one hundred guineas. They set fire to all the papers and books in his study. I heard that a man and a woman – dead drunk – lay down on his best bed and were burned alive with the house. Then the rioters moved on to Kenwood, Mansfield's country house, intending to burn it too (with my work within). They stopped to drink at the nearby Spaniards Inn, where the landlord kept them drinking until soldiers arrived.

Many rioters were shot or hanged and Lord Gordon himself was imprisoned. Later, I heard, he converted to the Jewish faith. Was he a madman? It did not reassure me to know that a lunatic could turn London upside down. My adopted city looked as if it had been sacked by an army. So many houses were smouldering or demolished – the very sun was black from all the smoke, as if Vesuvius had erupted in the midst of London.

All that summer, Rome came to me in dreams that lingered behind my eyes when I woke up: the Palatino at sunset – the view over the city from the top of the Spanish Steps (the panorama that I own now) – the quiet lanes of the Aventino. The beauty in store for us was balm to my anguished heart. After fifteen years, London seemed bigger and more incomprehensible than ever, while Rome shrank to become more knowable. A city where I will be welcomed, thought I, small enough to walk across in a few hours. I shall know everybody I want to know, and I shall be able to sell my religious and historical paintings, not just tedious portraits. We can live more cheaply there – Zucchi and Papa will no longer suffer from constant sore throats and coughs due to London's damp, miserable climate.

Best of all, we shall be safe.

# PART THREE

# ITALY

# 12

---

Venice is not as ancient as Rome, but she guards her secrets more jealously. It was not until I returned there with Zucchi that I began to understand Venice. You soon forget the rest of the world there, living inside a mother-of-pearl horizon, breathing shimmering, watery air. As we approached the enchanted isle from Mestre in a fleet of black gondolas, my new husband put his arms around me and murmured the names of the buildings that floated toward us in the dazzling light. I saw that this sternly practical man had another, more lyrical, side to him, and I was glad of it.

Once, Zucchi's family had had gondolas waiting at the door of their palazzo and servants in livery. But now they lived in a few rooms of their mortgaged palazzo with lodgers in all the others. They were a clever, shabby family of artists and engravers, very pleased to welcome the rich couple from England. My husband felt rejuvenated by his native city. How he delighted in showing me her hidden beauties. We two, newly married, walked around in a fog of joy. It was the honeymoon we had both been working too hard to enjoy before; we even talked of spending the rest of our lives in Venice.

We moved to a house just north of St Mark's with my father and his sister, my kind aunt, who crossed the Alps from Austria to be with us. My cousin Rosa, who had married the architect Giuseppe Bonomi and had a little boy, was also to live with us. Venice was much cheaper than London; we talked of buying a magnificent palazzo on the Grand Canal that would be my studio and gallery, as well as a salon where we could entertain our many friends.

Together, Zucchi and I revisited the Tintorettos in the Scuola Grande di San Rocco, almost as black as the gondolas outside but dazzling in their ambition. Zucchi loved Veronese's enormous, richly coloured crowd scenes and revered him because when he was summoned by the Inquisition he defended his independence, saying, 'We painters take the same liberties as poets and madmen.' I admired Tiepolo's frescoes with their spirit and fire, not yet blackened by time like the older paintings, but modern and full of light. I believed I would never tire of Venice's riches as I sat for hours in San Marco on an old, red marble bench, contemplating the deeply worn malachite and porphyry floor, gazing at the Byzantine mosaics and gems set in the walls. At concerts we listened to the music of Vivaldi and Gabrieli; at La Fenice we heard operas by Monteverdi. There was art and music and all the people I loved most – I believed I could live in Venice forever.

Zucchi explained his city to me: the strange mixture of formality and freedom, the ingenious ways Venetians evaded the inflexible code that regulated public life. One night he took me to a casino, a pleasure house owned by a rich patron who had just commissioned a portrait from me. When we stepped from our gondola onto the jetty, the building looked quite plain from the outside. He knocked three times at the unmarked door – a face appeared at a peephole – my husband whispered our names and we were admitted to one of the most luxurious interiors I have ever seen. Gaudy chandeliers illuminated painted rooms furnished with velvet couches and oriental rugs, where elegant, masked people drank and gambled wildly. Zucchi and I were too frugal to risk our hard-earned money but we watched, fascinated.

'That man weeping over there is descended from a Byzantine Emperor. He has just lost all his estates and his wife's jewellery.'

'What will they do if the police come?'

'There's a back entrance leading to a different canal where gondolas wait, just in case.'

Everybody wanted to meet me. The Tsarevitch Paul and his wife bought three paintings, including my *Leonardo da Vinci Expiring in the Arms of Francis I*. The Empress Catherine's agent ordered more work from me. All day I worked in my new studio and every night we were invited to dinners and salons. Thought I, at last I can make money from my historical paintings.

We two longed for peace alone together. One misty November afternoon, we had ourselves rowed across the lagoon to Torcello. My Zucchi laid on a handsome gondolier in a white shirt who improvised a tune to a poem by Tasso. As we lay back together on velvet cushions and listened, his chanting was heard by another boatman across the lagoon, who joined in. We floated on music through a liquid universe of silver and gold... I think I was never so happy. There were black gondolas that looked as if they might fly – barges carrying food – red boats taking bodies to be buried. I felt that I could never tire of such floating beauty. Torcello embraced us in green silence as we stood on the grassy campo in front of the tiny, ruined church that was once the Cathedral of the little city that gave birth to Venice.

Christmas passed in feasts with Zucchi's enormous family, in the pleasure of churchgoing in a Catholic country where I did not have to hide my religion. The city wore a dusting of snow on her lovely face. I looked forward to knowing her in every season and mood. The bells that rang in a hundred churches to celebrate the birth of Christ seemed to be telling me, 'you are welcome here'. In my surprising happiness as an elderly bride, I wanted only to be alone with my Zucchi.

I was so busy that I barely registered Papa's illness. On January the eleventh he died of influenza – he who had seemed as immortal as this city. With his strictness and interference and loving criticism of all I did – he could not die – yet he did. One of the red boats carried us with his body to the ancient burial ground near the Zucchis' parish church. As my black veil flapped in the icy wind, I finally believed in Papa's death. Zucchi gripped my arm as if afraid I would jump into the lagoon – in fact, I hardly knew what I was doing or who I was without my father.

Less than a month later my dear aunt died. The sorrow in my soul for the loss of such a beloved father and aunt has barely lessened, if at all. It is a wound in my heart which will never heal as long as I live.

I had masses said for them both as Carnival raged around us. Venice showed me again her cruel, melancholy face, a grotesque, rotting whore who partied night and day and cared not the snuff of a candle that my eyes were swelled with crying. Patrons flocked to order my work – I was elected to the Venice Accademia. But I could not stay in the city that had killed my father. My husband and I bought this jewel of a house in Rome, and just when we believed our future lay there, the Queen of Naples beckoned.

# 13

---

What a dance she led me, though at first I imagined I was leading her and was flattered by the commission to paint the royal family. After all my years in grey London, Naples was a shout of colour and joy. Such a beautiful city – far bigger than Rome – opening up to the sea as if the earth could not contain all her vitality. Neapolitans sang, laughed, robbed and did not seem to care a fig that they were desperately poor. Slums jostled palaces and pastel-coloured houses sparkled between sea and sky. Zucchi and I bought majolica pottery and inlaid marble for our house in Rome and I moved my harpsichord to Naples, believing I could happily spend my life between these two cities. All that year I was grieving for Papa, but amongst such brilliant colours my mind could not wear mourning for long. Bright ships filled the bay and Vesuvius introduced the note of melancholy that perfected the scene. Wherever you walked you fell over landscape artists at their easels.

I, however, have always wanted people in my scenery, and Queen Maria Carolina is powerful enough to fill any canvas. Not that she is fat. Despite countless pregnancies, her scheming mind has kept her muscles firm. They were a remarkably ugly family – an unappetising cocktail of Habsburg chins and Bourbon noses. Her husband Ferdinand looked and behaved like an overgrown ass and is known as *il re nasone*, or King Big Nose. That commission was my largest and most difficult painting. I had to make a perfect family of them – to preserve my flattery in syrup. It was almost impossible to persuade the King to sit at all. In my painting he stands reluctantly behind his wife, impatient to be off hunting or fishing. Our sittings were interrupted by his infantile giggles as he released rats and mice from cages and hunted them all over the marble floors of the palace.

My painting was to serve as an advertisement for the charms of the two older princesses – I forget their names – they're both Maria Something. One plays the harp to demonstrate her soulfulness while the other sits with a baby prince on her lap to show she is good childbearing material. Poor little Prince Joseph was dying and had to be left out of my final portrait. The children were amusing and loved their dogs, which I included in an attempt to warm my canvas.

Everybody in the palace was terrified of the Queen, who tried to impose her Austrian efficiency on the easygoing Neapolitans. Whenever she was angry (every day) children and maids fled in tears. Despising her boorish husband, she grasped the reins of power he was too childlike to hang on to. Her favourite – many say her lover – was Captain John Acton. And to my surprise, she took a fancy to me.

'You and I, Angelica, work day and night. These lazy Neapolitans with their *dolce fa niente*! Thank God I can speak to you in German, a civilised language. The Spanish influence here in the South has been a disaster. I am determined to introduce some British common sense and pragmatism here – some Austrian discipline.'

I did not tell her that she was fighting a doomed battle. She had a good brain but was very inflexible. Naturally, I did not point out that I am not really Austrian at all – I speak English and Italian more fluently than German. Since her husband could hardly even speak Italian – sliding into the contorted vowels of Neapolitan dialect – the Queen prized my company. During our sittings she barked her orders at her children, servants and dogs. Once they were all obedient, trembling whenever her glance fell on them, she turned to me with a beam.

'There! Peace at last! You know, Angelica, a family is very much like a nation. There must be rules, goals, incessant watchfulness. My mother used to say "a monarch never sleeps. I wish to meet my death awake." She suffered from insomnia just as I do.'

She persisted in the charade that the Holy Roman Empress Maria Theresa and my father, an itinerant painter, both of whom had recently died, were similar, and that we two, as grieving daughters, had much in common. I thought this absurd. Only now do I wonder if she was lonely and actually sincere in her protestations of friendship.

'You and I, Angelica, both had remarkable parents. Mama wrote long letters of advice to all of us – thirteen children scattered all over Europe. All pawns in her chess game. She only married me to this idiotic Ferdinand because my older sister died of the smallpox.'

I looked at the two princesses who sat beside her, staring down at their embroidery, but I could not catch any sign of embarrassment at their mother's indiscretions. The Queen's eyes filled and she sniffed. I wished it was permitted to show her like this, as an ordinary woman with human feelings – but of course nobody would pay for such a portrait.

'I shall miss being scolded by Mama. She told me off for my political activities and wrote to my silly Ferdinand to chide him for being so lazy and disorganised. She told us girls that had she not been almost always pregnant, she would have gone into battle herself. When my darling sister Maria Antonia did not conceive a child for seven years after her marriage, Mama wrote constantly to tell her she was frivolous and undutiful. Of course, my beautiful sister could not bear to consummate her marriage with that clownish Dauphin. She and I were both married off to Bourbon coxcombs when we were very young girls.'

Again I glanced at the princesses, whose facial muscles did not move. Perhaps royal children are trained in the art of being waxworks.

'Yet she and my papa married for love. She tyrannised him but adored him. When he died, she was devastated and spent the rest of her life in mourning for him. She painted her rooms black and lost all interest in life.'

A brief chuckle invited me to agree that it would be absurd for her to mourn her husband. I said little. Friendships with the great are never equal.

She insisted that Zucchi and I should dine with them. 'Just a little intimate family supper, nothing formal.'

We were very glad that we wore our grandest clothes, for the Queen's idea of littleness was not ours. Including servants, there were forty people in the room, and miles of polished mahogany accentuated the distance between the King and Queen. Zucchi attempted valiantly to make sensible conversation with the

King and tried not to stare when Ferdinand ate with his fingers. But my Zucchi knew nothing about hunting and his Venetian accent was almost incomprehensible to the King who, I remember, played an infantile practical joke on the butler, tripping him up with his foot so that he spilt the wine. The Queen was in a bad mood; she shouted at the servants because the soup was not hot enough and the ices were too sweet. I hardly opened my mouth, staring out of the window of the magnificent dining room. Through the trees the bay smouldered and glowed in the sunset.

Back at our rooms in the Hotel Reale, Zucchi and I embraced. 'I'm very glad we are made of common clay and do not have to marry people we detest,' said he. Lying there safe in his arms, I felt content with our life.

My father taught me to be submissive to all my royal and aristocratic patrons, but Zucchi was not so respectful. In Naples he collected pamphlets and we laughed together at the caricatures of the Queen. She was accused of being an Amazon and a Messalina from the North, and the King was portrayed as a drivelling idiot of a puppet, controlled by the half-naked figures of the Queen and Acton, who caressed each other over his head. We laughed – yet we were very careful to burn these seditious lampoons as soon as we had seen them, for we knew the Queen had secret police all over Naples who reported back to her daily.

The Queen was one who had to own what she loved and, for a brief dangerous time, she loved me. At the end of one of our sittings I said, 'Tomorrow I must return to Rome to supervise the repairs to our house there.'

'Nonsense! You have no need to live in some shabby little house. You are a great artist, Angelica. Besides, Rome is unhealthy – you may die of malaria.' Her face reddened as it always did when she was thwarted. 'Come! I have something to show you.'

I followed as she strode imperiously through the palace and demanded her carriage. 'Where are we going, Your Majesty?'

She ignored my questions. Her rudeness annoyed me so much that I almost made my excuses and ran back home. Almost – but a queen is a queen.

We galloped through the narrow streets of Naples in her golden carriage. Even her horses were cruel, trained to crush all opposition. Beggars, ragamuffins and market women leapt out of her way or were kicked.

'This filthy city – dunghills everywhere. Look at them pouring out of their hovels like vermin. Men lounging around on the streets in the middle of the afternoon. Lazy pigs!'

I saw richly coloured beauty; she saw only moral failings. By the time we reached her Palazzo Francavilla I was ready to open the door of the carriage and jump out, for she was in such a violent pet that I could hardly breathe.

We stopped outside the elegant palace, which was that shade of rose I have always loved: deep and warm and mellow. Unlike the palace at Caserta, which has over a thousand rooms, the Palazzo Francavilla is built on a domestic scale – for people, not for show. Clucking with impatience, the Queen shooed me into the building. Servants jumped to attention, frightened by her sudden appearance. She led me up the marble staircase.

'Don't dawdle! You see what I can do for you?'

She marched me into a suite of rooms with inlaid marble floors and walls painted with frescoes of vines and fountains. Large windows overlooked the bay and there was a fine terrace planted with olive, orange and lemon trees in terracotta pots. At the end of the terrace a flight of marble steps led down to terraced gardens, where statues of nymphs and satyrs overlooked the sea.

'There! Your apartment. You can move in whenever you like. This large salon can be your studio. If you don't like the furnishings you can change them – a carriage will be at your disposal. With my patronage you will soon be the foremost painter in Naples. *My* genius.'

Your creature, thought I, and my knees went knicky-knocky as I wondered how to extricate myself from her stifling goodwill. The apartment was delightful. A few years earlier, with my father bowing and scraping beside me and less money behind me, I would have gratefully accepted. But now I had Zucchi – savings – a magnificent house in Rome at the top of the Spanish Steps waiting for me.

So, I rejected Arcadia. Yet in my painting I set the royal family there, in lovely parkland like the gardens of the Palazzo Francavilla. Then the Queen commissioned a portrait of herself alone, and when I went to make the preparatory drawings, she made her displeasure very clear. 'A foolish decision. You will regret it! I am never wrong. That house of yours in Rome belonged to Mengs – you know I made his career? He died there. It is an unlucky house and you will not be happy there.'

In fact, Zucchi and I were both healthier and happier here in Rome than in Naples. We loved – I still love – this jewel of a house. The Queen offered me pensions – a larger apartment – a well-paid post as the Princesses's drawing teacher – more commissions. But, thank the Lord, my circumstances allowed me to preserve my independence.

At last I finished that difficult painting that is imbued with the contrary spirit of the Queen. My paintbrush seemed to rebel against the lies I was telling the canvas. I delivered it myself to the palace, very nervous as I unrolled the canvas in the throne room, watched by the entire royal family.

'Charming!' said the Queen.

'I like the dogs,' said the King.

The princes and princesses were also contented – as well they might have been, considering the way I had improved upon their reality. I was paid over four thousand Neapolitan ducats and the Queen also gave me an exquisite jewelled cross with her initials in diamonds, surrounded by twelve bigger diamonds. I must remember to hide it from the French when they invade.

She is a most extraordinary woman. Nelson adores her – Napoleon detests her – she is not a woman one can be indifferent to. Wars and revolutions cannot kill her. Although I have avoided her for years, I hear many stories about her. In Naples now the people hate her; they say her friendship with Emma Hamilton was an unnatural passion, and her secret police still tyrannise the city. Since her beloved sister, the Queen of France, was murdered, Maria Carolina has changed, and her caprices have become more vicious.

Six years back, she and the King fled to Palermo when the French seized Naples and gave it one of their ridiculous names: the Parthenopean Republic – named for the siren who drowned herself when Odysseus would not be seduced by her singing. In mythology, her body was washed up at the place that became Naples. It is a very long name for something that lasted six months.

Then the King and Queen returned to Naples. She vowed to revenge the death of her beloved sister Marie Antoinette, and although there was a peace agreement, the Queen violated it. All those who supported the Republic were persecuted and massacred; any man who had cut his hair short and wore plain, modern clothes was pursued by the mob as a Jacobin. Men started to wear fake pigtails – but the mob pulled them to see if they were real hair and, if they came off, the poor fellows were murdered just the same. I have heard that the lovely Emma showed a most unlovely side of her character. She had herself rowed out to sea to gloat over the hanged body of Caracciolo, a passionate Republican sentenced by Nelson to be hanged from his own ship. So many terrible stories! Heads kicked around the streets of Naples as footballs or waved around on pikes – human flesh roasted alive and eaten – women forced to pose naked as Liberty and then raped by gangs. Is this what we can look forward to here in Rome?

Much as I detest the French, there are many good people who support their cause. Revolution – counter revolution – executions – confusion – civil war – a reign of terror. What times we live in! Captain Acton is Lord Acton now. Nelson is also become a Lord – Romans call me Contessa, although I am not. How we all acquire titles these days, like actors trying on masks. The King and Queen have regained the throne of Naples, but it is soaked in blood.

# 14

---

I never shall be contented in one place. When I lived in London, Rome was always in my thoughts – her fountains, her warmth and colour, her miraculous golden light. Now it is Naples that lives behind my eyes. I have no energy to go there, but often travel there in memory, to walk beside the sea again and glory in the sweep of that great bay, to return to a shattered mosaic that exists now only in my mind. I can see Emma and her gentle old knight – dead now. I hope she did not break his tender heart when she drew them into that strange and notorious triangle between she, her husband and Nelson.

Dear Cornelia writes me from London that my old friend Ben West sat next to Nelson at dinner in London. The Hero of the Nile asked why Ben had painted no more pictures like *The Death of Wolfe*. Says Ben: 'Because, my lord, there are no more subjects.'

'Damn it, I didn't think of that.'

'But, my lord, I fear your intrepidity may yet furnish me with such another scene and, if it should, I shall certainly avail myself of it.'

'Will you, Mr West? Then I hope I shall die in the next battle.'

Cornelia writes that Emma Hamilton is quite plump now and something of a tosspot. She sits next to Nelson and cuts up his meat for him, for he has but one arm, having lost the other to the surgeon's knife at Tenerife. There are whispers that he and Emma have a secret lovechild. Cornelia believes that Nelson will rout Napoleon, but I have no such faith. That ogre will devour all Europe and his appalling relations will rule over us all.

Is it possible that delicious nymph has run to fat? When first I met her in Sir William Hamilton's house in Naples, she was Mrs Emma Hart, twenty-one years old and accompanied by her mother, Mrs Cadogan. I have a nose for ambitious parents, having been pushed and pulled by my own papa, and saw at once that the beautiful girl was controlled by her silent smiling mama. I never did discover who Mr Hart and Mr Cadogan were.

Emma's fame had spread to Italy long before she arrived here. Her lover, Greville, had her painted a hundred times and poor Romney was obsessed by her. He painted her again and again, in a straw hat and as Circe. Joshua, who despised Romney, went straight to the point and painted her as a bacchante.

'O Angelica, I'm so glad you've come,' she said. 'All the men are after me to paint me; all the artists come from Rome, but I want to see what a woman makes of me.' Emma strode forward to take my hand and I saw that hers were red and worn. But the rest of her! Never have I seen such beauty combined with such energy and eros.

'I'm delighted to meet you, Mrs Hart, but I'm afraid I am only in Naples for a few days. I cannot take on any more commissions just now.'

Behind Emma, her mother embroidered flowers, watching us silently. Sir William stared at Emma as she leaned against a priceless Greek vase.

'Don't be afeared, Sir William. I'll not crack your jug.'

He laughed nervously in that silly English way, like a horse whinnying. 'My dear young lady, my house is your house. How graceful you are!'

I overheard other guests at the Palazzo Sessa sneering at the vulgarity of Emma and her mother.

'She is a great beauty – until she opens her mouth and becomes a dairymaid again.'

'As for the mother, they say she was married to a blacksmith.'

I liked Emma for her directness and understood why Romney, who also grew up in poverty, adored her. *Femmes fatales* do not usually like their own sex, but Emma was determined to confide in me. One evening after dinner, when her mother had gone to bed and the other guests were playing cards, she pursued me onto the terrace. All the glory of the Bay of Naples was spread out below us in the velvety moonlight.

She took my arm and whispered desperately, 'It's all very fine here, but I want my Charlie. He packed me off here to his uncle. Ma says it's for my own good; she says Sir William will look after us. She says Charlie will come for me when he's had his holiday – he's in Scotland on business, you know – and fetch me back. But we've been apart ever so long, and he doesn't write. O Angelica! You know London, you know life. Do you think Charlie still loves me?'

I made soothing noises, said I had a headache and went to bed. I could not bear to tell her the story circulating in Rome and Naples – that Charles Greville had tired of Emma and was planning to marry an heiress. He had passed Emma on to his rich Uncle William who, recently widowed, wanted to add a living statue to his remarkable collection. He was having Emma taught Italian, French and singing.

Goethe came back from Naples fascinated by Emma and could not stop talking about her. 'Those Attitudes of hers! She is a great actress, without words. Who needs words? Her beautiful, dark eyes can express anything. Old Hamilton has actually made a gilded frame for his so-called ward. In her, Angelica, he has found all the antiques, all the profiles of the Sicilian coins. Even the Apollo Belvedere.'

'But what does she actually *do*?'

'She stands against this black background in dresses of various colours to imitate the paintings of Pompeii. She delights us all by striking the poses of famous figures from religion and mythology. Hamilton has had a Greek costume made for her, which becomes her extremely. She lets down her beautiful hair and, with just a few shawls, gives so much variety to her poses, gestures, expressions that – I could hardly believe my eyes – I saw what thousands of artists would have liked to express: a Sibyl, a Niobe, a Bacchante. All realised before me in movements and surprising transformations – standing, kneeling, sitting, reclining, serious, sad, playful, ecstatic, contrite, alluring, threatening, anxious. One pose follows another without a break.'

I wanted to scream with jealousy but, instead, I went to Naples to see Emma's Attitudes for myself. I was so impressed that at the end of her performance I kissed her hand again and again. We were all weeping, for her Attitudes really were great art and had the power to go straight to one's heart. Emma and Vesuvius – the two wonders of Naples everybody wanted to see.

Even the Queen of Naples, that formidable Maria Carolina who had tried to buy me, made an intimate of her.

When I finally did paint Emma, she was passing through Rome on her way to England, to marry her besotted old knight and become Lady Hamilton. Her eyes and jewels glittered with a hardness that was not there when she was younger. Mrs Cadogan sat quietly in a corner of my studio embroidering – her daughter's fate, perhaps. I asked Emma if she would like to read aloud to me while I worked, but she flung the book of Petrarch's sonnets onto the floor. I congratulated her on her engagement.

'Aye, I've not done badly.'

'You have dazzled the world. You look radiant; you must be very happy.'

'Must I? Do you remember a certain conversation we had on the terrace of our house in Naples?'

'Of course.'

'Well – Ma will tell me off later, but I must talk to someone about it or I shall burst.' Mrs Cadogan's smile became even more opaque. 'Charlie jilted me. He sold me on to poor old Sir Billy like a bloody slave girl to pay off his debts. He used me very harshly, Angelica. But I can bear malice. I hate the bastard now! I hope he chokes on his heiress's millions and all their children die of the pox.'

She shed a few angry tears, but I could not see her as a tragic figure. 'Well, what are you going to do me as? One of your goddesses? Lizzie Le Brun had me as Ariadne in all but my birthday suit.'

'I never insult the dignity of my sitters by painting them naked.'

I painted her as Thalia, the Muse of Comedy, as a performer just about to lift a curtain and appear to her admiring public. She holds up a smiling mask and on her belt there is a cameo portrait of Sir William. Soon, thought I, that mask will become her face. I hope old Sir William enjoyed a few contented years with his muse before she let Admiral Nelson board her. What power Emma had – has? Beauty is just as much of a talent as painting or music. To have it – to know how to use it – to train it as the mysterious Mrs Cadogan trained her daughter – that is an art. The society ladies who despise Emma cannot hold a candle to her. I also have been celebrated, but O how hard I had to work for my pennyworth of fame! How careful I have had to be. Emma does not care a fig for decorum, yet all the men have been at her feet. Now she has become a kind of queen after breaking all the rules.

# 15

---

By the time I met Johann Wolfgang von Goethe twenty years after my disastrous first marriage, I was a model of decorum. Like plaster, my face was set in the correct emotions, my tongue was cautious, and the hot, salty spring behind my eyes had dried up. All that I have of Wolfgang now is the umbrella pine he planted in my garden, a few books, and this portrait I painted of him.

'That's not me at all!' he said. 'You make me look like a girl, a pretty boy with frills on my shirt and soft, weak eyes just about to shed tears!'

I was kind to him as I always am to my sitters. I disguised his smallpox scars and protuberant eyes, softened his big nose, strengthened his full lips and weak chin – generally, I idealised him. Beneath his soft, brown hair, he has close-set brown eyes that often look black as his mood changes and his pupils expand. His left eye is slightly bigger than his right. He must be in his fifties now, but for me he will always be young. Perhaps I did this portrait for myself; I will keep it here with me until I die. Wolfgang has as many sides to him as a prism, and the one I captured was his sentimental side. He frequently cried – indeed, he used to say, 'I despise people whose hearts and eyes are dry.' I kept my own tears to myself when he rejected my modest oval and raved about the enormous portrait his friend Tischbein did of him. I have not seen that painting of Tischbein's for years, but jealous knives etched it into my mind.

How handsome Wolfgang was – is? – in his soft, grey hat and the cashmere cloak I bought him when he complained of the cold. On the Via Appia he gazes out over the Campagna, where we often walked together among the ivy-covered ruins. He leans back on a tomb, wearing his timeless cloak like a toga, as relaxed as if he is lying on a chaise longue. In the background is the circular tomb of Caecilia Metella; behind him a marble relief – overgrown with ivy – depicts the famous recognition scene from Euripedes's *Iphigenia*. The young princess, who has escaped from being sacrificed to Artemis by her father Agamemnon, has been spirited by the goddess herself to Tauris, where she becomes a priestess in Artemis's temple. Having escaped sacrifice, it is now her duty to ritually murder any foreigners who land there. Her brother Orestes, who has murdered their mother, arrives in Taurus. Because they have not seen each other for twenty years and because Iphigenia has just dreamt of his death, at first they do not recognise each other. Then, beautifully, just as Iphigenia is about to sacrifice her brother, they do.

How often Wolfgang and I read this scene aloud together with tears and gales of emotion. Zucchi, that old cynic, laughed at us and called us a couple of schoolgirls. I was thrilled that Wolfgang was writing his own play, *Iphigenie auf Tauris*. I loved to talk to him about it and was so proud when it was performed here in my house.

'I shall never rest until I know that all my ideas are derived, not from hearsay or tradition, but from my real living contact with the things themselves. From my earliest youth, this has been my ambition and my torment.' When he spoke like this, I felt he swept me up into his world of high art. I showed him my Rome, the ruins and paintings and sculptures and stories that inspired him. But he could be cruel – I was devastated by his criticism of my portrait as he stared at Tischbein's.

'This is what a portrait should be: the landscape of my soul. I look like a man – a poet, a philosopher, contemplating the classical world,' he declaimed in his resonant baritone voice.

Wolfgang was so used to admiration and attention that he often spoke as if he was in public. Tischbein's portrait, far more ambitious than my own love offering, has flown away to become famous, while my own little pigeon has stayed in its nest.

Why should a man be ashamed and angry to show his feminine side? If I have been called a man in petticoats, I sometimes saw him as a woman in trousers – he could not forgive me for that. Yet we are all many people. When I look in the mirror or at my self-portraits on the wall opposite, I see a young girl, a muse, an Austrian peasant, a businessman, a wife, a widow, a hostess, a *grande dame*, a shy old woman... always a painter.

While grasping my presents, hospitality, love and all I could teach him about art with one hand, Wolfgang slapped me hard with the other. After I gave him a magnificent luncheon here, he asked to visit my studio and stared at my work in excruciating silence. Then, 'You are a remarkable artist, Angelica. For one of your sex.'

'You despise us?

'How can you say such a thing? You know how I adore women. But you are an undulist – your work seduces. It is soft and pleasant, but lacks character and significance, just like this portrait you've done of me.'

'I would remind you that every distinguished foreign visitor who comes to Rome begs to be painted by me.'

'Of course. You have so many commissions that one can't buy a pen stroke from you for gold dust. You're talented, clever, good, and have a delightful house. Nevertheless, your people have no bones. It's not your fault that women are not allowed to study anatomy.'

'As a matter of fact, when I was a young girl I sometimes used to dress as a boy to attend anatomy lectures in Florence.'

He laughed. 'Perhaps you should have continued the masquerade, like one of those faithful women who follow their lovers into the army. Angelo Kauffman.'

'Then you would not be able to patronise me.'

'Dear Angelica, it would be indecent to expose women to naked male models.'

'I suppose you think we marry and have children in total ignorance of human anatomy?'

Such arrogance, when his own drawings, which I tried to be kind about, were not as good as mine when I was ten years old! Today I am angry with him and glare at his portrait. 'You're as bad as Napoleon! Using people, always in need of courtiers, abandoning those who love you.' I hiss the words, but I would shout them if I did not fear to bring my maid Alba running.

'Rome,' said Wolfgang, 'is where I am completely happy.'

He seemed so relieved to have escaped from Weimar. Once, when we were discussing patriotism, he said, 'It's something frightful to be displayed someday by us Germans in the form of the crassest follies.'

Wolfgang said he loved the Romans for their easy manners, their indifference to rules and power. He adored our food and put on weight here, encouraged by me. *Mangia, mangia* – eat, eat – I played the indulgent mother (disguising my incestuous longings). When I saw how he feared marriage I persuaded myself: he will stay among us forever, pursuing other women but always returning to the loving security of my house.

So many women. There were constant letters from Charlotte in Weimar, which he read aloud to me with amused contempt. Then there was Faustina, a Roman girl of the people who shared his bed; Emma Hamilton, who he adored and who I tried to adore too, in nervous collusion; Maddalena, whose story nearly ended in tragedy – all of them many years younger than him, while the eight years between Wolfgang and me were an abyss I could never cross. My sweet Zucchi was in his sixties by then; he watched my infatuation with hooded eyes and Venetian detachment. I did not want to hurt him, and I do hope I did not. He had observed so many hopeless loves – I think my little comedy entertained him.

Wolfgang made his reputation with his novel *The Sorrows of Young Werther* – who shot himself for love, starting a fashion for suicide all over Europe. But Wolfgang himself never contemplated pulling the trigger. Again and again, I had to watch that pattern of him falling in love with a woman, then leaving her when she showed too much interest and indulging in histrionic remorse, all the while insisting that what he really wanted was *einsamkeit* – loneliness.

Maddalena Riggi was staying in Thomas Jenkins's magnificent villa at Castel Gandolfo. Maddalena, the sister of one of Thomas's master forgers, was a young girl from Milan with light brown hair, clear, delicate skin and deep blue eyes. It is one of the crueller jokes the gods play on us – you always know when your beloved is attracted to another woman.

Wolfgang, Zucchi and I were invited to dinner by Thomas. Wolfgang always had to dominate any gathering; he loved to tease and soon had the entire table in fits of laughter. The flirtation between Maddalena and Wolfgang was so obvious that I could not eat. It was an excellent meal I missed, for the fruits of banking and forgery are delicious. By the time our champagne ices were served, their two beautiful heads were so close together that the rest of the company could only exchange mocking smiles. I could see that it was the first time Maddalena had felt Cupid's dart, while Wolfgang was as scarred as San Sebastian. She was complaining about a woman's lot, a subject dear to Wolfgang's heart. He saw himself as a knight, galloping in to rescue women from prejudice and ignorance.

'We're not taught to write for fear we would write love letters. We are only taught to read our prayer books. Nobody would dream of teaching us foreign languages. I see the English newspapers here in Mr Jenkins's house and long to read them,' she said.

'Of course you must! I shall teach you English, my dear,' said Wolfgang.

They arranged to meet the following day. There were other meetings – I did not spy on him, but people began to gossip. Maddalena was *fidanzata* to an engraver called Volpato. Naturally, kind friends told him that his future wife was having intimate conversations and private lessons with a famous poet, so he broke off the engagement.

Wolfgang ran to me in terror. 'She has been sobbing and wailing all morning! She says I've ruined her life, that she is dishonoured. This Volpato fellow may appear at any moment to challenge me to a duel. I can't bear it, Angelica. Why do they always spoil it by getting so serious?'

'Because you make them fall in love with you. There is always a price to pay for such flirtations and this is a Catholic country. Virginity is a currency, like gold or *scudi*.'

Before I could lecture him any more on the subtleties of Italian morality, Wolfgang fled back to Rome, leaving me to comfort Maddalena. She came to stay with us in our little villa at Castel Gandolfo, where I had the agonising pleasure of listening to all her confidences.

She regarded me as her mother, her own having disowned her for her scandalous behaviour.

'O Signora – Contessa –'

'Please, call me Angelica.' It was not sensible to be formal when she lay sobbing in my arms. Zucchi, who disliked raw emotions, had gone to bed. Maddalena and I were on the sofa in our salon, with its beautiful views over Lake Albano. The summer day was fading like the romance that had broken her heart, and fireflies lit the terrace beyond the window.

'Everybody despises me! My parents, my *fidanzato*...'

'You can stay here with me until they all calm down.'

'Yet he did love me. I am not mad. He said I was his destiny.'

Wolfgang met his destiny at least once a month. 'I'm sure he was sincere.'

'He said I am the loveliest creature he has ever seen.'

'Of course you are.' Her delicate features and slanting, long-lashed eyes will be given to one of his romantic heroines.

'Now I'm ugly! I can't stop crying.'

'Cry as much as you want, my dear.'

My dress was wet from her tears, which made my own eyes brim with my old grief for Horn and my present one for Wolfgang... all hopeless love flows from the same pool. Clinging to my dignity – afraid of hurting Zucchi – I refused to let myself cry. I plumbed the depths of her terrible innocence.

'I'm so worried. I let him kiss me. It's a sin, isn't it?'

'You must not feel guilty.'

'But I might have a baby. That's what they said at my convent.'

'Babies don't come from kissing.' Trying not to laugh, I gently let her sink down into the cushions and went over to the window. The Pope, whose summer palace was visible in the moonlight, was to blame for this. Purity or ignorance? Wolfgang was always rude about the Vicar of Rome, but for good Catholics like me, his authority is supreme. I thought about the way religion demands too much of women – also about the world before Christianity. Arcadia still feels very close in that landscape of aqueducts, shepherds, oxen and mules. It was easy to see Wolfgang as a satyr or lecherous god who had swooped down to ruin the life of a mortal girl.

But Maddalena's life was not ruined. Ten years ago, I painted her – Signora Volpato, a substantial Milanese matron.

# 16

---

Alba tells me that Romans are determined to have their Carnival as usual next year. The French tried to turn our Roman Carnival into a *fête révolutionnaire*; they censored all the bawdy jokes and banned the ceremony of the lights. Since then, each year, the Romans' instinct for pleasure has revived Carnival a little, but Alba tells me it is not what it once was. People enjoy themselves more cautiously now, always fearing the arrival of Napoleon's army. But in those days, nearly twenty years ago, Carnival took over the whole city.

'Is it really as wild as they say?' Wolfgang asked one day when we had invited him to our house for luncheon. We sat on the terrace – I can hardly climb up there now – drinking our coffee and watching revellers in fancy dress in the Piazza di Spagna far below us, brilliantly coloured ants whirling to the faint music of drums, pipes and guitars.

'I have never been,' said I primly.

'I used to go, when I was young,' said Zucchi. He always spoke of the time before I knew him with a dreamy smile, and I did not interrogate him about his old loves.

'I've read that your modern Carnival descends from the Saturnalia, when masters became slaves and men dressed as women.' Wolfgang's handsome face shone with excitement. I imagined him going down to lose himself in that crowd, where he would dance with younger women and forget his German inhibitions.

'You should go and see for yourself,' said Zucchi tolerantly. 'This is the last night.'

We had drunk a lot of wine. I felt restless and could not bear to think of Wolfgang leaving me. 'You men have so much freedom,' said I bitterly. 'You can change constantly, from Weimar to Rome – from statesman to artist – you can even dress as a woman if you feel like it. But I must always be Angelica – respectable and staid.' Close to tears, I stood up and turned to run into the house.

'Where are you going, *carissima*?' asked Zucchi in surprise.

'Into my studio. To work and be dull and make money.'

'No!' Laughing, Zucchi and Wolfgang pulled me back to the dining table. Wolfgang's touch burned my arm; I could not take my eyes off him.

'You know, Wolfgang, when my wife was a young girl she often dressed as a boy. Her father, my dear old friend, told me it was the only way she could study anatomy,' said Zucchi.

Wolfgang was charmed by this idea. 'Really? How I would have adored you then.'

'You were about ten years old.'

'And now? Why don't you dress as a man and come down to Carnival with me? You will be quite invisible in the crowd.'

'But I'm old and fat.'

'You don't look a day over thirty-five.' Again, my eyes were locked onto his smiling ones.

It is only now that I realise my wise old husband saw it all. We must have been very drunk that afternoon. Zucchi dug out a suit of shabby, brown, velvet clothes and a couple of black velvet masks. They made me put the costume on and when I came out to display myself, they teased me and laughed.

'I shall call you Angelo,' says Wolfgang.

'My dear, I've always known that there is something masculine about you. How does it feel?'

'It feels wonderful not to have to wear a corset.'

What will the servants think? would be my first thought now. We had so many servants in those days – an Italian manservant, a cook, two maids, a coachman and a gardener. Alba was not yet with me, but those others must have tittered and gossiped. Memory has edited out everything – except Wolfgang's excitement and my own, as our practical joke became a delicious reality.

Said Zucchi, 'I shall stay here and rest.'

For months I had longed to be alone with Wolfgang. Yet now that the opportunity was upon me, I was afraid and clung to Zucchi's hand. 'Please come with us.'

'No, you young people go and enjoy yourselves.'

'What will your disguise be?' I asked Wolfgang.

'I shall wear only a mask. My attempt to disguise myself in Rome has been a dismal failure.' When Wolfgang first arrived here, he called himself Herr Muller and insisted he wished to live among us incognito as a student of art. A false name was necessary because his novel, *Young Werther*, had made him so embarrassingly famous. Even then, I noticed his fury if anyone failed to be impressed by his real identity – yes, I already knew how vain he was. *Young Werther* was banned by the Church which, of course, made Wolfgang even more of a hero to young people in Italy.

'Please come,' I said again, but Zucchi laughed and pushed me out of the door.

Then I stood with Wolfgang in our Via Sistina. My confessor passed us, bowed to Wolfgang and ignored me. Rome was a different city now that I was invisible in my dull suit. I felt younger – as young as Wolfgang, who took my arm and led me down the Spanish Steps. Masked figures rushed down to join the Carnival madness.

My thoughts were drowned by the joyful roar of music. A brass band playing love songs made my feet itch to dance. Drums reverberated and penny whistles squeaked; everybody was dancing laughing shouting. Clowns, Pulcinellas, Harlequins, bears, cats, unicorns, lions, devils, skeletons, a giant of a woman in a crinoline – all were masked. Some Romans were dressed as foreign artists – us – in long, black coats with enormous pencils. Others wore ghostly sheets and haunted with loud "whooos!". A wizard in a pointed hat hit passers-by with his wand and there were men dressed in elegant black and white as Quakers – the Romans' idea of Protestants. There were many versions of Pulcinello, who is so much more complex than his English cousin, Mr Punch. With his humpback, huge nose, potbelly and gangly legs, he personifies the bawdy anarchy of this Carnival crowd. I could see another Pulcinello with a large horn dangling from coloured strings between his thighs. Yet another was a *cornuto* or cuckold, with horns on his forehead and bells attached. When he stopped under couples' bedroom windows, he moved his horns in and out like a snail to mock them. Safe behind my mask, I could roar with laughter with the rest of them.

Everyone stared at a beautiful woman in a carriage who wore no mask. A coachman dressed as a woman with enormous breasts lifted his disreputable friends up into the aristocratic carriage he was driving. We watched a battle with cardboard daggers between two ghosts and three skeletons, the mock coronation of a crippled beggar, a man with a bird cage on his head who opened the door to release a brilliant yellow-and-green cloud of budgerigars, a pregnant nine-feet-tall "woman" who gave birth to a three-headed green monster. Children played all around, the rich ones in adorable costumes and the poor ones in their usual rags.

The familiar Corso also wore a mask, this one of confetti and flowers. All the palaces were decorated with carpets and tapestries, with brocades hanging out of the windows and from balconies. A long procession of carriages and carts, gay with flowers, blocked the street. Masked aristocrats leaned out of their coaches to throw sugar plums, sugared almonds, and flour bombs, popping guns into the crowd.

On every street corner, I noticed, hung a *corde*, the instrument of torture used by the *sbirri* or secret papal police, a reminder of the consequences of any theft or violence. All this apparent jollity was another mask, to disguise rigid control. The masks people wore were little masterpieces of wax or velvet or papier-maché. Some imitated ancient statues of Zeus or Minerva or Bacchus or the double face of Janus, while others sprouted cats' whiskers, elephants' trunks, crocodiles' jaws, Pulcinello's vast nose, Harlequin's melancholy face, cuckolds' horns or asses' ears. Men were dressed as women with yellow wigs, melon breasts and obscene gestures, while many women wore beards and breeches. They flaunted enormous cocks and carried switches made of rushes to tickle the men with. My own disguise seemed very feeble by comparison.

Just before dusk, people started to yell 'The Barbary race!' Wolfgang and I were pushed towards the Porta di Popolo. Pressed tight against him in the heaving, stinking crowd, I felt both fear and delight. I considered pretending to faint so that he would have to carry me up to his apartment nearby and then… but the moment passed.

Arm-in-arm we walked to the stand, where Wolfgang bribed our way to two seats high up above the little riderless horses. Each was covered in a white linen sheet hung with tinsel and brightly coloured ribbons. A troop of horsemen played fanfares on their trumpets as they strutted around the piazza, displaying the *palio* or prize: a piece of long, gold cloth attached to a painted pole like a flag. The shouting and arguing were deafening as the horses' grooms, in splendid liveries, lined them up at the obelisk that was to be the starting point. I saw that the terrified little creatures had spiked lead balls attached to their harnesses to make them run faster.

Then we heard a shot – and the barbary horses galloped off down the Corso, the street that took its name from this race. The horses had to run down the narrow space between the carriages and the screaming crowd. Fireworks – hysteria from the gamblers who had placed bets – all around us, people stood up to yell and swear. I felt only pity for the poor little horses who looked drugged and frightened as they raced chaotically through the frenzied crowd. A few minutes later, the horses arrived at the finishing line at Piazza Venezia. More pandemonium – triumphant music – screams of rage and jubilation. A wine-soaked Harlequin sitting beside us was jubilant because the horse he was backing had won the golden saddle cloth.

Then it was dark, and the atmosphere changed completely. It was still permitted to wear costumes, but masks were forbidden. All around us lamps and torches were lit as people stared at each other's naked faces. Behind us a band tuned up for one of the *festini*, public dances that went on until dawn. Harlequin rushed off to an elegant fancy-dress ball at the Teatro Aliberti. Because it was the last night of Carnival, the Corso was candlelit; paper lanterns appeared on the stand where we were sitting and on all the balconies around us. Carriages were illuminated and pedestrians carried lanterns on their heads or on poles. Thousands of voices roared, '*Si ammazzato chi non porta moccolo!*' – death to anyone who isn't carrying a light. The game is that you have to blow out the candle next to you. The noise and heat increased as a candle was thrust into my hand.

I sat there, staring into Wolfgang's passionate blue eyes. His skin was golden in the candlelight and his face wore its poetic look – that expression I captured in my portrait of him. He disliked my painting because he thought it made him look effeminate. On this night, when men could be women and women could be men, I knew only that this was a face I loved. I wanted to dance with him all night. He, who was never lost for words, stared back at me in silence while the hot wax dripped down onto my fingers.

Then someone blew out my candle. I was glad that Wolfgang could no longer see my wrinkles and my drab old clothes that made me look more like a middle-aged merchant than a fairy tale princess. He stood up. I clung to his arm and knew I would follow wherever he wanted to go – into the dance, or back to his apartment, or back to my sedate home. I put my hand on his arm and tried to sense the mood of this unpredictable man.

We moved together down the Corso through the screaming crowd. Now that it was dark, their joy became menacing – ghosts and skeletons jostled us. Looking up at Wolfgang's face, I saw a hard, wild expression I mistrusted. My grip on his arm tightened as I tried to lead him back home towards the Piazza di Spagna. But he broke away from me and turned down a narrow alley where I thought I saw him disappear into a house. A bordello? There are so many in Rome and during Carnival their business thrives.

Suddenly I was alone in the roaring, bellowing night. Candles, lanterns and braziers illuminated the frenzied crowd – but there was no sign of the one face I wanted. Bewildered, I tried to push through the pressing bodies. Was that him, that dark figure darting down one of the alleys off the Corso and disappearing into a building?

Without Wolfgang, the noise was hateful. Cruel laughter – stupid music – pressing, groping, stinking, bodies. My hat came off and my hair poured down. Without my mask, I feared I would be recognised and laughed at. I fought to escape their brutal jollity. All the narrow streets off the Corso were human traffic locks where drunks yelled and spewed and tried to kiss me. Stumbling, crying with humiliation, I slunk home.

My household was silent. I could not face Zucchi if he was still awake, so I went upstairs to the terrace where our adventure began. There were still lights down there and the muted roar of laughter and music. Despite the cold, I stayed up there until midnight struck on a hundred tinny bells all over the city. Carnival was over – all the lights were extinguished – the Church grasped the Romans again just as I gripped the balustrade of my solid terrace. Tomorrow, Shrove Tuesday, we would all go to church and then go home to eat meat for the last time before Lent. I shivered as I thought, he has rejected me, although nothing was said.

The next time I saw Wolfgang, we went together to the Vatican Museums. When I mentioned the Carnival he said, 'Where did you get to? I lost you in that disgusting mob of lunatics.'

'You didn't look disgusted. I thought you enjoyed it.'

'Not at all. There was no genuine merriment. It's like a very old joke that has been told too often.'

He was a German scholar again, cool and dry.

# 17

---

When Wolfgang left Rome, he gave me that plaster cast of the Juno Ludovisi over there in the corner of my studio. It was in his bedroom and at the end of each meeting he used to say, 'I must go home to my Juno.' I knew there was a flesh and blood Juno waiting for him, Faustina, the daughter of a Roman tavern-keeper. When Wolfgang returned to Weimar, he paid her off with four hundred scudi. He never felt guilty; he was in revolt against the strict Lutheranism of his youth and despised moral scruples.

There were other girls, too. 'Those little Italian minxes,' he said with a laugh. He admired curves and curly, black hair – blondes did not attract him, perhaps because they looked like German women. One day he and Zucchi made an appointment to see *The Erotic History of Venus*, the frescoes Raphael painted in Cardinal Bibbiena's bedroom. Then Wolfgang rushed down to Naples to see the salacious wall paintings that had just been discovered in Pompeii. A respectable matron like me is not supposed to know such things exist. Wolfgang liked to shock me. He used to go to the Sistine chapel with other artists to make watercolour copies of the frescoes. The custodian, if tipped, would let them in through the back door behind the altar and allow them to picnic there.

Said Wolfgang, 'Yesterday I snatched a noon nap on the Papal throne.'

'But that's blasphemous! Tell me you're joking.'

'No, really, I did. It's only a chair, after all, and I'm only an old Protestant Diogenes. Come with me to the Capitoline museum this evening.'

'I must work.'

'You work too hard, Angelica. That husband of yours is too fond of money.'

Together we visited the Vatican and Capitoline museums by torchlight. Sculpture should not be seen in the banal light of day. Each work comes to life when it springs at you out of the shadows and you see it alone in the timeless night. Polished marble glows with inner life, details sharpen, the carved fauns and satyrs behind you rustle and whisper. Wolfgang was at his simplest and nicest when he stood with me in front of the Laocoon in its niche and sighed, 'Well, I am too old to do any more than dabble in the visual arts.'

One day he sent me a note, inviting me to his apartment that evening at eight. I called his lodgings at the Casa Moscatelli – The German Academy – because it was always full of young German artists. When Zucchi and I arrived, we saw that his windows were illuminated, and as we climbed the stairs we heard music. It was one of my favourite pieces, from Mozart's *Die Entführung aus dem Serail*, when Constanze sings of her tortures. When I entered there was a burst of applause. There, smiling, waiting to embrace me, stood Wolfgang and a dozen of my dearest friends: Cornelia, her mother, Antonio Canova, Thomas Jenkins, Tischbein – I cannot remember them all now.

I saw only his dear face in the doorway, heard only a secret whispering in my soul: he does love me. I burst into tears when I realised all this was for me.

Wolfgang, who was always praising silence but could never resist making a speech, took my arm. 'She has arrived! My dear friend Angelica, the Mother of the Arts, who mothers and feeds and gives advice to all the foreign artists in Rome, whose astonishing talent is praised all over Europe but who is still as modest as a schoolgirl. Look at her blushing now! Without your help, Angelica, I would never have begun to understand what art is or how to look at a painting. This year in Rome I feel as if I have been reborn. You give but never take, so this evening is a gift for you, dearest Angelica, a chance for you to be frivolous for once.'

Then the hired musicians struck up again. There was dancing, singing and laughter as Wolfgang dominated us all with his charm and wit. That night he conjured the best out of us all. When I looked out of the window, I saw a crowd staring enviously up at our improvised concert and remembered how I used to stand in such crowds as a young girl, looking up at parties I had not been invited to. Turning back to my friends, I let Wolfgang persuade me to sing. Perhaps I have never been so happy.

Was *he* happy? I thought so at the time. Rome both fascinated and repelled him. He was appalled by the smells and filth. One Sunday he arrived at my house for luncheon, carrying a nosegay of lavender.

'I'm afraid these flowers are not for you. I bury my nostrils in them to disguise some of the stink in the streets. Garbage and filth everywhere, pigs rooting in it. Your house is so clean – we northerners have some virtues at least. How can they bear it, to *da per tutto dove vuoi?* I can't say it in German, it's too disgusting. Not only the poor, who have some excuse, but people of all classes. Last night I was invited to a grand reception at the Palazzo Colonna. You know how I hate being drawn out of my solitary shell, but the Principessa insisted.' Wolfgang loved the myth that he was a hermit, too involved in his work to venture out, but took umbrage if he was not invited to the best houses. 'Such an elegant assembly waiting to go up: aristocrats, cardinals, beautiful women, an army of footmen. The staircase leading up to the drawing rooms was lined with carpets, tubs of myrtle and orange trees. There was an enormous antique vase at the bottom of the stairs. One by one the men queued – don't be shocked, Angelica – to piss into it.'

'Of course I'm not shocked. I know the customs of the Romans. Haven't you noticed the "R" chalked on our front door? It stands for respect.'

'Ah, so they piss down the street instead? Such beauty alongside such squalor!'

Other aspects of our city delighted him. He used to talk to Alba for hours about superstitions and legends, taking notes as he snorted with laughter. One evening in June he rushed into my studio, accompanied by his gang of young German artists.

'Angelica, you must come with us. Tomorrow is the Feast of John the Baptist.'

'Have you converted to Catholicism?'

'Never! But I want to see your religion at its craziest.'

They carried me off to San Giovanni in Laterano. There is a legend that the ghosts of Salome and her mother Herodias fly to Rome on their broomsticks the night before the feast of the man they murdered is celebrated. On the huge field in front of the church they lure other witches to their sabbath. The faithful camp out all night in front of the church to protect their beloved saint and their church against the evil influence of the witches.

When we arrived it was getting dark. Several hundred men, women and children were putting up makeshift tents and sitting around bonfires. I heard the rhythmic chant of many voices praying – the clattering of hundreds of pots and pans – kitchen noises to ward off the supernatural. People threw salt onto the bonfires and the fires replied by shooting up blue and green flames that were believed to keep away bad spirits. Many people were using their pans to boil snails, whose horns are a symbol of the devil.

It was such a beautiful moonlit night. Silvery light washed over their faces and over the Scala Santa, the staircase Saint Helena brought back from Pontius Pilate's palace in Jerusalem – the very steps Christ walked down before he was crucified. That night the great story of Christ's death and passion was as timeless as the moon that bleached the facade of San Giovanni, which is the real cathedral in the hearts of Romans, not San Pietro, despite all its pomp. Thought I, the beheading of Saint John, the murder of the Son of God – these events are still happening and will echo forever down the centuries. I love these people for their simple faith and their courage in fighting the evil that is as real to them as their pots and pans.

We foreigners stood in an outer circle and watched this scene as all around me I heard sniggers, the cold voices of the enlightenment.

'Poor fools. They are priest-ridden and believe all this nonsense.'

'I do hope Salome does her seductive dance of the veils for us.'

'This is such a bore. Let's find a trattoria and go to eat.'

If Wolfgang had joined in their chorus of sneers, I believe I would have stopped loving him. But he caught the numinous atmosphere and felt the poetry that shone as brightly as the moon. Slowly, he moved towards the crowd, looking up at the sky as if expecting to see the diabolical mother and daughter swooping down on their broomsticks. Moonbeams danced on his handsome face as he measured the power of the religion he did not want to believe in.

'The Romans built for eternity,' he used to say admiringly, as we explored the city together. But his own attention span was quite short. Soon I realised he had made up his mind to leave Rome – having devoured the feast of beauty I offered, he was ready to move on. He knew he had no real talent as an artist. For all his philosophy, his knowledge of art history and clever theories about colour, he could not do it – that mysterious "it" that I, with a quarter of his intelligence, have devoted my life to.

I was devastated when he left Rome. He wrote to me from Weimar of his relief in finding himself again after love and travel. Meanwhile I lost myself. For months I was too depressed to work. Wolfgang condescended to send me German books to improve my German which, he said, was very bad.

When the Duchess Anna Amalia arrived next door in the Villa Malta, like a messenger from the gods, I interrogated her about his life on Olympus. She told me that the Duke, her son, bought a house for Wolfgang to bribe him to stay in Weimar. Wolfgang created a palazzo there, an Italian courtyard with plashing fountain and shallow stone steps leading to the upper rooms. In a letter to me he said, childlike, that he "could never tire of going up and down" his new staircase. How I have longed to see that German palazzo. But I know now that I never shall.

"I feared you would say that I wrote too often…" I wrote to him. "I can only say that I live and hope to live in your memory as you do in mine, where the remembrance of you will always and forever be dear." My need howls out of my letters to Wolfgang. I copied them out again and again before I dared to post them.

Yet my heart is such a fool that I dream of him still. Just now, during my siesta, I dreamt I was in a large room, bathing a man in a shallow, marble basin. We were both naked, and although I could not see his face, I knew it was Wolfgang, still young and golden. Suddenly I realised I could be seen from the piazza outside where a mob was laughing, mocking, baying at me. Humiliated, I fled into an inner room.

When I woke up just now, I could not recall the details of that dream room. Was it Wolfgang's studio in Rome? I remember it so well – the plaster casts of ancient heads – a double bed with two pillows – a cat and many books. That was the scenery where he played at being an artist. What did he play at in that double bed?

I shut my eyes and allow myself to imagine our reunion in Weimar. This scene has been painted over so many times that it is varnished with age and lost hope: one burnished autumn afternoon, my carriage arrives in Weimar. Wolfgang has built himself an imitation Italian palazzo where he reigns, a Prince of Intellect. He runs down a flight of stone stairs to meet me in the courtyard and we embrace. I feel again that flame of vitality that warms my brain and flickers behind my eyes. Hand in hand, we climb the stairs to a shared life…

Such fiddlesticks. He has had a hundred mistresses since we last met; from all over Europe his admirers flock to Weimar. He can barely remember who I am – his last letter must have been written by his secretary, a formulaic reply to one of the hundreds of adoring letters he receives every day: "Most Honoured Friend… Farewell and kindly answer either yourself or through others."

# 18

---

As I lay abed just now, I seemed to see my dear Zucchi's head beside mine. As I grow old, time plays such tricks upon me – how often do I live more in my past than in my present? All through his long illness I nursed him and prayed that he might live. 'Don't leave me,' I whispered again and again, hoping that my dearest friend and companion would somehow cheat death. I made great plans to celebrate his seventieth birthday – but death cheated me of it. It was the will of God to whom we must submit.

While I was still in mourning, we began to hear rumours that the French were coming to sack Rome. A widow, alone, I was more fearful than I would have been when Zucchi lived. That was when I invited Cousin Johann to come to live here and deal with my household management and business affairs. He has done so, but I cannot talk to him – laugh with him – open my soul to him. Much of myself died with Zucchi.

Barely two years later, the Roman Republic was declared. I was almost glad my husband was nor forced to see the humiliation of the city we both loved. They speak of the Terror in France – my own terror of the French shook me so profoundly that those days will never end.

Behind my eyes, they play the same hurdy-gurdy tune of fear and misery.

Says Cousin Johann, 'Everyone is fleeing the city. We must go, cousin.'

'Where can we go? Nowhere is safe,' I said. I stand at the door of my studio, arms outstretched, guarding all that is most precious: my own paintings, my art collection, this house I have worked so hard for.

Alba comes running in. 'Contessa, in the market they say the French soldiers are looting the Quirinale. They haven't even left the doors on their hinges. And they're looting all the palaces and churches. O, let's escape while we still can!'

'No!'

'But they may billet their soldiers here and then we will all be raped.'

After many sleepless nights and begging letters, I learn that my friends here have asked the French authorities not to billet soldiers in my house. The commander of the garrison, General de Lespinasse, is to live here.

Fearfully, I stand at my front door to greet him. The streets around us ring with shooting, screams and smashing glass. I force myself to behave like the Contessa I am not and, strangely, the man who dismounts from his horse is willing to play this game with me, as if the revolution has never happened.

I see at once that Augustin de Lespinasse is a cultivated man, a relation of Julie de Lespinasse, who once ran a great salon in Paris. As soon as he has settled into the suite of rooms I give to him and his *aide-de-camp*, he asks to see my studio. A man of about sixty, he has the leathery skin of a soldier and the hard body of a man who spends much of his life in the saddle. To me, the short hair these modern men wear is barbarous. To be "natural" is to be crude and underdressed. Wigs and powder covered so many defects and flattered the faces of both men and women. Yet the man himself is not a barbarian.

We converse in French; mine is rusty but servicable.

'Contessa, it is so kind of you to allow us to stay in your beautiful house,' he says.

As if I have any choice. I curtsey, he bows, it is like a minuet danced on the grave of the civilised world he has helped to destroy. Then he hands me a letter, guaranteeing, in elaborate French, that my house will not be interfered with.

Dizzy with relief, I allow him to roam around my studio. He looks at my work with interest and intelligence and then, to my horror, draws back the curtains to reveal my Leonardo, my Titian, my Van Dyke and my Veronese hanging nearby. 'Copies I did as a student,' I lie. 'Don't you think they are very like?'

'I would not know, Contessa. I have spent my life campaigning, not looking at paintings. Certainly they are beautiful.'

Who is the cat and who the mouse? In my house the General and I dine together. We speak of gardening, music, architecture – anything except politics or religion. He plays the harpsichord well and sometimes accompanies me in the evenings. After a few days, a kind of friendship develops between us.

I feel guilty as the rest of Rome suffers. There are bread riots while we sit in my dining room eating the quails and asparagus the Colonel has procured.

Says Alba, 'Our Pope, our Holy Father, is a prisoner in his own palace. An old man of eighty. The French have forced him to sign a truce, giving the French hundreds of rare manuscripts and works of art. And millions in cash, says the baker.'

Here on my terrace, I stand and watch an enormous anti-French demonstration winding from the Aracoeli to the Vatican: barefoot monks in mourning for Rome's dignity, the poor in mourning for the religious charities that no longer have the money to feed them.

Our city is ransacked. Paintings, marbles and statues all disappear. The Romans are furious; they hate to see the excommunicated French received politely by their Pope. The mob have always hated the French, but some of the great families love them and even hold balls for them. The art students at the French Academy are all Jacobins and freemasons. They tear down the statue of Louis XIV, remove portraits of popes and cardinals and replace the royal fleur-de-lys with republican flags.

When the French envoys' carriage appears on the Corso flaunting tricolours, it is stoned and attacked by the mob. One of the envoys, Basseville, dies from a razor slash. Then the French Embassy and the French Academy are sacked by the Roman mob. Alba says it is a victory for the Church over the devil.

Art dealers from France swoop like vultures. They set up improvised auctions – hundreds of holy relics are sold off. The French atheists respect nothing. They seize our olive wood *bambino* from the Ara Coeli, our own baby Jesus that the Roman people have worshipped for centuries. They strip our holy infant of his robes and jewels and toss him aside to be burned for fuel. But one of our Roman aristocrats pays a ransom for him. He

gives our holy wooden infant to some nuns who shelter him in
their convent.

The men of Trastevere march on the French with knives and
rocks. A few days later, we hear that many of them have been
executed down there at the Porta di Popolo. Carnival is can-
celled. People say that the street madonnas weep for our city.

Says my cousin, 'Berthier had to rent a crowd for his triumphant procession to the capital yesterday. He stood wearing a
laurel wreath in front of the statue of Marcus Aurelius's gilded
horse, tricolours in its mane, and made a pompous speech.'

Says Alba, 'Our bronze angel on Castel Sant'Angelo, who
guards our city, has been made to wear a Liberty bonnet and
wave a tricolour flag after those wicked Frenchies liberated all the
gold and silver from the vaults. Now they've filled the dungeons
with brave men loyal to our Pope. Liberty trees replace our
crucifixes and busts of Cato and Brutus usurp our beloved statues
of the saints.'

Meanwhile, de Lespinasse lives here with me. Just when I
foolishly come to believe that I shall miraculously escape the
worst outrages of the French occupation, he asks to visit my
studio again. Terrified, I watch as he prowls around. He pauses
for so long in front of my art collection that I feel certain he will
steal it and cart it off to Paris with all our other Roman treasures.
Then he draws a sheet of parchment from his breast pocket.

'Contessa, I received this today. We have lived here in mutual
trust for months. Now I trust you to tell me if this information
is correct?'

He hands me a list of all the paintings that have been commissioned by my German, Russian and English patrons – a

great number, as I have not been able to send them abroad due to the wars.

'Yes,' I confess with tears in my eyes. Suddenly, nationality is a matter of life and death. I am very grateful to my Swiss mother for giving birth to me in Chur. Were I English or German, my studio would be emptied.

I watch in horror when his soldiers come to seize my paintings the next day – yet it might have been far worse. In gratitude for what I have been spared, I offer to paint his portrait.

How strange to be painting this man I ought to hate, yet when I look into his face, I see kindness and humour there, as if he too is aware of the irony of our situation. Despite myself, I enjoy the splendour of his uniform with its magnificent scarlet collar, cuffs and cummerbund, all embroidered with gold. I do not talk to him as much as I usually talk to my sitters. While I paint, he works his way through piles of documents, signing each one. Are they death warrants for priests or rebels, for friends of mine, perhaps?

'Tis impossible to paint your hands, for they are never still,' I say.

Polite as always, he stops his fidgets. In my portrait he sits with both hands on his sword – sensitive, manicured hands, on a sword that must have killed so many.

And so for eighteen months we lived together under this roof. My terror did not fade, but it became dormant like a volcano smouldering in its crater. This time, thought I, providence has been kind to me, but next time Napoleon himself will come to destroy us. *That* terror has never left me.

After the French troops left, King Ferdinand of Naples came to "liberate" Rome and stole more of our treasures. He wanted to merge Rome with his kingdom of Naples. Then soldiers from Prussia and England and Russia marched into the city. There was confusion, more looting, murder and fear. They entered Rome by one gate; Ferdinand fled by another. As Pasquino joked, '*Veni, vidi, e fuggi*' – he came, he saw, he fled. We heard of a great victory over Napoleon at Marengo – we all celebrated – then a few days later we heard that the French had won the battle after all. Now he calls himself the ruler of Italy; soon he will be master of the world. A new pope has been elected, Pius the Seventh, our little Braschi scholar. Many people here have changed sides. I've no idea who they support now. Romans don't want to fight – they're too fickle, too cynical and pleasure loving to admire martial valour. They want only peace, that elusive dove that shuns our age.

# 19

The doctor says I must not paint because it brings back my fever, but I ignore him – for what is the point of life without work? I grew up in my father's studio and always feel most at home in my own. As long as I can put on my old painting smock and come here each day I will be truly myself, even though my painting hand is stiff and swollen now. At the end of my vista of elegant salons, I allow my studio to be messy. Here is a glorious muddle of easels, palettes, brushes, stones for grinding pigment, jars of oil, mannequins. Here are costumes: baggy Turkish trousers, turbans, old crinolines, togas, Highland costumes, cloaks and hats. Propped up against the wall are empty frames, doors I will never walk through. Every studio is a theatre and my audience are my own self-portraits, together with unfinished or unclaimed portraits whose subjects have left Rome because of the wars. So many faces. Wolfgang is here of course, and my sweet Zucchi. Sir Joshua still bosses me about from the wall over there; I hear his voice lecturing me on the grand manner: 'You must not paint ignoble subjects, Angelica, but always show us some eminent instance of heroic action or heroic suffering.'

Yes, Zucchi and I came to Rome because we believed we would be safe, but now I realise that nowhere is safe. Another revolution is on its way to Rome – mindless, screaming violence. Soon the *canaglia* will come for me.

Yet even after all these years in Rome, I never tire of my beautiful view. I have only to open my shutters to look down over the city: brilliant green umbrella pines – red roofs – golden domes – oranges, pinks, yellows, ochres, burnt sienna – all the colours and light I pined for in London. Morning shouts with joy in the azure above the swollen dome of Saint Peter's, as carriages crawl up the Via del Babuino. When Napoleon finally arrives, will he destroy all this to build himself a palace even bigger than Nero's Golden House? Just below me is the Piazza di Spagna, where models sprawl on the steps and try to look picturesque.

I remember those short, dark London days when I had to paint by candlelight even in the morning, when colours were ghosts of themselves, wraiths I struggled to remember. In London I bought my paints from the colourman in St Martin's Lane, ground and tied up – ultramarine at three guineas an ounce, burnt sienna at sixpence a bladder. Here in Rome, colour is free and colours are alive.

'Coffee, Contessa?' says my young friend Lucia with pre-tended humility.

This is a peace offering after our quarrel yesterday. Argument, rather, she would say – we cannot even agree about what to call our differences of opinion. Lucia has opinions about every-thing, far too many for a young girl. She stands beside me at the window, gasping at the view. I hope she will not gush or quote poetry, but for once she is silent.

When I have inhaled enough beauty to face another day, I close the shutters. The green silk hangings deepen from emerald to pine as I move over to my chaise longue. There is always pain now when I walk, and a giddiness that makes the words dance when I try to read. Lucia sits beside me on a hard, gilt chair, vibrating with youth and health as we sip our coffee.

'In the Caffè degli Inglesi last night they were saying the French will come back soon. They'll have to find a new name for the caffè as most of the English artists have left now. The Caffè dei Francesi?'

I examine her with my phizmonger eyes and see that her complexion is fading; she has allowed the sun to coarsen it and roses have fled from her cheeks to her nose. Her green eyes are still charmingly intelligent above the flimsy white nightgown that is supposed to be a dress.

'Nobody offered me work,' she adds petulantly.

'What will you do when I'm dead and you can no longer earn a crown or two as a model?'

'Perhaps I'll become a painter like you – like Papa,' she says. 'Or write poems in praise of Napoleon,' she adds mischievously. 'But don't die just yet.' She reaches over to hug me, her clear eyes smiling into my rheumy ones.

'I won't leave you any money. It's all going to my relations and to the poor.'

'So you tell me every day.'

Lucia infuriates me – entertains me – makes me say indiscreet things. If there had been children, would they have disrupted my life as she does? She brings me the latest jokes and the tittle-tattle I am supposed to be too dignified to care about. 'What does Pasquino say about the French?' I ask.

'I don't know. Who is Pasquino, anyway?'

'He was a tailor in the Piazza Navona, a famous gossip. When he died, people missed his filthy stories about popes and cardinals and aristocrats, so they found a mutilated classical statue, propped him up in the street, and started posting satires and lampoons on him. The Pope couldn't punish them because nobody knew who'd insulted him,' I explain.

'So Romans don't really love the Pope, as you say they do?'

'Perhaps they're like children who obey their teacher as long as they can laugh at him behind his back.'

My cousin Johann comes in to remind me that Mrs Taylor is coming at ten to sit for her portrait. He tries to persuade me to eat some bread, but I am not hungry, so Lucia, as usual, gobbles up my breakfast. He watches disapprovingly; he will throw her out onto the streets when I am gone. I must protect her while I can, because dear Cornelia asked me to.

Lucia's father was an unsuccessful English painter who, unwisely, fell in love with his beautiful model – a peasant girl from Amalfi – and married her. When they both died of malaria – because of our bad Roman air that too many people have breathed for too many centuries – Lucia was left quite alone in Rome at just eighteen years old. Cornelia was friendly with the girl's father and wanted to help, remembering, as I do, how it feels to be young and penniless. And so I have agreed to give her a room in my house.

Mrs Taylor arrives, shivering, her baby wrapped in her only shawl. 'It's always so warm in your house!'

'I sent for our good Austrian stoves from Bregenz. The Romans don't know how to be comfortable in winter,' I say.

'In our room this morning it was so cold that there was ice on the window. I thought Italy was always sunny.'

Baby Rosina has a feeble little cry and is pale as a white mouse. Mrs Taylor is a dark, oval-faced beauty. I want her for a Madonna, in case I ever have enough energy to work on another religious painting. It always moves me to see her suckle Rosina – the little mouth so hungry for life, the mother so patient, as a madonna should be. I pay her to sit for me and give her some of the sketches I have done of her to sell. The family are desperate. I call them "the moths", these young artists who flock from all over Europe to the flame of art in Rome. Most have left now due to the wars that madman has unleashed on us all, but the Taylors have been stranded here like Lucia.

'My husband has written to his uncle again,' says Mrs Taylor. His uncle is some fatpurse city merchant who thinks his nephew a great fool to pursue the sublime when he could be sitting in a counting office.

'The post from England is not reliable. I've been waiting for an important letter for months,' I say. I am waiting for information about the income from my stocks and shares, dwindled since the wars.

'Every morning I tell my husband we should leave,' says she.

'It is not safe to travel now. Napoleon's spies are everywhere, and they hate the English.'

She looks so sad that I am afraid she will weep and spoil her face just as I am painting it. I want to show the beautiful curves of her cheeks and breasts, but if she gets any thinner those curves will disappear. The old monks never saw a naked woman or a baby, so their madonnas are angular and wooden, their babies like shrivelled old men. I love the Flemish madonnas, those strong young girls with fleshy breasts crammed into the mouths of real babies.

Usually I ask my sitters to read poetry to me while I paint, but Mrs Taylor is so distracted by her baby's needs that it would be cruel to demand any more of her. The little creature mewls and pukes and shits, then enslaves us both with her smiles. I want to ask her how it feels to be eaten like that but do not dare – so delicate is the threshold between sitter and artist. I do not know her first name. She calls me Contessa as they all do, even though I am not.

'May I borrow you for another hour?'

'My husband will be only too glad of the peace. I wonder, if it is not too much trouble – he is really very good, you know. His teacher in Clapham said he had quite a spark of genius and only wanted Rome to give him some polish. We should be so pleased – honoured – if you would come to our room, to his studio, to look at his work.'

I see that she has been practising this speech for hours. It would be churlish to refuse. Perhaps he is indeed an undiscovered genius, but even if he is a clod, I will have to buy something. Though I rarely venture down into the city now, I agree to visit them this afternoon.

Cousin Johann insists on accompanying me down the Spanish Steps, because he is afraid I might have one of my dizzy fits and fall. People greet me at every step, for Rome is like a village – everybody knows me. This is the dear Piazza di Spagna that thrilled me so much when I first saw it as a young girl, the very pulse of the world of art I yearned to belong to. The pulse is weaker now, but there are still models lying on the steps, trying to look interesting enough to be engaged by artists: Italian French German Spanish Scandinavian Dutch – human statues for hire – all of them with strikingly beautiful or ugly faces. There are few artists left now to rent them, so they beg, in four languages, as we pass. I give them some loose change from my purse.

On that first visit to Rome when I was a young girl, my father and I stayed at Mengs's house at the top of the new Spanish Steps. It was the pleasantest place to live in all of Rome. Salvator Rosa lived in the same house before Mengs, so I felt it must be a lucky house for painters – as indeed it has been for me. How Papa would love to see me living in this very house, and how I wish he could.

All these streets are haunted by friends who have died or fled from Rome. In the sixties of the last century they swarmed with artists – good and bad, rich and poor, Grand Tourists and their bear leaders. There were dozens of drawing schools where young men ogled naked women and where I, as a woman, was not allowed. Even on this dull morning these stinking alleys are beautiful as they crumble richly in luscious pinks, yellows, oranges and ochres.

Here on Via Bocca di Leone reigned the king of all the painters, Pompeo Batoni, Mengs's great rival. His portraits were commissioned by the Pope – by the Emperor himself – by all the passing *milordi*. I was dazzled when he invited me to his studio and was kind to me, an unknown young girl. When Batoni died he left an elaborate will – but no money. His widow had to open a wine tavern on the ground floor of his studio; I see it is still here. Nobody would buy the paintings that all of

Rome had swooned over a few years before. O what a lesson! In this age, when kings and aristocrats can be murdered by the dozen, what is the reputation of a painter?

The Taylors have rented an attic above a butcher's shop; the rotting stairs are covered with slime and offal. Says Cousin Johann, 'I cannot allow you to risk your neck.' But I have given Mrs Taylor my word, so up we climb. How easily might I have ended up in this squalor: a tiny room littered with clothes, dirty plates, the baby's bottles, paints and canvasses.

As we enter, the handsome young couple stand to attention like recruits before a sergeant major. I try to ease the atmosphere by picking up Rosina, who wails and pulls my nose. We all laugh and Mr Taylor kisses my hand. He is a very nervous young man who shakes as he lays out his sketches and watercolours on the only table. They are views of the Colosseum and the Piazza Navona, with nothing to distinguish them from a thousand others. I see that I must buy a few and try to look enthusiastic while Johann glowers. He looks pained as I reach for my purse. It is not so much my person he wishes to protect as his interest in my will. Well, I have left him quite enough, and shall do as I please with my money while I am still here. Their room is indeed cold – their tiny grate is bare. I must send them up some firewood and food.

Johann supports me when I slip and nearly fall while descending the perilous stairs. I am very glad of his presence. How he reminds me of my father, his uncle. He has the same lack of humour combined with genuine moral uprightness. "Kauffman" means "a man of business", and I have need of one. Though he has lived with me in Rome for over ten years now he is still rigidly Austrian and suspicious of Roman frivolity. He speaks Italian with an atrocious accent and would like to domineer over me as Papa did – but he is younger and poorer than me, and must do as he is told. Every day I think of dismissing him, but then his good sense and honesty conquer me once more. This morning is such an instance.

'You cannot walk all the way home,' he says, taking my arm and leading me to the Caffè Greco on the Via dei Condotti, where the waiters fawn and half a dozen artists mob our table in the hope of advancement. The caffè is not what it was before the French occupation – it is older and shabbier like us all, the company less brilliant and the velvet upholstery in tatters. My cousin fetches a carriage. Exhausted, I sit back in the darkness and do not object when my cousin and Alba carry me upstairs to my bedchamber.

# 20

---

'Signor Canova,' says Alba, showing him in. I embrace him, but he senses my reserve.

'I tried to refuse, Angelica. I made excuses; I really did.'

I have to control my absurd anger. The very thought of those vile Napoleons boils my blood. Yet how many despots have I flattered and painted? We artists cannot afford principles – go where the money is, as my father used to say. I return to Antonio's face, to this portrait of him that has taken so long and is still unfinished. It's been so long that since I started it his face has aged, become more worldly and contented. His big, obstinate, peasant chin and nose have settled into a cushion of pampered flesh. He has at least two chins – my brush will melt them away, for even old friends must be flattered. It is easier to observe his face than to shout my sense of betrayal. Even he has gone over to them.

He senses my hurt and justifies himself eloquently. 'La Paolina sent for me as soon as they arrived in Rome. They insisted on coming to my studio to see the statue of her brother I'm working on. She simply burst in and commanded us all – says she has to have a sculpture of herself to give to her prince as a present. "Something dignified and graceful," says I, "lying down in a beautiful classical robe? Or perhaps I could do you as the virgin huntress, Diana?" She doesn't even smile at this for she has no sense of irony. "No!" says she. "If my brother is going to be Mars, I must be Venus. Venus victrix!" It was not so much a commission as a royal command. Ask your cousin, for he was there.'

I had wanted to help my cousin and *Landsmann*, Peter Kauffman, who shows some artistic talent, so I'd persuaded Antonio to give the young man work in his studio.

'Is La Paolina really such a great beauty?' I ask.

'She is tiny but exquisite, full of vitality, a pocket termagant.'

I know that look in his eyes. Zucchi used to say, 'Antonio will fuck anything.' He is still under fifty and at the peak of his powers. Who could count the lovers he has had? He has never married; says he does not believe in marrying them. How I envy the freedom of these male artists.

'What will your miniature Venus wear?'

'The same as her brother. Nothing.' He roars with laughter. 'Don't look so shocked, Angelica. It is the fashion to portray these great folk as naked classical gods and goddesses, not draped in coy veils as in the old days.'

My days. 'I would not dream of flaunting those parts that are best hidden. The vulgarity – the indecency!'

Antonio laughs again. 'Times change and 'tis best to change with them. I didn't want to like La Paolina. Josephine detests her and you know how I adore Josephine. She's such an amusing woman, so stylish and beautiful, with a genius for friendship. Napoleon would be nothing without her, still a little general in the French army –' Antonio gasps at his own indiscretion and looks around, as we all do now.

'There are no spies in my studio, Antonio. Yet.'

'Anyway, Josephine is a natural goddess, an empress – as she may very well become. La Paolina will have all her fire and grace someday, but as yet she wants polish. She's a coarse little wildcat from Corsica, vain and spitting with rage.'

His dark, deep, visionary eyes shine with lust. Has he slept with all the Bonaparte women? Our conversation is becoming dangerous. 'Do you want to read some poetry to me while you sit? I have an Italian translation of Schiller here.'

'O no, Angelica. I'd far rather talk to you.'

There is so much to talk about – indeed, that is one of the reasons it has taken so long to paint his portrait. 'I rarely go out now, but I would love to visit your studio and see what you are doing,' I say.

'Despite your disapproval?' he asks.

'Who am I to disapprove of Pygmalion? Take care you don't fall in love with your Galatea.'

'I always fall in love with them, but it does no harm.'

'My Zucchi used to say you capture their souls in marble. Those who have souls.'

'*Basta*, Angelica. Who can choose their patrons? When I have a moment I still work on my classical sculptures, like my *Hercules* and *Lica* that you loved.'

'I thought it quite wonderful. Ovid is such a great poet and you bring out the tragedy of the situation – that Hercules thinks his poor servant has betrayed him, when really it is the centaur. Is it finished yet?'

'Sometimes I think I'll never finish it. Or that when I do, I'll drop down dead.'

'Your Hercules is so alive in his rage and power. No other sculptor alive now comes near you. This portrait is not going well! I shall change it and paint you instead at work on your Hercules. Next time I visit your studio I'll make more drawings of it – that's the kind of work you ought to be doing.'

'It's all very well to lecture me from your angelic heights, here in this glorious house, surrounded by your art collection and your adoring servants,' says Antonio. 'But I have still a career to make, patrons to please, official duties to pursue.'

'Ah yes, Inspector-General of Antiquities and Fine Art of the Papal State. Like Raphael.'

'Like, but not equal to. But you – I've always thought of you as a Raphael among women.'

He knows how to soothe me, yet I cannot resist a few more dagger thrusts. He is the last person left I can speak to freely, for we have known each other so long.

'You must not throw your talent away, Antonio. Such a talent! When you were a boy your Theseus and the Minotaur astonished all Rome. Everyone thought it must be a copy of a Greek original. How Winckelmann would have loved your work.'

'How I wish I'd known him, as you did. I would have loved to discuss Ovid with him. He was right when he said the antique is the ideal.'

'It would break his heart to see how the French barbarians have looted Rome,' I say. 'He worshipped The Apollo Belvedere. Do you remember how he described his hair as like the tendrils of a noble vine? It would have killed him to see his beloved Apollo abducted from the Vatican and taken to Paris.'

'We have all died a little in these last few years,' says Antonio. I can see that he is not really so changed from the man who used to rage with me against the French. When they destroyed the independence of his Venice and set up their loathsome republic here, Antonio went into exile, back to Possagno. Then off he went to Vienna, to try to gain support for the deposed Pope. At heart he is still a Venetian patriot and as staunch a Catholic as I am – but the heart grows colder.

'I forgot! Your Perseus has filled the plinth the Apollo once stood on. Holding the severed head of Medusa – did you mean it as a political allegory, Antonio? I've often wondered. Who is the gorgon?'

He leans forward and whispers intensely. I put my brush down and lean towards him to hear what he is saying. 'If only real politics came clearly labelled like Greek mythology. If only one could say, "I am Perseus and Napoleon is a monster who must be slain." When he carried off our bronze horses of San Marco to Paris, I dreamt of assassinating him. But he has done good things too. He has almost unified our chaotic Italy, has abolished many stupid laws and traditions, and kicked us all into the nineteenth century.'

'Where I have no desire to be.' He looks at me with pity and I read his unspoken thought: she will die soon. 'But you are a natural courtier. You will survive all this and have even more success.' I try not to sound resentful.

'I love Rome just as much as you do. For a little longer it will be the centre of the art world, then Paris will overtake us as an ambitious apprentice outruns his master. In a few years all the talented young artists will go there, not here. Napoleon says he will make Paris the most beautiful city in the world. You should see it now.'

'I shall never go. For me, Rome will always be more beautiful.'

He walks over to the smaller window in my studio to look down on the sweep of the Piazza Barberini. Our sitting is over, but I want our conversation to continue. 'Ah yes – so beautiful. If Napoleon had been able to steal our Pantheon and Colosseum, he would have done.'

'I wonder what will become of Rome after I die.'

'I hope you will be with us for many more years, dear Angelica.'

'Always tactful. But what do you really think?'

'Perhaps it will become what Greece once was for the ancient Romans: dreams, ideals, fragments of a lost past. Tombs and majestic skeletons, a wonderful museum.'

'No! Far more than that,' I say. 'Artists will always need this dazzling light and air. Those of us who fall in love with this city acquire a deep sensibility to beauty that couldn't possibly develop in the fog and smoke of Paris or London.'

'Well. Perhaps.' He has already moved on from me, impatient to go to his next appointment – to his splendid future. Most of my sitters wear their best clothes, but he is wearing an open white shirt with a simple brown jacket. They are working clothes; for Antonio, work will always come first, and that is the great bond between us. I clasp his hands in both of mine as we make a date for his next sitting, which will probably not happen because his days are much fuller than mine. When we part, he embraces me as if I were his mother. I almost could be. Strange that I do not think of him in any other light, despite his vigorous masculinity. The gap in age is not so much greater than between Wolfgang and me. At last I am too old for such nonsense – old age has its compensations.

# 21

————————

Sleep flees at night, so I must catch it when I can. I must have slept, for the short day is fading behind my shutters when I hear a tapping at my door. Into my silence bursts Lucia like a Roman candle.

'I hope I don't disturb you,' says she, bouncing onto the chair beside my bed. 'Alba's sister, the one who works in the Borghese kitchen, came to see us. And I know you'll want to hear all about them.'

'I cannot approve of gossip.'

'O but *such* gossip!' Lucia giggles, tripping over her words in her eagerness to share her sugarplums. 'La Paolina treats her servants abominably; they call the Borghese Palace the Ministry of Caprices. She uses her ladies-in-waiting as footstools and insists on being carried to her bath by her enormous African footman. At first she was nice to Prince Camillo, but now that she's got her hands on his titles and jewels she calls him His Serene Idiot, tells him he'd be nothing were he not married to Napoleon's sister. Even in front of her servants she says these things! But she's dazzlingly beautiful. I wish I could see her. I wish I could work in her household.'

'To be used as a footstool?'

'I wouldn't mind! I would write a book about her and become famous. They say she can't read or write properly in French or Italian, so I could teach her.' Lucia is an excellent linguist, like me, having picked up three languages in her wandering childhood. She rushes on. 'She's trying to learn how to behave in Roman society. She's having lessons in deportment and dancing. She wants to be liked.'

'Then she has failed miserably, for she is hated. In Rome the nobles have always allowed the people to use the gatehouses of their palaces as a kind of caffè, where they can get free coffee or ices, and so they have dampened any revolutionary nonsense. Your Messalina has locked them out of her palaces.'

'French aristocrats are very proud.'

'French aristocrats indeed! The Bonapartes are Corsican peasants, pursuing vendettas and nepotism. Corsica only became part of France after the revolution. I've heard that your hero Napoleon has never even mastered the French accent, and as for his mother and sisters –'

'Really? O Contessa, *do* tell!'

I ought not to say these things, but my anger has been festering for so long. 'When the Napoleone women fled from Corsica to the south of France, they had to take in washing. And worse.'

'Whatever do you mean?' Lucia's excitement glows in the darkening room. Alba comes in to light the lamps and stays to listen. She has picked up a great deal of German and English from her years with me. I should be more discreet, but I cannot bear to hear these loathsome upstarts admired.

'I've heard so many rumours. That Paoletta had a thousand lovers including her brother Napoleon – that Madame Mere ran a bordello in Marseilles with Paoletta as a fourteen-year-old prostitute.' Did I really say that? 'Lucia, I do apologise. I should not speak of such matters in front of a young girl.'

In the lamplight Alba's wrinkled, brown face and Lucia's green eyes are avid for more. I cannot stop myself. 'When his mother was pregnant with Napoleon, she hid in the mountains after the Corsicans' revolt against Genoa. The father of that dreadful brood, Carlo, was ennobled, but they had no money. When Napoleon was sent off to a French military academy, he couldn't speak a word of French.'

Says Alba in Italian, 'My sister says that though La Paolina spends a sack of money on her clothes, she and her mother send back yesterday's stale bread and demand a discount on today's. That must be because they were born poor, like me.'

'Then why did Prince Camillo marry her?' says Lucia. 'He's *Romano dei Romani* – so rich – he owns all those wonderful palaces and that magnificent art collection. He could have married a real princess.'

'He and his brother have always supported revolution. When the French invaded six years ago, the Borghese boys pulled the crest off their family's palazzo and threw it onto a bonfire together with cardinals' hats and Inquisition decrees – just down there in the Piazza di Spagna. Three boys with wings carrying torches came down the steps to light the bonfire. Then a naked woman appeared. Truth, they announced – the French will use any excuse to strip a woman of her clothes. Such vulgar nonsense. The watching mob screamed and threw stones. Most Roman nobles sided with the Pope, but Camillo was too stupid to see where his best interests lay.'

Says Alba, shaking her head, 'My sister says the Princess hates her husband now and blames him for the death of little Dermide. Only six years old, so sad. The *poverino* died of fever and convulsions. So now she hates Rome and wants to go back to France.'

'If she married the Prince last year, how could she have a six-year-old son?' asks Lucia.

'She was married first to General Leclerc,' I explained. 'Then when he died, her monstrous brother told her to marry the prince. He wants his family to marry into half the aristocratic and royal families in Europe.'

Alba smiles toothlessly. 'My sister says La Paolina inherited seven hundred thousand francs from her first husband.'

'Alba, tell the Contessa what you told me. About that musician.' Lucia nudges Alba, who comes forward and whispers in Italian, so close to my ear that I can smell her hot garlic breath. 'My sister says la Principessa has a hundred lovers including Paganini, that famous violinist. The prince is wildly jealous, but he can do nothing. What a crazy household!'

Suddenly impatient with this indecorous conversation, I shout at them to leave me alone.

Lucia and Alba flee. In my solitude, all I can think of is that terrible family who have ruined my life and torn Europe apart to satisfy their vanity. That whore's brother will come soon – his soldiers will return – perhaps this time they will loot my house, as they have looted so many of our Roman palaces and churches. I must talk to Johann about the best way to hide my treasures. They shall not have my Leonardo or my Titian or my Van Dyke or my Veronese. Everything I own I have gained through my own hard work and effort.

How dreadful the last French occupation was! How many dear friends I lost. Gavin Hamilton died of shock when the French troops came to plunder his house. They stole Thomas Jenkins's art collection; he fled to England but died soon afterwards of a broken heart.

The wonderful collection Winckelmann put together for his patron, Cardinal Albani, was carted off to Paris. Winckelmann was kind to me when I was young and painted his portrait. Looking into his face, I saw the suffering of his early years writ there. He was a cobbler's son who taught himself Latin and Greek, then fell in love with their cultures. Like so many romantic Germans, he came here to Rome where he found a generous patron in Cardinal Albani. Winckelmann converted to our Catholic faith and spoke perfect Italian. I learnt much from listening to him. He used to say that the only hope we modern artists have of greatness is to imitate the ancients. He taught me to see the noble simplicity and quiet grandeur of Greek sculpture. I loved his idea that the works of great sculptors like Praxiteles have souls, but I was intimidated by his mania for the perfection of the male body. How he ranted on about delectable young boys – attractive manliness – he made me feel quite plain. Well, the poor dear man was murdered by his own enthusiasm. In Trieste he took a fancy to a young man called Arcangeli, showed him some valuable coins and was stabbed by his archangel.

When I came back to Rome with Zucchi, I was sad that Winckelmann was no longer alive to advise me. After escaping from the horror of the Gordon Riots in London, I felt safe in Rome. So foolish – one is never safe. There are bullet marks on the houses opposite and blood-splashed walls.

# 22

When I open my eyes, blood is glowing behind my shutters – dawn – I often see it now. I open my shutters and lie in bed to watch the day break over my garden. God is a better colourist than I am – every morning a different variation. Here is pure colour and form: valleys, bays, burning peaks, tiers of monuments in the sky. Always new as I grow old. One day soon I will not be here to see it. God's crayon outlines clouds with light and fire, capriciously He builds towers and cities only to demolish them. Then, after that burst of rebellion and passion, the sky calms down to become dull and staid, as most of us do.

Suddenly there are splutters and gasps, like an animal in distress. A cat in my garden? No, a human sound. I put on my cashmere dressing gown to go in search of the invalid down the corridor of closed doors. Once, my house buzzed with visitors, Zucchi's family from Venice, mine from Bregenz Woods, and old friends from London. But now most of these rooms are empty.

The fourth on the left is Lucia's. I enter to find her kneeling at her commode, spewing. She is very pale and grows even whiter when she sees me.

'Contessa – so sorry – disgusting – I will clean it up.'

'My dear child, you are ill. The servants have not lit the stoves yet and it is bitterly cold. Come into my room.' I sit her on the green chaise longue by the window under one of my good Austrian eiderdowns. 'Go back to sleep if you can.'

I get dressed. Alba will be cross – she thinks it beneath my dignity to dress myself. I have not told her of all the years when I had no maid. Down in the icy kitchen I struggle to light the stove, for it is a long time since I have cooked for myself. I will not be defeated by a lump of metal. At last I succeed and one of the little keys I wear on my belt opens the Japanese enamel canister where our coffee is kept. I fill the *caffettiera* up to the nail with water, put coffee in the top part and screw it all together again. Then I find the little almond *biscotti* Sabina, our cook, baked yesterday and put them on a plate on the breakfast tray. All this takes so long that the wintry sun has risen by the time I return to find Lucia sitting on my chaise longue, beaming. We enjoy our little picnic.

'Do you think Napoleon really will come soon?' How quickly the young recover. Her face is radiant in the sun that gilds my bedchamber.

'Yes. He has sent his vulgar sister as a John the Baptist to herald his coming.'

'You are very sarcastic about the champion of the people,' says Lucia.

'I have terrible memories of the last time the champion of the people sent his murderous rabble to Rome,' say I.

'The republic, you mean? I wish I'd been here then. I was living with my grandmother in Amalfi.'

'We heard rumours of the revolution, of course. Many courtiers who had fled Versailles came here to Rome, where they were admired for their style and elegance. Then we heard that King Louis had escaped and was fleeing to Rome. Such excitement! Huge crowds around the French embassy, drums and fireworks and *vive le roi*. Until we heard the poor King had been guillotined.'

'He was a despot,' says Lucia.

'God had chosen him. We heard that in France all the Church properties had been confiscated. Thousands of priests had been executed, killed by the mob or exiled. We did not believe it could happen here. But now I know it could.'

'Voltaire said, "superstition sets the whole world in flames, but philosophy quenches them." There's a new religion now: Theophilanthropism.'

'I have no need of your godless philosophy,' I say. 'My darling Zucchi was old and ill by then. I nursed him. We sat here in this room, waiting for the French soldiers to break into our house. When my husband died, I was almost glad he did not have to see these evil times. Romans generally thought the new French ideas were moonshine. They thought Voltaire was a lunatic – they still cross themselves when mentioning his name.'

'The poor Romans have lived in superstition and ignorance for centuries. They need to be liberated.'

'The French liberated us by stealing our property and looting our palaces and churches.'

'Yesterday I met an artist in the Caffè degli Inglesi who has been to Paris to see the wonderful Museo Centrale Napoleon is making there,' says Lucia.

'O yes, I remember how artists flocked to Paris after the Treaty of Amiens. The French call their stolen goods *les fruits de nos victoires*. My friends in England wrote to tell me about it. Italy is in Paris now, they said, and in this new century Paris will be the capital of art, the most beautiful city in the world. Do you know how much the French love art? When they seized Milan, Napoleon's soldiers amused themselves by using Leonardo's *Last Supper* for shooting practice.'

'Many of those artworks were neglected in Italy. Napoleon will give us a Europe where there are no hereditary tyrants and all the borders are free.'

'Poppycock!' I say. 'Like all his promises. What does it matter if power is inherited or not? Some ruthless man will always hold it – not you nor I. Do you know the story about the boatman?'

'No.'

'After William of Orange won the Battle of the Boyne, he escaped by boat and the boatman congratulated him on his victory. The King said, 'What's it to you? You'll still be a boatman.''

'But what about you? Why did you stay in Rome after your husband died?' asks Lucia.

'I had nowhere to go and did not dare to leave my house empty to be looted. My friends and patrons all started to leave; there were no more commissions or great parties or *conversazioni*. Then, six years ago, we all expected the ogre himself to come and swallow us for breakfast, but instead he sent General Berthier. The French proclaimed the *Repubblica per ridere* – the ridiculous republic – that's what the Romans called it.'

'I've heard that many people supported it,' says Lucia.

'You have no idea how terrifying it was. Such hatred and violence.'

'The republic is the victory of reason over superstition.'

'Of greed over faith!'

'Did you suffer?'

'I was fortunate, for I am neither English nor Italian nor Russian nor German.'

'What are you, then?'

'I am Swiss, like my mother, and was born in Chur. The Swiss, thank heaven, have had the good sense to remain neutral in these horrible wars.'

'Then you didn't suffer at all!'

'Not in regard to my person, but I'm much impoverished by inflation and the loss of my patrons. My investments in London bring in far less than once they did.'

Lucia laughs bitterly. 'You don't know what it is to be poor.'

'That's not true. As a child I was as poor as you – but I do not intend to be so again. If the French return now there will be more fear, looting, and nights of screaming, shooting and burning.'

'What happened to the Pope?'

'The godless French deposed him. Poor Pius the Sixth – *Il Papa Bello* – handsome and very vain. When he said he wanted to die in Rome, they laughed and jeered and told him that one can die anywhere. So he died in Valence the following year at eighty-one, a French prisoner. Eighteen hundred years of sacred tradition violated. The whole city mourned our martyred Pope.'

Lucia explains as if to an idiot, 'We are in a new world now. Wherever Napoleon goes he brings modernity and sweeps away hereditary privilege and dead traditions like your old Pope. He will emancipate the Jews and the serfs.'

'O yes. He liberates men and then conscripts them into his armies to die like cattle.'

'He will free us all from religion and give us opportunities for advancement because we're talented, not because our parents have titles. Soon he will invade Britain and sweep away their aristocracy.'

'Then I will lose my remaining income and will no longer be able to offer you shelter here,' I say.

'We must not think only of our own little lives! Napoleon is a great man, perhaps the greatest ever. We must admire his free spirit.'

For a moment I wonder if my zealous young friend could be a spy for her beloved ogre. But no, she is too indiscreet.

'Well, the Romans were too much for him. They hated the silly new street names, the new calendar and the new coins. The Church used to feed everybody, but the republic only fed those who could prove they were destitute. So your ridiculous republic died with the century. Who knows how it will end?'

'It will end well, dear Contessa. Napoleon will bring truth and justice.'

'How young you are.' I look at Lucia more gently, remembering I am old enough to be her grandmother. 'Are you feeling better?'

'A little dizzy.'

'Go and lie down. I must work.'

After she leaves me I do no work, but sit here terrifying myself with phantasies and bitter memories of the French occupation. When the French return, when Napoleon looms over our city like Leviathan over the Hebrews and the four horsemen of the Apocalypse come galloping up the Via Sistina, where shall I go? I imagine a balloon outside my window, manned by my benign Zucchi. Smiling, he helps me into the basket and away we fly, like eagles swooping over the smouldering ruins of Europe.

Alba knocks. 'Contessa! Today is a saint's day. You should not work.' In Rome there are a hundred and twenty official religious holidays, every one of them an excuse for idleness.

'Go away! I must work.'

# 23

I still say that, yet it is not true. The sham Contessa rarely works now. My hands are too swollen and painful to hold a paintbrush for long or play my pianoforte. I sit here alone in my studio talking to my paintings – not aloud, of course, else Alba will come running – but in the theatre of my mind. No more grand *conversazioni* with music and cards and famous men and cardinals. These silent conversations have no witnesses.

Lucia tells me the coffee houses are seething with the news. People talk of nothing else. Alba joins us in my studio to gossip and even my sober cousin Johann hovers in the doorway to listen and gasp.

Lucia is shrill, breathless with the pleasure of knowing more than us. 'Then the Pope handed him the crown.'

I am close to tears. 'Our Holy Father! It was Camillo Borghese, that hussy's husband, who dragged him to Paris. What a disgrace for the scion of a Roman papal house!'

'O, Camillo is a booby,' says Lucia as if she knows him well. We all talk of these dreadful people as if they live in the next room. All Europe is their house now and we shrink as they expand.

'Paolina didn't want to go to Paris. Madame Mere and Lucien refused. They've stayed in Rome.'

'Bravo Lucien! The only decent Bonaparte.'

'The only failure! He married a French merchant's widow when he might have married a duchess,' says Lucia with contempt.

'He had the good sense to marry for love, he despises his brother's imperial ambitions.'

'They say all he does is dig up old statues,' says Alba.

'A very important occupation. He's a scholar and a gentleman, unlike his murdering braggart of a brother.'

'And *la diva* Paolina, was she at the coronation?' Even my austere cousin has been bewitched by her.

'Paolina detests Josephine,' says Lucia with her knowing air.

'We have no need of an infallible pope, for we have an infallible Signorina.'

Lucia ignores my sarcasm and gallops on: 'Paolina would have liked her brother to divorce Josephine because she can't produce an heir. She disapproved of the coronation but, in the end, she went to Paris. She and her sisters carried Josephine's train at the coronation; they say the velvet weighed a ton. There was gold everywhere – jewels, lace, satin, silk, brilliance. How I wish I'd been there instead of in boring old Rome.'

Were it not for me she would be in neither city, but in a ditch somewhere. I hardly know whether to be amused or annoyed by Lucia's ingratitude. 'How can you possibly know all this?'

'I read the newspaper in the Caffè degli Inglesi.'

'Those dreadful lying French newspapers!' Yet I cannot resist listening as she produces one – she must have stolen it from the coffee house, for she is quite unscrupulous. She reads aloud, translating as she goes into fluent Italian for the benefit of Alba.

'Listen to this: "11 Frimaire, An XIII –"'

'O spare us their ridiculous calendar!'

'December the second, if you must be so old fashioned. "The pontifical procession, accompanied by one hundred and eight dragoons, set out from the Tuileries Palace. Pope Pius VII rode in the second carriage and the procession was led by the Nuncio Speroni, riding an ass and carrying the cross. This piece of absurd pontifical protocol greatly amused bystanders –"'

'Stop! I cannot bear it.' Lucia looks up at me in surprise and shrugs. As a little protestant barbarian, she does not care that centuries of papal dignity have been sabotaged.

'Have you heard what Pasquino says?' Alba smirks. 'To save his faith, one Pius lost his throne. To save his throne, another Pius lost his faith.'

'When your tawdry Emperor comes to Rome there will be no more Pasquino, no more freedom of speech.'

Says Lucia in a swoon of delight, 'Do you think he really will come? Now he's a Holy Roman Emperor like Charlemagne – the greatest man in the world. How I'd love to see him! Do you know, he took the crown from the Pope's hands and set it on his own head? Then he crowned Josephine.'

'He makes the Emperor Nero look like a paragon of modesty.'

'O Contessa, you're so severe. If he does come to Rome, will you meet him? All the artists in the caffè were saying that David is to paint the coronation. Perhaps Napoleon will ask you to paint his portrait and he will come here, to your studio. I shall hide behind the curtain – he will glimpse me and ask you who that beautiful girl is.'

'I shall say, she's a very foolish little flibbertigibbet. Or rather I shall say nothing, for I shall never, never permit a Bonaparte to cross my threshold.'

'But you could be really famous again, like David.'

Then the anger that has been simmering in me all morning boils over and I turn on Lucia. 'Why would I want to be like him? I remember when Jacques-Louis David was only too glad to accept invitations to my salon. He's an opportunist who wallows in violence. During the days of the terror he posted placards all over Paris, telling good citizens to run priests through with a sword – signed the death warrant of his king – made no comment as the tumbrils took away his former friends. Such a republican he used to be! He used to say people should live as they did in Sparta. Yet now he is to paint Napoleon's coronation!'

'I think his *Death of Marat* is wonderful,' says Lucia. 'I saw it in Paris. Such colours!'

'He paints in blood, but not his own. Marat as a revolutionary martyr bathed in soft glowing light. Ridiculous! I knew Marat when he was a penniless doctor with strange ideas in Soho. My darling Zucchi met him at Slaughter's Coffee House in St Martin's Lane. He was one of the least heroic looking men I ever saw – tiny, sallow, pockmarked, with lank, black hair and a twitching mouth. Before we were married, he ate at Zucchi's house almost every day and borrowed a great deal of money from him. Never paid back a penny of it, of course. He used to write sitting in the bath because of his hideous psoriasis.'

'You've known everyone,' says Lucia enviously.

I say nothing because it is true. I do not add that Marat bragged all over London that he had seduced me. I was so angry that I would gladly have killed him and spared Charlotte Corday the bother. Lucia loves such gossip; she would rush straight down to the coffee houses to spread it. I must not tell her too much about my past.

'Your old friend David, who you despise so much, designed the costumes,' Lucia gloats over her newspaper again. 'How glorious it must have been. Listen to this: "The Emperor wore a white velvet vest with gold embroidery and diamond buttons, a crimson velvet tunic and a wreath of laurel. Before entering Notre Dame, the Emperor was vested in a long, white, satin tunic embroidered in gold thread. Josephine wore a white satin empire style dress embroidered in gold thread."'

Says Alba, 'The cook at the Palazzo Borghese told my sister that the three Bonaparte sisters made a big scene before his coronation. They refused to carry Josephine's train. Then their brother lost his temper and threatened to take away all their titles and money, so they sulked and, just to spite their brother, they pulled Josephine back so that she stumbled.'

I laugh with the others. Then Johann snatches the newspaper from Lucia and translates haltingly from the French. '"The police esteem – estimate? – that some two million people were present in Paris. Hundreds of church bells rang out, followed by illuminations, artificial fires – fireworks? – formal balls and dancing in the streets. A balloon ablaze with three thousand lights was launched from the front of Notre Dame during the celebration..." *Mein Gott*, how much money this man squanders.'

My frugal cousin sounds pained. I try to raise the tone of the conversation. 'And how many lives! He is a monster, He will murder a whole generation of young men and bankrupt us all.'

'But how magnificent it all is.' Lucia's green eyes sparkle. She twists a chestnut curl around her finger as she imagines dancing with the Corsican ogre. She is still very pretty despite the weight she has put on lately. This silly fashion for waists that are tucked beneath the arms shows me that she no longer has a waist. O how stupid I have been – I dismiss Johann and Alba, who stares hard at Lucia as she goes out.

Lucia is about to follow them, but I ask her to stay. Alone with me she becomes nervous and sits awkwardly on the throne my sitters use. She's too fat to be paintable now.

'How many months since your little friend has visited you?' She pretends not to understand. 'Come now. Your *règles* – your curse – the red king – the red road?'

She is sullen and will not look at me. 'Lucia? Have you seen a doctor?'

She bursts into tears and insists there is nothing wrong with her. I tell Alba to fetch Doctor Morici.

The girl lies on the daybed in my studio to be examined, eyes shut, looking terrified as he probes. He, who is usually so charming, looks down at her with cold eyes as he invades her body and addresses all his remarks to me.

'Contessa, the signora – signorina...?'

'The *signora*'s husband has tragically died in the wars in France,' I lie blithely, and he looks relieved.

'The signora is with child. I estimate it will be born in the early summer. Is she a servant here?'

'A friend.' My voice is firm despite the quivering jelly of my doubts. This is the scandal I have been avoiding all my life. Alba knows. I must send Lucia to the nuns or to one of the butchers in the city below.

# 24

---

This last week has passed in fever and sickness. Alba wrote many letters to the saints, praying for my recovery. Unable to sleep I lie abed, waiting for the dawn. Just now I opened my shutters and fetched a carafe of water from the icy kitchen. It is not fair to disturb Alba; her name means "dawn" and every day she works from sunrise until late at night, as once I did. She needs her sleep. I envy her ability to lie down and forget herself. Are those her snores I can hear down the corridor?

How long the nights are at this time of year; too long, each one a dark tunnel I must walk through blindly – sleeping waking remembering dreaming.

Rossi hovers. He asks too many questions – flummers me shamelessly – speaks of writing my life for publication. But I am writing my own here – for the bonfire. After death, who can control what they say about you? I say as little as possible.

'Esteemed Contessa, what a joy to enter again in your temple of the muses. I have come to wish you a most joyful and wondrous new year. May I call you by your Arcadian name? Amaryllis, painter of souls. Please address me by mine.'

'I can't remember what it was.'

'Perinto Sceo. Can you in your modesty have forgotten the verses I composed in admiration of you?' He flings his arms around as he declaims in our old Arcadian manner – once so passionate, but now so silly. 'You return and Rome, difficult Rome / Spying in your sweet, sacred refuge / the Parthenopean deities and their / Divine offspring reborn, thanks to your creator brush, and happily applauds –'

If I do not stop him, he will recite all morning. 'Please, Giovanni – Perinto – you are too kind.' Far too kind. What does he want of me?

'I am so desolated to hear you have been ill. Yet still you have your fiery eye and flaming gaze.'

This was the florid language of the Arcadian Academy, of which we are both members. I rarely attend their meetings now; ill-health has its uses. Rossi used to spout his dreadful poems. We all did – we were younger then. Before Rome was ravaged and looted, all that seemed quite natural – even delightful – but now it feels artificial. Rossi was Minister for Finance under the Ridiculous Republic a few years ago. It feathered his nest, but he went on warbling about truth and beauty and classical ideals. Zucchi used to say his plays were a very feeble imitation of Goldoni's.

'Still an enchantress! No wonder the great Sir Joshua used to call you Miss Angel. Tell me again, how did you meet him?'

'It was so long ago. I can hardly remember.'

'In London, was it not? Is it true he had the tenderest feelings for you?'

'Your gossip is almost as ancient as Arcadia. Speaking of which, dear Fortunata Fantastici wrote to me recently. She sent me charming drawings by one of her little daughters.'

'The divine Fortunata! Or Temira Parriside, as we called her in our Arcadian circle. To think that such an ethereal creature could mother human babies! I hope she is not grown fat. How beautifully she read my verses and how inspired her improvisations were.'

Were they? All this talk of the past embarrasses me. I plead an appointment with an imaginary sitter. After Rossi leaves, I go through to my studio and sit alone. I do not think I can bear to attempt another self-portrait. There have been so many – there they all are on the wall. The story of my life in pictures. Better to end it a few years back when my face was tired and lined but not yet utterly wrecked. My eyes are failing, but the mirror reveals quite enough.

How proud I used to be of my naturally white complexion. It is like parchment now covered with furrows and crinkles as if scribbled on by a crazed monkey. After my eyebrows disappeared, I stuck on mouse-skin imitations which overhang my rheumy eyes. In honour of Rossi's visit I wore false teeth made of elephant ivory. My gums are sore and my mouth is full of blood. I tear out my expensive teeth and watch as my face collapses like a cake withdrawn too soon from an oven. There will be no more self-portraits.

Lucia knocks in her newfound politeness. I whip my teeth back in – for vanity is the last thing to go. I have been avoiding her these last few days because I do not know what to do about her.

'Come in.'

I have given her a grey cashmere shawl to hide her condition – but it does not. My eyes are drawn to the future bulging inconveniently out of her. Remembering my manners, I look into her face, which has grown lovelier as her troubles make her more complex. Her green eyes meet mine with doubt as a nervous hand goes up to play with her hair.

'Sit down, child. Will you read to me while I draw you?'

'Poetry?'

'Whatever you will.'

She holds a book in her other hand. 'I will read this.'

I try to relax into the familiar rhythm, the delicate charcoal between my fingers in my womblike studio. The mystery of the other's face is offered up – the multifarious decisions: to make a nose or a mouth smaller – to smooth out a double chin. But Lucia is not paying, so I do not have to flatter her. And besides, her features are almost perfect. How I envy her delicate flush and even, white teeth. It is pointless to compare these things to peaches, cream, emeralds and pearls, for they are uniquely human, each beauty a miracle that will be dissolved by time.

At first, I do not listen to what she is reading.

'"If an innocent girl become a prey to love, she is degraded forever, though her mind was not polluted by the arts which married women, under the convenient cloak of marriage, practise. Nor has she violated any duty – but the duty of respecting herself –"'

'What is this tosh you are reading?'

'*A Vindication of the Rights of Women* by Mary Wollstonecraft. A very great book that every woman should read.'

'I knew her in London.'

'You knew everyone in London.'

'She was a very wild young woman. People said she was an unsexed female. Hopelessly in love with Fuseli – a fascinating man, but quite indifferent to her.' He was a pornographer, once in love with me – but I do not like to talk too freely with Lucia.

'I admire her so much. She defied the conventions of society and lived as a free woman.'

'She died before she was forty, if I remember rightly. One child out of wedlock and a second with that amiable lunatic Godwin. Dead of puerperal fever after her second child. Poor creature.'

There. We have introduced the subject and there is no turning back. She closes her book and there are tears on her long eyelashes. Her nose is red too – no use drawing her now. I put down my charcoal so that there are no barriers between us. She does not dissolve like some spoilt young miss but sits up and swallows her tears as she looks at me very straight.

'I may not be considerate enough to die in childbirth.'

'Have you thought about where to go?'

'Where can I go?'

'There are convents.'

'I detest nuns. I was taught by them in Florence – we had to bathe in our shifts that we may not ever see our own bodies. They spoke of women who had babies out of wedlock as sinners and whores. The other girls said the nuns sold off the babies of the unfortunate girls who came to them *in cinta*.'

'Some of the kindest women I have known have been nuns.'

'Kind to you. Rich, famous, virtuous, pious.'

'You still refuse to say who the father is?'

'If I tell you, will you help me?'

'I will try. Was it someone I know?' I have been so worried. Is it Cousin Johann, with his buttoned-up ways? Antonio Canova, who cannot see a pretty girl without trying to seduce her? Or is it that fat old hypocrite Rossi?

She squirms. I try to make the moment less embarrassing by tidying my paper and crayons. We do not look at each other while she speaks.

'You have no idea what it's like to have no family or friends. Only eyes staring at me – looking to see what they can get out of me. Artists paid me to sit, but they always pawed and groped me. After a while I got used to it and stopped minding. I became a goddess or nymph or saint or martyr, and I took their money. When I left their studio, I was still Lucia. But then – O Contessa, it was terrible.'

'You fell in love?'

'He was younger than the others, quite shy. His father was English and his mother was French. He had grown up all over Europe like me. When I undressed the first time to put on Niobe's drapes, he turned his back. When I left his studio, he insisted on accompanying me to the top of the Spanish Steps. After each sitting our walks grew longer. We walked all over Rome together, talking about everything. Politics and art and music. Then, one afternoon in the Borghese Gardens we kissed. And then.' She is silent.

'Does he know you are with child?'

'He left Rome before I knew. To join his wife in Paris. So he told me the last afternoon we spent together. I wept and screamed and raged and watched as all the love went out of him like air out of a balloon.'

'So there is no possibility of marrying him?'

'I don't want to marry. My parents did nothing but quarrel – the men in the caffès talk about their wives as chains and pests. The only women I've known who have some dignity – like you – have no husbands to order them around. To be the property of some man! I've seen the advertisements in the newspapers in London: Mrs So-and-So has absconded from her husband. Any person harbouring her is menaced with the utmost severity of the law.'

I also used to marvel at those advertisements.

Just then I see Lucia in profile, her face so young and her belly in full sail. She's younger than I was. It all comes back. I have to shut my eyes to keep out my humiliation – my father's harsh orders – the massacre of the innocent.

'Are you ill?'

'A little giddy.'

'I've tired you out with my problems.' Lucia jumps up, frightened. I remember that fear too: that my friends in London would drop me and I would become an outcast.

When Lucia leaves, I ring the bell for Alba to ask her to help me through to my *salone*, my classical room full of plaster casts of gods that stare at me reproachfully. Apollo Belvedere, Jove as an Eagle with Ganymede – so cold and white in the wintry air. They are offended because they are neglected now – all their admirers dead or fled. My reception rooms are freezing, for it would be wasteful to heat them. Once they were full of people, music, laughter and conversation until three in the morning. Everybody who mattered in Rome came here to my house: David, Flaxman, cardinals, monsignori and aristocrats from all over Europe. I shiver as I stand at the big window, looking down at Rome. The green silk drapes are frayed and dusty, but I will not replace them now. Down there are beggars and prostitutes and cutthroats – I cannot throw her out into those bitter streets. Inside every palazzo in Rome there are women far worse than Lucia who have copulated in cynicism instead of in love.

I wonder if Rome remembers the French occupation. Have her buildings absorbed all that has happened to them? If cities have souls, Rome's is golden – a treasure I cannot let go of. Over there is the empty Quirinale. Perhaps the Pope will never return. His palace will fall into ruins like the imperial palaces on the Palatine. Like all of us, the city is waiting for Napoleon.

# 25

---

Today I have a long letter from dear Cornelia. What a journey it must have had! Delivered from her hand to a palace servant – through the London fog down to Dover – across the sea to France, past innumerable spies and censors – over the snowy Alps to Milan – and finally down here to Rome. Tossed in a sack and carried by post horse, mule, donkey, ferry and handcart. It's easier now for a letter to make that journey than for a human being.

Cornelia and I write in our private Italian-English code, referring to the French as landscape painters and to the English as historical painters. Napoleon's spies are everywhere. So many friends are dead now and many of the living ones like her are beyond my reach, on the other side of the Alps. In London, says Cornelia, they ask if I am dead.

O, those happy years when Cornelia and her mother lived here in Rome. After the Admiral died they had ten languages between them, but no money. I admired their courage: they lived on a pittance, made their own clothes and even cooked for themselves. Cornelia was always busy drawing and writing – women who work are more to my taste than ladies of leisure. People laughed at Cornelia because she was a blue stocking, but I respected her and invited her to all my *conversazioni*. I painted her with a pencil in her hand and her novel, *Marcus Flaminius*, beside her. Some thought she was *jolie laide*, but most people said she was plain, with her large, sensible features and dark, untidy hair. I can always find beauty in intelligent faces and detest the common way of describing a woman only in terms of her good or bad looks. A plain man is "distinguished" or "has a face full of character" (if he be rich) but a woman must win golden apples. Here in Rome, *bellezza* rules. A woman like that debauched little Paolina Borghese can do as she pleases because she is beautiful.

Cornelia and I became such close friends that she asked me to alter the portrait cameo of Minerva on her painted girdle to a portrait of me. She is a staunch Protestant, a Tory and Bourbonist with no sympathy for republican principles. She and her mama fled to Naples when the Ridiculous Republic arrived in Rome. The following year Lady Knight died. Over forty – unmarried – cultivated – penniless – what choice does a woman have? Cornelia wisely placed herself under the protection of Sir William and Lady Hamilton, choosing to ignore the unconventional relations between the lovely Emma and Nelson, who accompanied them back to England. Had she money, she would shine at her own salon and dazzle London society, for she is cultivated and has a well-stocked mind. Having not a sou, she has become Lady Companion to Queen Charlotte. The Queen is the kindest lady – she saved my reputation after the fiasco with H – but the royal household is not erudite.

Cornelia's letter is full of veiled complaints. She must be unhappy, for she has forgotten to use our usual code. "We are very quiet here. The Queen no longer appears much in public.

She has given up the musical concerts she once enjoyed so much.... My duties require me to be always at hand, whether at dawn or midnight, and I have hardly a moment to read or write.... the King's illness has caused us all great distress and the Queen has been in very low spirits.... They say the King is mad as a hatter at times.... The Queen has been very busy with her botanical pursuits." Poor Cornelia. She used to yawn uncontrollably when I talked about my garden. "The dear princesses are very dull at Frogmore.... We daily expect Napoleon's invasion and the King has reviewed our volunteer troops."

No corner of Europe is free of the shadow of that ogre. Queen Charlotte and Queen Marie Antoinette never met, but they wrote to each other and shared their horror at the events in France. Kind Queen Charlotte was quite sure the French royal family would be able to flee to safety in England, and she even arranged apartments for them.

"The Queen wept this morning, saying that we shall all be murdered like the poor Bourbons.... The King says that when Bonaparte invades, he will take the field and lead his troops. The Queen says he is too ill and old and that if she is widowed, she will die of grief."

Poverty has taught Cornelia diplomacy so she must be desperate indeed when she writes "the classical taste and sober dignity of Italy, with the grandeur of its spacious habitations, eclipse in my mind all I have seen elsewhere and render C H nothing more than a nobleman's dwelling, expensively furnished." It is obvious that C H is Carlton House. Well, she entreats me to burn her letter as soon as I have read it. I will do so, of course – as we all do in these precarious times. She misses Rome, just as

I did when I lived in London. Yet sometimes I pine for England. We polyglots are never happy.

Cornelia brings news of the fascinating Maria Hadfield. I first knew her when she was a little girl in Florence, where Papa and I rented an apartment in her father's inn. I saw at once that the child drew and sang quite beautifully. They are a strange family, the Hadfields, half-Italian and quite eccentric. There were eight children, but only four have survived because a crazed nursemaid murdered four of them. She was overheard to say that Maria would be the next to be despatched to heaven. As a result, Maria has always been excessively religious.

She grew up to be a beauty. I made her my protégée and I am proud of her. In Rome I arranged for her to be taught art by Mengs and Batoni. When her beloved father died, Maria announced her intention to enter a convent, but I persuaded her that her gifts were of this world, so she moved to London. Maria's marriage to Richard Cosway did not please me, for I knew him for a libertine – ugly as a monkey and twenty years older than Maria. His heart is as small as the miniatures he paints.

Why do brilliant women choose so badly? It is a painful subject.

When he saw that his bride had more talent than him, Richard was jealous and forbade her to accept payment for her paintings. To my horror, Maria gave up painting. I went to see her in great distress, to argue that she had a duty to God to develop her talent.

'No,' said she. 'All my duty is to my husband.'

'O Maria,' said I. 'Please don't abandon the muses who have given you such gifts.'

'My husband says that paintresses attract gossip,' said she, with a hard look so that I would know she was referring to me. 'Please don't speak to me in Italian, Angelica. My husband says my foreign manners are an embarrassment to him and I must live here in seclusion until I master the English language.'

She did master it, and she became a great society hostess – the Goddess of Pall Mall, they called her. How much easier it was to be a fashionable goddess than a hard-working painter.

Soon after her marriage I left England. I must have offended her – she no longer confides in me – but I wonder if she named her daughter for me: Louisa Paolina Angelica. The poor child died when she was only ten.

I have always followed Maria's career with great interest. She conquered many hearts, though never her husband's shrivelled organ. Thomas Jefferson was quite smitten by her in Paris when he served as the American envoy to France. I hope her triumphs have outweighed her pain, for Richard betrayed her shame-lessly. He travelled for six months with Mary Moser – another woman of talent who has poor judgement of men. It was a sketching tour, or so they said. Both of them were married, but not to each other. Mary and I were once great friends. In those exciting days when the Academy was newly founded, she and I were the only women among so many men.

When I heard of Mary's disgracefully public affair with Richard, I took Maria's part – but have not seen either of them since I left London. We few women who attempt to play an active role in this man's world should never quarrel with one another, for we are blood sisters in the eternal war between the sexes.

I have seen so many women bullied out of their talent like Maria. 'Tis love that undoes us. Most women need only human love, but a woman who loves her art must marry it. Joshua – Canova – how many male artists say this and are admired for their single-mindedness? Yet a woman who dares to say it is accused of being cold and unnatural. I can see now that I was weakest when I loved most. For H or Wolfgang would I have given up painting? Never!

Maria must be about five and forty now. How ancient that makes me feel. Cornelia writes me that since her separation from Richard, Maria has gone to France. I have heard that she admires Napoleon – even meets with the monster. She has resumed her career as a painter and copies stolen Italian paintings in that vast museum, that shameful warehouse of stolen goods Napoleon has opened in Paris. It has the Veroneses, Titians and Tintorettos he stole from Venice, our own *Apollo Belvedere*, *The Laocoon*, *The Dying Gaul*, the Medici Venus, Titian's *Sacra Conversazione*... I feel as if they have been torn from my own soul.

Cornelia tells me that through her friendship with Cardinal Fesch, the ogre's uncle, Maria has established a college for young ladies. Now Fesch has become the French ambassador here. He has invited me to a reception, but I have no wish to meet him. I hope Maria's work as a teacher has mended the heart that was broken when her own little daughter died. Politics have divided us, yet Maria is always close to my heart and I am very pleased to have this news of her.

Cornelia also writes that Frances Reynolds is grown old and ill. I did not like the manner in which Joshua threw his sister out after she had kept house for him so many years. Frances taught

Cornelia to paint and might have been a distinguished artist herself. Another female talent fallen by the wayside! O, when will girls and boys receive the same education? Only then will women truly shine – women generals, bishops, judges, doctors, priests – a day will come when none of these will seem remarkable, and women will no longer be told that their ambition is unfeminine. But I shall not see it.

# 26

---

My sitter sweeps into my studio – and immediately I feel dowdy. That Parisian style is more like a weapon than a refinement. Even her compliments sound barbed as her clever lisp moves effortlessly between French, Italian and German.

'Dearest Angelica! I know we haven't met before, but we ought to have done, for we have so much in common. Now, do with me as you will. Where will you put me? Forgive my scruffy clothes, just some old things I pulled on.'

She still wears mourning for her beloved father, the crooked financier Necker, who died a few months ago. Her hat and gown are a symphony of black, perfectly orchestrated. She must have spent hours in front of the mirror with her maid fussing around her. Her black velvet dress is cut low and her dark hair falls in waves beneath her wonderful black hat, so elegant that one hardly notices her coarse, red features. Of course, I will refine them. Her eyes are good, and she knows how to play them. My hand goes awkwardly to my untidy grey hair as I remember my breakfast coffee has joined the other stains on my painting smock.

'Would you like to read some poetry aloud while I draw you, Madame?'

'O, please call me Germaine. Much as I adore poetry, I had far rather talk to you, for I have heard so much about you. My mother told me of the days when all of Europe was Angelicamad.'

'And your reputation for wit precedes you. Are you writing a book at the moment?'

'Always writing. Which reminds me.' She takes a book out of her reticule and hands it to me. 'Wolfgang asked me to give this to you. I was in Weimar last year.'

At the sound of his name I gasp. My hand trembles as I open Friedrich von Schiller's *Wilhelm Tell* and read the inscription on the flyleaf: "For Angelica the Good" – *die Gute* was his name for me. Even when he was here with me in Rome, I knew that men do not fall in love with good women. Germaine takes all this in with a quizzical smile, like a cat watching a very naive mouse.

I have longed to meet her for years. She grew up in her mother's Paris salon and was famous for her wit before she was twenty. Then she married the Swedish ambassador – as it occurs to me that she might know about H my heart tumbles. Her connection with both men is too much excitement for one morning and I have to sit down to recover my breath.

'Thank you so much. Tell me about Weimar.'

'Isn't it an extraordinary place?'

'I have never been there.' Except in my imagination. A thousand times.

'O! They all seemed to know you so well.'

'They spoke of me?'

'Wolfgang called you his good angel of art and the old Duchess said you were the kindest woman she knew.'

'Dear Anna Amalia! We lived here like sisters for a few months. She took the Villa Malta just next door, and we visited each other daily. How is she?'

'Old and frail. They were all very sad about the death of the poet, von Herder.'

'Another good friend. He also lived here in Rome for a while.' He and Anna Amelia were my consolation prizes when Wolfgang left.

'The national genius of Germany can learn so much from the warmth and spontaneity of the South. Personally, I adore classical ideals, but they are basically opposed to the Nordic, where the future lies. Our friend Goethe has understood that his work must express the moral and historical reality – the zeitgeist of the nation in which it is conceived. As for Napoleon...'

My French limps behind her swift bon mots. She has opinions about everything and everyone – she makes me feel quite insipid. Germaine is famous for these arias on national differences, but I am not interested in the general. I guide our conversation back to the particular.

'Did you go to the theatre in Weimar?' I ask.

'I had the great good fortune to attend the first performance of this very play, Schiller's *Wilhelm Tell*, at the exquisite little jewel box of a theatre they have made there. Such a brilliant young man! Wolfgang directed it and the friendship between those two geniuses is so wonderfully unselfish.' Wolfgang's latest infatuation.

'I think I will have to ask you to come for a second sitting, Germaine. I cannot draw with my usual speed, for you distract me by talking about my favourite subjects – Wolfgang and the Corsican ogre.'

'Both monsters!' she declares with her usual brio. 'But in life one must choose between boredom and suffering. These monsters make us suffer – and we women are fascinated by them.'

People talk of her duel with Napoleon. 'Forgive my curiosity, but is it true that Napoleon has exiled you from Paris?'

'Yes, I may not go within forty leagues of Paris. He hopes to crush me, but I am not so easily destroyed. I love to travel. But one can have too much of a good thing.'

'So does he. We live in daily fear that he will come here.'

'Perhaps. Already he has what he wants from Rome.'

'Yes, he has stolen the lifeblood of our city.'

'He justifies his plunder – says those treasures belong to the people of France now, rather than to foreign despots. A few years ago, I watched as a triumphant procession passed beneath my window in Paris. I saw the four copper horses from the facade of St Marks in Venice. Thirty carts loaded with classical sculptures – Raphaels – Titians – Tintorettos – what a magnificent museum he is building!'

'And filling with stolen goods.'

'Those Venetian horses were originally looted from Constantinople. Great art goes to the victors. There is no morality involved, as long as the owners respect it. It is true that Italians are often careless custodians of works of art.'

I hesitate to argue with her about politics – to cross swords with a woman who has challenged Napoleon to a duel. At the beginning of the revolution in France Germaine was a Jacobin, but later she supported the moderate Girondin faction. I see only individuals, not nationalities or grand, abstract ideas. She is a brilliant woman and it is a pleasure to talk with her.

'I long to know what you think of Rome.'

'Your Rome is the land of tombs. It offers a dreamy melancholy pleasure but, if I stayed here, I would get secretly and nobly bored. Society amounts to virtually nothing – although of course there are charming exceptions, like you and Canova.'

I feel obliged to defend my beloved city. 'You are not seeing Rome at its best. So many distinguished people have left – or died.'

'Even in Paris people die. I am speaking of the vitality of this city, which is sapped by an oriental indolence and flexibility of character. One can only eat so many lotuses.'

'You must miss Paris greatly.'

'It is the city of the future. May I trouble you to ask for more coffee? I only slept for three hours last night, for I was busy writing.' She looks around my studio greedily, as if recording every detail to use in one of her books.

'I wish you'd seen our Rome a few years ago, before it was looted and ravaged. What you see now is a kind of shell. Why, even our Holy Father has been stolen by Napoleon.'

'I don't share your adulation for the Bishop of Rome.'

'We Romans need him – Rome is my city now. Perhaps the city you know best is always more real than any other.'

'There is nothing real in the world but love.'

For a moment I am tempted to ask her about that, about the rumours that even before she separated from her husband, Benjamin Constant and many others were her lovers – that

Constant is the father of one of the children she has brought to Rome – that their young tutor shares her bed. But an aphorism is not a confidence, so I merely ask, 'Where do you go next?'

She sighs. 'I suppose we may see more of Italy. Then I shall return to Coppet, where my father has left me his chateau. Travel is one of the saddest pleasures in life.'

'I also feel that I belong nowhere. But to understand why I love Rome, you have only to look out of the window. Even on this dull February morning there is a golden light here you see nowhere else. Looking out at these domes and obelisks and those hills in mist or sunset or at dawn – well, I am an artist. I live through my eyes.'

'A pretty view might distract me for half an hour, but not for a lifetime.' Seeing that I look wounded she adds, 'How right you were to choose to live here rather than in England. I admire their parliamentary democracy and their education but living in England develops only the critical intellect. One needs imagination to appreciate Italy.'

'Yes, I found London very interesting – but ugly. English women do not benefit from either democracy or education.'

'Absolutely! Do you know, when I was very young my parents thought of marrying me to that fellow Pitt. Even then he thought of nothing but politics, and now he is their Prime Minister again. When I visited England I was appalled by the way they treat their women.'

'I do agree. Most Englishmen love their horses and dogs more than their wives.'

'Englishwomen are imprisoned in the domestic sphere.'

I remember that dreadful visit to Nathaniel Dance's family. 'I too narrowly escaped marriage to an Englishman, a young artist I met here who assured me he would always respect my work and regard me as his equal. Then, when I went to England, I was invited to meet his relations, summoned to some vast, damp house in the middle of nowhere. At dinner I joined in the conversation *con brio* and saw him frown at me. Young ladies are not supposed to express opinions.'

'Dear Angelica! I also endured a visit to such a morgue. And were the ladies banished to the drawing room after dinner?'

'Just so, and they sat in silence with their embroidery. Eventually, some old woman said, "The men will be up soon."'

'Yes! Then, after another long silence, "Shall we put the kettle on for their tea?"' Germaine mimics the genteel voice perfectly.

'I knew then that I could never marry him. In the morning I fled back to London.'

'Why, in Paris or Rome, men would find the idea of an evening without the company of women unbearable.'

'They would run after us into the drawing room!'

We are giggling like two schoolgirls. Says Germaine with warmth, 'You and I are cosmopolitan; we belong all over Europe. Where were you born? Are you not Swiss like me?'

'My mother was Swiss. I was born in Chur but think of myself as Austrian, although I have spent very little time there. My father was Austrian.'

'Women like us are formed by exceptional fathers, who encourage their daughters' intelligence instead of crushing it.' She looks sad and I see that she truly mourns that old rogue, her father. I still miss mine after all these years.

The bells of *mezzogiorno* chime all around us, the joyful shout to heaven that the French atheists have not been able to stifle.

'Midday already?' She jumps up. 'I have invited guests for luncheon – I must supervise my children's lessons and write another chapter.'

'I hope you will be able to fit in another sitting while you are in Rome.'

'Perhaps. But I am so busy. May I kiss you, dear Angelica? A delightful morning!'

She rushes out. I envy her free spirit as I look down sadly at my feeble sketch. I am no longer able to work well, but she has enough energy to carry her on for another hundred years.

I must write to Cornelia about Germaine's visit. She will be fascinated, for Germaine is considered very scandalous in England. Fanny Burney visited her at Coppet but was so shocked by her morals and politics that she had to leave. Cornelia and I have always had to work for our living; we must fear the censorious tongues of those who pay us. But Germaine is rich, she soars above such considerations like Vesuvius. This morning she was in a good mood, but I have heard that she erupts volcanically if anybody displeases her.

After she leaves, my studio does not feel empty. It is still imbued with her extraordinary personality – her confident ringing voice and explosive vitality hang in the air. Unable to work,

I go to the window to look out over my garden. The pine tree Wolfgang gave me seventeen years ago has survived another winter and is quite tall now. When it was a baby – a sapling – I used to run out whenever there was a storm to swaddle it in a cloth. In the middle of the night I would wake choked with fear that it had died. His pine tree will outlive us both.

# 27

---

When Alba brings my breakfast tray, Johann accompanies her. From their long faces I see they are a deputation come to bother me. I am weak after days of fever and coughing, trapped in bed. I have no stomach for argument or even breakfast – I have no choice but to listen. Alba opens the shutters, lets in the day with heavy disapproval and does not amuse me with her usual kitchen gossip. She pours my coffee in silence, then takes an ominous breath.

'Contessa, you know that I have served you well and have always been proud that this is a respectable house,' says Alba.

'Dear cousin, I have not been with you as long as Alba, but I bear your name and promised your husband before he died that I would protect you,' says Johann.

Their faces loom over me. Johann's is so thin you could cut yourself on his nose and chin. Alba's black eyes are angry in her pudding face. I sit up to feel less like a child who has displeased her parents and the effort makes me breathless.

'What is it that has upset you both?'

'That little whore must go,' says Alba.

'I appreciate your charitable impulse, dear cousin, but that girl's bastard cannot be born under your roof.'

'I've spoken to the Sisters on the Aventino, and they will accept her,' says Alba firmly.

I have heard rumours that the healthy babies born there are sold – that there is a hidden cemetery where wild flowers are fertilised by the bones of mothers and babies. Lucia is afraid of nuns and would be miserable in a convent. But what shall I do if Alba and Johann leave me? I start to cough. My breakfast tray rattles on my knees. Alba mops up the coffee I have spilt, but her face is still slammed shut.

'I will speak to Lucia. Alba, you have no right to go behind my back like that. But I thank you both for coming to talk to me frankly like this. I have told the doctor that Lucia is a young widow and I suggest we all accept this pretense. It is what my confessor would call a kindly lie.'

Alba turns to go without looking at me. 'Signor Rossi is waiting to see you, Contessa.'

Not again. If only they would all leave me alone, I would get better. As it is, I must fight them all as well as the disease. One cannot have a satisfactory battle lying down – three days in bed are quite enough. So I ring for Alba, who forgets to be angry when she sees me on my feet.

'Contessa! No! You must be careful, for you were not born in Rome, our *aria cattiva* kills so many foreigners.'

It is comforting inside her sweaty embrace. 'I must get dressed now, Alba.'

She fusses around me. 'I will pray for you when I go to the Aracoeli to pray to win the lottery. What did you dream of last night?'

'I can hardly remember. I think I was lost again and struggling across a deep river.'

Alba takes her *Libro di Sogni* out of the pocket in her apron and consults it. 'Ah, drowning! That is a bad dream and it means I should back number eighty-eight on Saturday.'

The weekly lottery is integrated into Romans' religion. The Pope runs it – or used to – perhaps he still does, from France. Statues of the Virgin preside over the counters where lottery tickets are sold and every Saturday the city erupts with excitement when the winning numbers are announced.

As she laces me Alba says, 'Perhaps we can help that wicked Lucia to get a dowry so that she can find a husband to cover her shame.'

'I am not rich, Alba.'

'But you know so many cardinals. They might tell you the winning numbers. Perhaps God tells them? Every week ninety poor girls like her are given free tickets.' If one of them gets five winning numbers, she is given fifty crowns as a dowry. 'Lucia could marry a nice little husband – or become a bride of Jesus.'

I do not shock Alba by telling her that Lucia does not want a husband, least of all a sacred one. 'I will talk to the girl. Tell her to come and see me.'

Lucia comes to me later in my studio. I have been avoiding her lately. The size of her belly is now quite indecorous – was I ever so unsightly? Above it her pretty face is swollen and blotchy. Poor Lucia reminds me of Poor Maria from *Tristram Shandy*. Years ago, my pictures of Poor Maria were reproduced on watch cases and tea caddies all over Europe. Her story touched me: once, Maria was happy, pretty and charming. But after she lost her father and her lover, she became crazed and wandered the countryside, playing the pipes, accompanied by only her pet goat and a little dog. Lucia is an *anima vagabonda*, a wandering soul – I can imagine her wandering all over Europe with her baby.

'You sent for me, Contessa?'

Now that she is here, I do not know what I want to say to her, and my confusion pours out of my mouth as anger. 'You are disrupting my household! I can't have my servants being upset like this.'

Lucia disconcerts me by staying very calm. 'Do you want me to go away?'

'No. You can stay until the child is born. But you must not draw attention to yourself.'

'I live here like a nun. I stay in my room and write and draw.' She looks around my studio. 'What a wonderful place this is.'

The envy in her voice provokes me. 'Founded on hard work, many years of it. When I was your age I worked from dawn until dusk – then often by candlelight. Everything that I have I have worked for. If you want to change your situation, you must work for it.'

'I do work, but I don't suppose anyone will want to buy it.'

'Show me your drawings.'

She comes back with a battered green leather portfolio. 'This belonged to my father; it is all I inherited from him. All the rest was sold to pay his debts.'

Inside are a dozen angry, startling drawings. The charcoal is so thickly worked that the white paper beneath is buried and even has holes in it where her wild heart has worked through. Skulls, skeletons, masks, eyes and chains leap up at me in chaos. They remind me a little of the crazier work of my old teacher, Piranesi.

'O dear.'

'You don't like them. I knew you wouldn't. I'm no good, am I?'

I try to be both honest and comforting. 'You do have talent, Lucia. Really. But these drawings are all about your feelings – such rage. You must control your passions and think of pleasing your public. The ladies who buy drawings want prettiness, soft colours, agreeable subjects. Not this – *terribilità*. You may of course portray distressing stories, but do try to be more restrained. If you can do that, I will show your work to my visitors and I'm sure I will manage to sell some for you.'

Lucia still looks mortified, so I pick up one of her less shocking drawings. A veiled young lady confronts a monstrous serpent. 'How much do you want for this one?'

'Fifty scudi.' It is far too much, but I hand her the money and see that she will be a good businesswoman someday. Well brought up young ladies are too delicate to ask for money.

'May I ask you for one more favour, Contessa?'

I grunt. I do not want to be ungracious but beneath her pretended meekness, she is quite ruthless.

'May I borrow some paper and charcoal, please? Also some of those sickly – those soft colours like the ones you use?'

I have cupboards full of supplies. Her productivity is an affront when I cannot even finish my sketch of Germaine – then I remember that one must always encourage talent.

'Of course.' I fetch them for her. 'This is a gift. Let us not talk of borrowing.'

'Thank you.' She does not look at me. Naturally, she hates me for being old and rich.

On my way through my drawing room I pass Rossi, asleep on a chair in the corner. He has been waiting for hours. I tiptoe past but he wakes with a start and puts on his humility like a coat that does not quite fit.

'Angelic Contessa! Your maid has told me that you were occupied by some errand of mercy.'

'I am busy today.'

'If I could just rob you of a few precious minutes to ask a couple of questions about your fascinating life?'

'My life has been quite uneventful.' How much does he know?

'I have reached the chapter about your arrival in London. I believe your devoted papa was not with you?'

'That's right. He stayed in Morbegno with his relations.'

'So you were all alone.'

'No. I stayed with Lady Wentworth who was extremely kind to me.'

'Having left her second husband, John Murray, when he became the British Ambassador in Constantinople?'

'Lady Wentworth was a most respectable person. I was not alone, for I soon made friends in London.'

'Ah yes, a host of admirers! Nathaniel Dance who pursued you from Rome. The great Sir Joshua. I have even heard whispers of a Duke?'

'I really can't remember. It was all so long ago.'

'Also a Swedish Count? De Horn?'

Can that be a blush heating my withered cheek? I glance at the mirror above his head and see a frightened old woman. 'If only I had kept a journal, I would remember these things.'

'The memoir your brother-in-law wrote of your life is charming, but somehow it seems to leave out more than it fills in.'

'I thought it very well written.' Zucchi and I approved every word.

'Have you never been inspired to write about your life?'

'Never. I can hardly remember what I had for dinner yesterday and have quite forgotten all these people you mention.'

# 28

---

If only I *could* forget. When Lucia knocks on my door I am softened by tender memories and forget to be grumpy with her. Lucia's heart is always seen in her face. Today she is afraid, her green eyes wide with the unknown danger swelling in her belly. She carries white knitting, trailing it as her child will someday drag its doll.

'Am I disturbing you? Were you asleep?'

'I'm awake now, and glad of the distraction. Come and sit down. What are you making?'

'A blanket. But when he – she – it – is born it will be summer, and too hot for anything except a sheet. If...'

That "if" opens up a silence between us. She sits on the chaise longue under the window as the late afternoon sun pushes through the shutters to paint stripes onto her face. She is a little pagan who does not know how to behave. She wears mourning now to support the polite lie of her widowhood and her face above her black gown is thin and pale.

'I don't want to die!' shouts Lucia angrily.

'Doctor Biagio is an excellent *accoucheur*.'

'Yesterday I walked to the Protestant cemetery and saw all the graves of women – many younger than me – with their babies.'

'Roman fever is a great danger to us foreigners, added to puerperal fever. You should not wander the city on your own. It is not safe.'

'I shall go mad if I stay in my room alone all day. When I venture out into the kitchen, Alba and your cousin glare at me. I can't go down to the coffee houses anymore because they all laugh at me. Nobody believes that silly tale about my dead husband.'

'Never mind. It allows me to keep you beneath my roof.'

'I am grateful,' she mutters sullenly. 'Did you sell any of my drawings?'

Her rudeness makes me smile inwardly, although I try not to let my amusement show. She is the girl I trained myself not to be.

'Yes, three of them.' Another kindly lie. I give her one hundred and fifty scudi from my purse.

She snatches the money. 'Thank God! I can buy some baby clothes. I hate sewing. Who bought my drawings? Perhaps they would like some more?'

If I mention names, she will rush out to force herself on them. 'I forget their names. They were a young German couple who were passing through Rome. They came to visit my studio and saw your drawings of the Colosseum.'

'So that's what sells. There was no feeling in those drawings, no part of myself. They look like a thousand others.'

'Yes, that's what sells,' I agree sadly.

We sit in silence as she knits ineptly. She drops all the stitches off one of her needles, stabs her failed blanket with it and flings the grubby white bundle onto the floor.

'We both need some fresh air. If it's fine tomorrow will you come out in the carriage with me?'

'I should like it of all things!' says she with her sudden brilliant smile.

This morning bright sunshine dried the murky rain of the last few weeks. I asked my coachman, Stefano, who is also the gardener, to prepare my coach and four. He was annoyed, for he has become used to passing his days gossiping and eating in the kitchen with Alba and Sabina. All morning I could hear Stefano and the stable boy through my open window, complaining in the stables below as they polished the harnesses and groomed my horses.

Lucia has banished her mulligrubs. 'What a magnificent carriage! Have you always had it?'

'I bought it from Thomas Jenkins, a great friend and a great rogue.'

As we drive off, she looks out of the window in delight. 'Everybody knows you! They're all waving and bowing. Where are we going?'

'I've asked Stefano to drive round the Villa Borghese Gardens, then down to the Piazza Navona, the Campo dei Fiori and over to the Colosseum, that we may see the wildflowers there.'

'Wonderful! Why do you say he was a rogue?'

'Thomas? I will tell you when we reach the Colosseum. He was a great friend of my husband's and also of my teacher, Piranesi. He was half a Roman, born here, who went to England and then returned to study art. Did some lifeless paintings he could not sell. Then he became a dealer – a collector – also a spy for the British government against the Jacobites. As the

Hanoverians could not send an Ambassador to the Holy See, Thomas took on that role as well, unofficially.'

I smile as my words conjure him back to life: a handsome man in old-fashioned powdered wig and elegant silk clothes, the friend of popes and kings. 'He was a great man here. Whenever I went out with him people kissed his hands and called him *illustrissimus*. Alba told me he once saved a man from the galleys – a word in the Pope's ear. Thomas was my banker and he knew even more about art than I did. He had splendid apartments on the Corso – also in Castel Gandolfo, where he lived with his niece and his dog. I will show you a copy of the portrait I did of them.'

'What happened to him?'

We are driving round the Villa Borghese gardens when she asks this. Lucia squeals with excitement as she catches glimpses through the hedges of fashionably dressed people. 'O do look! How elegant they are. Do you think that's Paolina Bonaparte with her friends?'

'Your beloved French murdered Thomas, as they have murdered so many people.'

'He was guillotined?'

'No, they only broke his heart. When the soldiers came seven years ago, Thomas was so terrified that he fled to England with what little he could carry: his collection of gems, his cameos and intaglios. He was an old man by then, in his seventies, quite frail. But after half a century in Rome, he could not breathe the damp, grey air of England. He died in Great Yarmouth.'

'And his art collection?'

'The French looted what they could, and the lawyers are still squabbling over the rest of his money.'

I am glad of Lucia's company, for she tugs me back into the present. Watery sunshine intensifies the pinks, golds, baked earth and ochres of the crumbling houses, transforming the spray from the fountains into crystal. We are like goddesses in our magnificent carriage – Ceres and Proserpine – returned from the underworld with the gift of the Spring. Were I younger I would paint us allegorically. But I have only enough energy to sit back and enjoy these moving pictures. As Stefano forces his way brutally through the narrow, stinking alleys, people smile and wave at us and beggars run after us. 'Why don't the poor hate the rich?' asks Lucia.

How wonderful it was to see Piazza Navona again. 'Are you crying, Contessa?'

'This was always my favourite place in the world. Do you know, this great space used to be flooded on summer nights?'

'Why?'

'Just for the joy of it. There were free ices, fireworks, pageants and jousts. The water came up to our horses' chests as our carriages plunged in. We lay back and laughed and ate ices. How happy we were! At midnight there was a huge outdoor supper under the moon. Musicians floated around in beautifully decorated boats, playing guitars and mandolins.'

'What are those enormous fountains *for*?'

'For water, for beauty, for the whim of Olimpia.'

'I thought that was a word for a prostitute.'

'Yes, because the Roman mob hated her. They called her *Olimpiaccia*, *La Dominante* or *La Papessa* because of her influence over her brother-in-law, Pope Innocent X. She liked Bernini's silver model of that fountain with the four river gods so much she made him create it – at enormous expense – and put it in front of her Palazzo Pamphili,'

'I suppose you knew her, too.'

'She died long ago. But they do say she comes back here when there's a full moon, driving her black carriage drawn by black horses with flaming eyes. Then she disappears through the gate of her palazzo.'

Our carriage is too wide to pass between the stalls at Campo dei Fiori, so we stop at the edge to admire the treasure the French have not yet stolen from us: the heaps of blazing oranges, lemons, apples, zucchini, artichokes, cabbages, leeks, garlic, spinach and cauliflowers like pale brains. The air is perfumed with rosemary, thyme, sorrel and horse shit. Baskets of olives lie seductively between pyramids of cured ham and truckles of sheep's cheese. Raucous voices haggle and yell. Up there at a window, a woman is singing a lullaby to her baby; men are being shaved at outdoor barbers' shops; a drum rolls to drown the shrieks of a man who is having his teeth pulled out; quacks sell miracle cures for liver complaints. A fortune teller, a leathery old crone who is probably younger than me, taps at the window of our carriage.

'O please,' says Lucia breathlessly. But I dismiss the gypsy because my fortune has come and gone. There is an unbearably delicious smell of fresh bread and hot cheese, so I send Stefano to buy focaccia still warm from the oven. Lucia and I eat it greedily in my carriage.

'The first time I saw this market I was twenty, younger than you are now, on foot with my father. We walked from our flea-ridden inn, carrying my portfolio of drawings and a bundle of

introductory letters. It was a hot morning and the only breakfast we could afford was water from a fountain and a loaf of
ciabatta. I tore at the bread as I stared at the luscious heaps of
fruit and vegetables. We had just been snubbed by a cardinal in
the Piazza Navona who we had expected to help us. Says my
father, "When the market closes, we will come back and pick up
the fruit they leave behind.""

'Were you ever really that poor?' And young? I hear her
think.

'O yes. Then Mengs took us in – he lived in the house I live
in now.'

Stefano drives us to the Colosseum. Narrow, rotting, modern
streets suddenly open their scrawny arms to embrace ancient
splendour. When the road ends, we have to get out of my
carriage to walk; we are followed by a goat, some hens, a dozen
barefoot children and a gang of beggars. When I give them a
few small coins Stefano, guarding my carriage, calls out, 'Be
careful, Contessa!'

Lucia and I walk over the carpet of wildflowers. There are
roses, honeysuckle, anemones, daisies, poppies, violets and broom.
Olive and fig trees flourish in the crazy generosity of the Roman
Spring. Lucia waddles in front of me, clutching her stomach as
the donor in an old painting clutches the church he has just paid
for. I have painted the Colosseum so often as a dignified stone
circle, yet when you are inside it you see that it is not exactly
round. The ancient walls are fallen or crumbling, encrusted
with moss. Near the hermitage a few pilgrims are following the
stations of the cross, praying fervently. A barber has set up shop
in a corner and his towels are drying on a washing line.

'Why did you call him a rogue?' asks Lucia.

'Thomas Jenkins? You see where that barber is shaving that man? Thomas had a factory there where his workmen churned out cameos, busts, sepulchres and urns. Then Thomas would age them – a few cracks – a head or an arm off a god – and stain them with tobacco juice. He used to bury them here and arrange for a passing collector to see them being dug up. One day Zucchi and I stood over there, by those cypress trees, laughing helplessly as a bear leader arrived with his young English milord. He winked at Thomas, who "found" a marble head of Jupiter and charged him a thousand scudi for it. No doubt it is proudly displayed still in some damp country house.'

Lucia roars with laughter. 'I'm glad he cheated them! I hate them, those rich, spoilt boys who only come to Rome to drink and gamble and chase whores. They've no more interest in art than that goat eating the poppies.'

'Well, they don't come any more. The wars have put a stop to the Grand Tourists. Only lost souls like you and me remain here now.'

'What about Thomas's own art collection? Was that fake too?'

'O no, he had a wonderful eye and bought only the best for himself. He paid for the portrait I did of him with antique jewels and an exquisite marble head. They were genuine – at least I hope so.'

'I would love to buy beautiful things like him – like you.'

'Yes, there is great satisfaction.'

I want to add that it is also quite pointless, because art outlives the owner. But I hold my tongue – I brought Lucia here

to banish her melancholy. My own returns as I stare up at the
larks soaring through the broken arches against the pure blue. It
is the same sky, the same birds, flowers and arches the ancients
saw. It took two thousand years to build this city – and a few
days to destroy it. Napoleon's army rages always behind my
eyes. Any day now they will come. He will be jealous because
Rome's power and *bellezza*, even now, are greater than his own
sham Paris. Then, like any infant in a tantrum, he will smash
and wreck and ransack and steal.

# 29

---

Our Holy Father has returned to us at last. Our *Papa-Re*, our Pope-King. At Easter the city was alive with rumours that Napoleon would not allow him to leave Paris – that he was on his way to Rome – that he would die a prisoner in France like our last pope. How different the city feels now that we have him back! When I look out of my window, I see that the Quirinale is alive once more; it is illuminated at night and the yellow and red papal flag flies again.

With great difficulty I obtained good tickets for his first high mass in St Peters. I drove there yesterday afternoon with my cousin Johann who, although a good Catholic, is more cynical than me.

After Castel Sant'Angelo, there was such a crush of carriages that we had to leave mine and walk. The great piazza was so crowded that we could hardly push our way through the peddlers, beggars, priests, nuns and aristocrats. Peasant women waved their babies in the air – as if the Pontiff could bless them from afar. We were all like children whose beloved father had been restored to them after a long absence. There were no immodest fashions to be seen, no bare arms or breasts. All the women wore proper veils and black dresses. As we stood in the enormous queue of elegant people waiting to be admitted to St Peter's, I listened to the gossip.

'What use is it to negotiate and compromise with a monster like Napoleon, who will never keep his word?'

'He will steal the papal throne and put himself at the head of or church like that *mascalzone* King Henry of England.'

'He should never have gone to Paris for that ogre's coronation.'

'He should have stayed here with us. The Pope is our father; Rome is his family.'

'But he thought he was acting in our best interests. Is it true that he had to escape from Paris by night, in disguise?'

I listened, fascinated, as their gossip continued. 'No! I was in Paris when he departed, a few weeks back. The streets were lined with men and women kneeling with their rosaries, awaiting his blessing.'

'So the French have not all become atheists?'

'You forget that *I* am French. I've been a refugee here these sixteen years. We Catholics were persecuted, our priests were murdered, and our churches and seminaries were closed. But we of the true faith cannot be cowed.'

I have heard that St Peter's can hold sixty thousand people. Yesterday it was full, the atmosphere febrile as sobs and wails rose to the glorious ceiling together with clouds of incense, rich organ music and the pure voices of the choir. Looking around, I recognised many cardinals who used to attend my *conversazioni* in happier times.

I stared at Cardinal York. If history had been kinder to the Stuarts, he would have been Henry IX of England now. Instead, he is a frail old man who lost all his money when the French came to Rome. He gave the Benediction of the Blessed Sacrament, then the Pope gave thanks to the Prince of the Apostles for his preservation from danger. He knelt at St Peter's tomb, just a few yards away from where we were sitting. When I brought godless little Lucia here a few months ago, she remarked that Bernini's magnificent *baldacchino*, which covers the place where St Peter is buried, is like a gigantic four-poster bed supported by black sticks of barley sugar.

My own faith is simple – I want nothing to do with filthy politics. For me the Pope has always been God's representative on Earth, not a man. But yesterday, as I watched him kneel, I did begin to wonder about Chiaramonti. He looked so vulnerable beneath his heavy ceremonial robes. I heard a woman behind me whisper, 'He's so small that the papal vestments don't fit him; they've had to be pinned up. His slippers are stuffed with straw.'

Perhaps Napoleon has succeeded in his wicked plot to destroy the supremacy of the Roman church, for this Pope is not quite an absolute sovereign. Five years ago when he was crowned, he had to wear a papier-mâché tiara. The French seized the original tiara when they arrested poor martyred Pius VI. Now, to replace that pasteboard tiara, Napoleon has given him a new one. We all strained to see it – I saw gold and emeralds flashing – who knows if they are real.

Johann mutters in my ear, 'I hear his new tiara has been made too small as deliberate insult and is covered with pictures of Napoleon.'

Chiaramonti is sixty-three now, almost my own age. It is a point in one's life when the future is very short and memory drives a long road through the tunnels of one's mind. I have never met him but have heard that he is obstinate and bad tempered. His present troubles are not likely to make him any sweeter.

Over to my right I can see Duke Luigi Braschi Onesti, the nephew of the last Pope. His uncle showered money and favours on him and Pasquino had fun with his name. Braschi's dishonesty made him hated when he made a fortune draining the Pontine marshes. His Palazzo Braschi is still unfinished; they say it has bankrupted him. When the French troops came to drag the last Pope off into exile, they arrested the Duke. Then they occupied the Palazzo Braschi, sending all his statues and antiquities to Paris. So many of these old aristocrats are impoverished now – these families who can trace their ancestry back to Romulus or even to Troy.

Although the Secretary of State, Cardinal Ercole Consalvi, gave me a thin smile, I know I am of no importance in their world. I so often asked both Popes for an audience and invited them to visit my studio – but they always refused me. Because I am a woman? An artist? Not quite respectable, despite all my efforts? Can they have heard some ancient gossip about my first marriage?

I allow myself a pleasant daydream: the Pope sees me here and is touched by my gentle air of piety. He asks his secretary who I am and commissions a large religious painting from me. It pleases him so much that he wishes to know me better. I become his favourite painter, his confidante… I must confess I was jealous when I heard the Pope was painted by David when he was in Paris.

All of us are faced with the same conundrum: how can we keep the Papal States out of the political and military turmoil all around us? Do we fight or forgive? A few years ago, Chiaramonti proclaimed an amnesty for those who held positions in the Roman Republic administration. That year of insanity – so many of those around me grovelled to the French that year. Now those same people are currying favour with Napoleon, a Holy Roman Emperor who is neither holy nor Roman nor an emperor.

There was plenty of time for my thoughts. The Pope continued to kneel there in prayer. At first people whispered and muttered. I heard a few ecstatic groans from the more histrionic females.

Then there came upon us all – thousands of us – the most extraordinary silence. The greatest church in Christendom felt less solid, as if its very walls were permeated by our doubts and fears. I would not have been surprised to see the *putti* and angels above me come to life and flutter above our heads. I knelt, shut my eyes and prayed to be shown how to follow Christ's teaching in these evil times. I think we all did, most of all the man kneeling beside St Peter's tomb, locked in silent dialogue with his God. It grew dark. Still he knelt there. Lights were called for – we all began to think he was ill.

'Napoleon has poisoned him,' I whispered to my cousin. 'The tiara!'

Two cardinals came forward to help the Pope to his feet, but he shook them off, as if rejuvenated by his long minutes of prayer. Then at last he stood up, a sovereign again. High Mass was celebrated as usual with music and splendour. Yet nothing felt usual anymore.

On the way out I nodded and smiled at fifty acquaintances and friends. Many had tears on their cheeks, for only an oaf could fail to be moved by what we had just been through together. As I walked back to my carriage through the crowds on my cousin's arm, he dragged me back into the cold evening – his dry voice would clip the wings of any angel.

'A magnificent show. In Rome they hardly need Carnival, for the church gives them so many spectacles to enjoy.'

'Surely you don't think our Holy Father was merely acting?'

'You think he prayed spontaneously? In front of sixty thousand people?'

'I felt that he was sharing his innermost thoughts with us all.'

'Of course. That is what he intended you to think. He knows he has lost face by giving in to Napoleon and now he has to win back the trust of the Romans.'

I sighed and touched my cross under my cloak. Johann is an excellent business manager but the abacus in his head calculates everything, always, even God.

This morning there is a letter from Anna Amalia to tell me that Schiller has died of consumption. She writes that Weimar is in turmoil – Wolfgang is devastated. Schiller was only forty-six and they all expected him to write many more great poems and plays. I never met him, but Germaine described his brilliance, charm and fashionably unkempt good looks. Our conservative Roman theatres refuse to perform Schiller's plays, but I have read them eagerly: *Marie Stuart* and *Don Carlos* seem to me incomparable in their intensity and emotional power.

Audiences weep – ladies swoon and have to be carried out. Genius. That word is like a slap on the face that is never applied to a woman.

Jealousy gored me when Germaine spoke of the close friendship between the two poets, how they argued vigorously, criticised each other's work and together made the tiny theatre in Weimar the centre of European drama. How often have I longed to fly over the mountains and join them. Such a joy it was when Wolfgang showed me his wonderful plays. He asked me for advice and loved the frontispiece I engraved for his tragic *Egmont*. He said my understanding of his work was deep and tender – said that in my paintings I captured "strange living heavenly figures in formless expanses of Nordic snow." Thought I, he will never find another soul so attuned to his, he will need me always. Yet he has no more need of me now than of a book he has read and returned to the circulating library.

Schiller had ten years with Wolfgang while I had only a few months. He was far too young to die; he leaves a wife and four children. Wolfgang also has a son now by his mistress. According to Germaine, Christiane Vulpius is a coarse woman who once worked in a factory. Anna Amalia has also written to me that this creature has loose morals and is often drunk. In Weimar they call her Wolfgang's "fatter half". He lives with her and their bastard quite openly.

After dashing off a reply to Anna Amalia, I struggle to write a letter to Wolfgang. A letter he cannot ignore, to show him that I am the only woman who can appreciate him in all his many-sidedness. He is a great poet – a Minister of State – a

Jove in his Olympus, which is the Athens of Germany. I long to share with him my thoughts about Napoleon, who threatens Weimar as he looms over all of us. Wolfgang used to despise ordinary people – perhaps, in his own way, just as much as Napoleon does. Anna Amalia tells me Wolfgang believes that after Napoleon has pacified Europe, our continent will at last be unified and at peace.

My brilliant letter remains unwritten. Blots – scratches – tear-stained spider tracks. I wonder if Germaine is right when she says that passion rules the world.

# 30

———————————

Thank goodness I kept copies and sketches of so many of my portraits. On lonely days they come to life to keep me company.

'Who is that fat, bald old man?' asks Lucia, following my eyes. She sits here in the studio with me, sewing lopsided dresses for her baby and listening to my stories.

'That's the Earl of Bristol, Bishop Hervey. He was once my neighbour here.'

'An earl and a bishop! He must have been a terrible prig.'

'On the contrary, people called him "the wicked prelate" because his conversation was full of blasphemy. He was Bishop of Derry, but people said he did not take his duties seriously enough. Once he filled the vacancies in his diocese by making the plumper candidates compete in a race.'

'Why is he staring at that piece of sculpture?'

'That's a bust of Maecenas. One of his nicknames. He owned many enormous houses and loved to fill them with art. Whenever he came to Rome all the artists here would flock to his door, but he didn't always pay for the paintings he commissioned.'

'Did he pay you for that one?'

'Yes, for my husband was an excellent business manager. But many other artists were not so fortunate. He commissioned a classical dog kennel from John Soane when he was quite a young man. Poor Soane wasted months designing a kennel that looked like an ancient Roman temple – but it was never built. The Bishop had an unpleasant habit of disappearing from Rome just as all the artists he had commissioned work from were expecting orders on his banker.'

'So he was a scoundrel?'

Lucia is young; she likes her characters drawn in black and white. 'Many thought so but I enjoyed his company. He was clever and witty – he knew so much about art, cared deeply about it as few people do. He fell in love with a Roman temple dedicated to Vesta and wanted to buy it – dismantle it – ship it back to Ireland and rebuild it. But the Pope wouldn't sell. So the Bishop told his architect to sketch the temple and he built his own copy, near his house in Ireland.'

'Where did he live in Rome?'

'Here on the Via Sistina. He used to come out of his house opposite wearing the most extraordinary clothes – a broad-brimmed white hat, gold chains, red breeches. "Why should I wear dreary black," said he, "when cardinals are given such splendid costumes?" He used to go out in a purple velvet night-cap with a golden tassel hanging over his shoulder above his wicked little face, holding a sort of mitre.' I laugh at the memory. 'Gold silk stockings, slippers and a short round petticoat fringed with gold above his knees. A great eccentric. I miss him.'

'I wish I was rich enough to be called an eccentric. If you have no money, people only call you mad.'

'They said that of him, too. He drank far too much and swore and blasphemed quite shockingly. Once, in Siena, he threw a tureen of pasta from the window of his hotel onto the heads of a passing procession of the Host. I expect he did not think it *al dente* enough, for he was a great gourmet. He ate and drank his way all over Europe – had such a reputation as a bon viveur that every hotel he stayed in renamed itself the Hotel Bristol. I think you are sewing the sleeves together, dear.'

'*Porca miseria! Merde*! I hate sewing.'

'Lucia, you must not swear like that.'

'No, because I'm not a man or a bishop or a lord, so I must pretend to be ladylike. Was his house full of beautiful things?'

'O yes, he was a great collector. He had many ancient mosaics and busts and marbles – Raphaels, Guidos, Carraccis. But my husband would not let me go there.'

'Why not?'

'Lord Bristol's morals were appalling. No modest woman could go up his staircase where the frescoes – so I heard – were disgraceful. The wives of the artists he patronised were painted as Venus in indecent poses all over the house.'

'Was he married?'

'He was – and a very bad husband. I never met his poor wife; she stayed in England while he travelled. He referred to her as a majestic ruin. He could be very cruel.'

'Did he have any children?'

'Dozens, I should imagine, but I only knew his daughter Bess. There she is, that young lady in the straw hat and the pale dress with a pensive expression. The cameo she wears at her waist is of the famous Georgiana who was – *is* – her great friend.' Despite the fact that Bess gave birth here to the Duke of Devonshire's by-blow, Caroline.

I do not wish to encourage Lucia to think that such immorality is normal or desirable. I would like these stories I tell her to teach her that virtue is its own reward – but somehow they do not.

'Bess was very young then, some twenty years ago. It was a pleasure to have her sit for me. She was a charming girl. Sometimes you remind me of her. She was very frank and amusing, but the Romans thought her scandalous. They said she wore too much perfume and flirted with all the men. She had many admirers, including the historian Gibbon and Count Skavronsky.'

'I heard about him in the Caffè Greco. I met a man who used to be his butler, but the Count dismissed him because he couldn't sing well enough. The Count's servants weren't allowed to talk. They all had to address their master in recitative.'

'There he is on my wall! Skavronsky was a great-nephew of the Empress Catherine, you know. He used to be Russian Ambassador here. When he sat for me we had a delightful time, singing arias from all the operas we knew. Rome used to be full of the most fascinating people.'

'What happened to the Earl Bishop?'

'His end was very sad. Your beloved French said he was a spy. They kept him in prison in Milan for eighteen months. Poor fellow – to be put on a diet of bread and water after a lifetime of quails and champagne. Two years ago, when he was released, he wanted to come back here to Rome where he still had many friends. On the journey, near Albano, he felt unwell. So he asked a peasant couple to shelter him for the night, but they were afraid to welcome a Protestant – a heretic – into their house. Such an irony, when all his life he campaigned for religious tolerance.'

'Did he ever come back to Rome?'

'No. They made him sleep in a cold damp outhouse. The poor fellow must have been about seventy by then, worn out by his imprisonment and bad food and anxiety about his art collection. He died in the outhouse like an old horse in a stable. His body was brought back here to Rome. Eight hundred artists, including me, attended his funeral.'

'What happened to his art collection?'

'The French looted it all.'

# 31

---

I cannot get to the truth of Antonio's face. I need to see him reigning in his studio, not sitting in mine looking nervous – that high, clever forehead ploughed with anxiety. He is such an old friend, almost the only person left in Rome to whom I can speak to freely now. My note to him is guarded. *Brucciate questo foglio* – burn this sheet of paper – we always write that now, for we are afraid. One of his studio assistants may be a spy, listening to our conversation in the hope of hearing anti-French insults. Then we will both be reported, put on the list of people to be arrested or executed when Napoleon finally invades. I am too old – it would kill me. I must be careful.

Antonio replies at once, warmly. 'Come whenever you like, dearest Angelica. I will be here all day tomorrow, before leaving for Possagno on Thursday morning. You know you are always welcome here. I look forward eagerly to our conversation.' He expresses himself well, although people call him an *uomo senza lettere* – an illiterate. They like to think we artists are stupid. Antonio is the son and grandson of stonemasons; like me, he never went to school. But there is a fine education to be had in studios and books and polite conversation.

I want to visit him alone, incognito in my old black dress, but Johann insists on accompanying me. 'It is not safe for you to walk the streets of Rome alone, cousin.'

It is not my safety that worries him but my purse; he does not want me to be lured into buying Antonio's work, looking its best in his magnificent studio like a flame dancing in its own hearth. Johann thinks I do not notice him creeping around, making an inventory of all my possessions. He knows how much I am worth to the nearest scudo – how much will be for him – for charities – for our relations in the Bregenz Woods. He does not want me to add to my collection now in case it is all looted.

For the time being I succumb and allow him to order the coach for five. Alba says I must have a rest before I go out. How they all fuss over me. They think me a worn-out old pussycat. One day I will show my claws, but not today, for I could not manage without Johann and Alba.

Alba will not allow me to go out in my old studio clothes. 'Contessa! He is such a famous gentleman. You can't go out with paint and tomato stains all over you. I've pressed your green silk.'

'His studio is filthy. I'll come home covered in dust.'

But she insists, whispering as she does my hair, 'Will you see that wicked statue of La Paolina naked?'

'I suppose so.' I do not admit that I long to see it.

As always, our coach and four attracts attention as we pass through the streets. It is gratifying to Johann but irritating to me. I would prefer to visit my old friend informally. The walls of his studio, just off the Corso on the Via di S. Giacomo, are encrusted with fragments of ancient carvings. Inside it is vast, a cave of wonders – it is such a joy to be here.

Antonio runs to embrace me, tells one of his assistants to make us coffee and returns to his scaffolding. I find a battered wooden chair to sit on, happy to gaze around me while he works away in silence. We two do not speak while his assistants shout orders to each other, hauling a large sculpture out on ropes to a waiting cart. Someone whistles a Neapolitan love song as chisels tap seductively at hard marble, coaxing out the life within. I gulp in the comforting smells of hard work – sweat, dust, wet clay, tobacco and sour wine.

Johann, who has brushed the dust off a chair just inside the door, perches there rigidly, just as my father used to do, guarding me – or protecting his own fragile self from the hurricanes of art. Our young cousin Peter, one of Antonio's many assistants, climbs down from La Paolina's hair to greet Johann and me. As they chat together in German, Johann becomes less wooden.

I tell myself: you must not fall into your stale old arguments about Napoleon. Put art above politics – where it has always been, for me. Far above. Antonio's Mars and his Venus will outlive their narcissistic models, for marble lasts forever as fame does not.

Glad of this chance to be alone with Antonio's immortals, I walk around his studio, observing them from different angles. Venus Paolina is a great beauty, her sumptuous limbs emerging from frothy marble like a wanton from her bath. Her nakedness embarrasses me – she is already so alive that I feel I have indeed intruded on her toilette.

Her brother Mars is nearly four metres tall (the original is almost a dwarf, they say, and putting on weight). Of course there is no sign of a pot belly; Mars Napoleon has perfect classical features and limbs Winckelmann would have swooned over. Even more absurdly, Antonio's statue is to be called *Mars the Peacemaker* – while all Europe trembles with fear. In his right hand this heroic creature holds a globe of the world with a gilded statue of Nike, winged goddess of victory, on top; in his left hand this monstrous hypocrite carries an enormous, threatening staff. A toga is draped over his shoulder while, on a tree stump beside him, his sword and belt wait to kill and thrash. It is a vast expanse of masculine nudity – I cannot look at the area between the long marble legs.

It is getting dark when Antonio at last climbs down from Napoleon's face and draws up a chair beside me. 'Well, Contessa?'

'Well, Ispettore Generale?'

We speak in low voices in Venetian dialect, just in case one of his assistants really is listening. I learnt it from hearing Zucchi speak with his family. My maestro, Piranesi, also came from Venice. She is the city of the imagination and her favoured children are born with keys to visions in their hands. Their language, with its exotic zeds and strings of consonants, is as wild as their architecture.

'You think him vulgar.'

'The man or the statue?'

'You know what I mean.'

'I think you have performed a great service for him. You deserve a dukedom in his new imperial order. Would it be so difficult to find a fig leaf?'

He laughs. 'Dear Angelica, you have lived too long in England. As a matter of fact, he wanted me to show him in a French General's uniform. It was I who insisted on the allusion to Mars. It isn't finished; it will be better than what you see here.'

Talking to him here in his kingdom I see Antonio's real face, the one that has eluded me as I attempt his portrait: his wit, vitality and energy. I take out my notebook to write those three words, underlined vigorously. He watches, expecting an attack, but instead I take his calloused hand in mine.

'It's true I'm not in sympathy with all your work. But I'm so proud of your success.' He looks doubtful. 'You think I'm jealous? No, because your talent belongs to Rome. While you are here, this city is still the centre of the world of culture. They all want your work – not just this barbaric emperor, but princesses, bankers and politicians. You carry the flame for Donatello – for Michelangelo – for Bernini – for all of us.'

Just then his assistants light the torches and we smile at this private joke. The glaring white marble looks softer and warmer; so does Antonio's face. Behind us the upstart Mars casts a vast, flickering shadow as all around gods and goddesses act out the golden age that survives only here. Safe from the age of chaos outside, they are still noble, pure, heroic. I stare up at the small clay models stacked on shelves right up to the ceiling.

'Your little statues remind me of toys in a shop.'

'They *were* my toys. Before I could read I was making them, and carving marble for my grandfather.'

'Like me. I always played with my father's paints, chalks and paper. He thought me a nuisance before he discovered I could earn more money than him.'

'A child prodigy.'

'A very old one now.'

'Your studio was one of the first I ever saw and envied. I remember thinking it was inspiring – anti-Medusan. I mean the atmosphere you created around you turned stone into life.'

'Can I see the model of your Hercules? My portrait of you needs a focus. Not this evening – it's too dark – but perhaps you could bring it to my house for our next sitting?'

Before my sentence has finished, he darts up the scaffolding like a sailor climbing the rigging of his ship and returns at once with the little clay model. 'A grey embryo – a foetus – I don't think I will ever manage to give birth to it.'

'O but you must. Such a wonderful subject! I read the story again in Ovid before I came here. Even the greatest hero of all could be unjust – not knowing that the centaur Nessus has sent him the poisoned shirt he blames his servant. Your Lichas is almost a child; he begs for mercy, but Hercules shows none. Even in miniature, your Hercules is so powerful.'

We chant the famous line together: '"The crazed Hero whirled him thrice and once again about his head, and hurled him, shot as by a catapult, into the waves of the Euboic Sea."'

'Your Hercules is far more brutal than the Farnese one. I think you admire these ferocious monsters – Napoleon and Mars and Hercules.' I detest these men with their bulging muscles who cause all the violence and wars, yet I understand why men want to possess them. Become them.

'Perhaps. They act in the world while I only play in it. You are still handsome, Angelica. If you come back in daylight, I will make a bust of you.'

'I'm a wreck, but perhaps the torchlight is kind to me.' It hides my blushes, for I am delighted to think my face could still interest him.

'Anyway, I prefer Venus to Mars. Let me show you my latest toy.' He shouts orders to his assistants and there is a grinding, whirring sound, like the moment between the acts at the opera when the scenery is changed. 'Look!'

We all turn towards the statue of La Paolina. Slowly she revolves – a carousel of vanity – impatience on a monument. Even Johann is riveted by the spectacle as the flickering light caresses her, licking her exquisite marble body. Again, I wonder about Antonio's feelings for her. Chuckles and giggles from his assistants seem to answer me. Well, it is none of my business.

'It's late – let's all go to La Bufala.'

Antonio claps his hands. The young men come leaping down from the scaffolding as the door opens onto the street, where the ideals of the ancient world are smothered by the drabness of the modern one. Beggars, drunks and whores all greet the great Canova. On our way to the restaurant, two hungry look-ing Spanish art students are invited to join us.

Fourteen of us sit down to dine. The wine is passed round; as pasta and ossobuco fill our bellies, our table grows raucous. As far as I know Antonio has no children, but he fathers all these young men who surround him. He feeds them, gives them work and leads rich patrons to the studios of less successful sculptors. As usual, I am the only woman here. I feel a little maternal towards them all as Antonio's generosity and charm illuminate our table. For a few hours we find our way back to the old Rome where artists were kings.

# 32

---

Rossi is sniffing around my first years in London like a dog that scents shit buried under leaves. If I tell Alba and Johann to ban him from my house, he will write vile things about me after I die. I plead illness – forgetfulness – tiredness – work. This morning I left him sitting in my empty salon for hours but when I pass through on my way to luncheon, he accosts me.

'Esteemed Contessa! I trust you have recovered from your migraine?'

Remembering my last excuse, I hold my head and groan. 'Signor Rossi –'

'Please, call me Giovanni. We are such old friends. When you have a moment, I have a few questions about your glorious career in London. I will call that chapter "Angelicamad" – for all the world adored and pursued you.'

Flummery. What does he mean by pursued? 'Was there a particular question, Signor Rossi?' Politeness demands that I should invite him to luncheon, but my instinct is to keep this man at a distance.

'Your devoted father did not go with you to London?'

'No.'

'How you must have missed him.'

'Yes.'

'So you were alone in London for a year before he joined you?'

'I really can't remember.'

'Alone, that is, apart from a throng of admirers.'

His smirk is too much. 'I worked from dawn until dusk and had no time for frivolities.'

In the corner above his head is the bell pull I installed years ago to summon help when guests at my *conversazioni* behaved badly. Rossi is not drunk or violent, but his questions trample on my soul. I pull it – Alba rushes in – I pretend to faint. Rossi leaves with fulsome apologies.

Luncheon passes in a trance of memory like some treacherous miasma that sneaks into cracks in the wall and in my mind. Lucia chooses a good moment to knock on my door. Her belly is a tight-curved drum that has been grafted onto her thin little body; her face is shrivelled with fear and sickness. Lately I have been abrupt with her – I do not know what to do with her – but today I sit her down on my chaise longue by the window where there is some air. Gently, I cajole her into eating some minestrone.

'I'm not hungry. It's too hot.'

'The little creature inside you must be nourished.'

'Creature, yes, a succubus that drains me of life.'

'Come, dip the bread in the soup to make it soft.' I feed her as I would a child – a child *with* child. Suddenly my doubts vanish and I see what I must do to help her, if her baby lives.

'Alba calls me a whore, a *putana*.'

'We speak many languages in this house.'

'You all laugh and sneer at me.'

'No, Lucia. I admire your spirit and do not judge you.'

'I should have fought him off. I should have rejected his advances like those silly girls in novels.'

'Love is not a crime.'

After she falls asleep on my chaise longue, I sit beside her in my green silk armchair to consider this. Rash, impulsive, passionate love in women is punished as if it were indeed a crime. Rakes, poets and musicians may sing of love, but they are the first to despise us women when we fall into their trap. So we women learn to sham and hide our real feelings. Then I fall asleep.

I am lost, alone in cavernous darkness, where spikes on the giant wheel wait for victims. These staircases lead nowhere. Up there, in that gallery, are the gallows where one shadow strings up another. On the wall to my left there is writing I cannot decipher, an important message for me. Silence, broken only by the groans and screams of slaves, men whose faces might be made of stone or shadow. There's a smell of charred flesh like the stink in the streets of Rome when Napoleon's soldiers came – no modern city, this, but an ancient underworld of broken spirits, columns and ruins.

I run up the great flight of stairs, run as I have not been able to for years. Is that a figure ahead of me on the stairs, a man who might help me escape? Perhaps he is the power behind all this. I can hear these shadows talking, whispering, oppressing each other. Over there, prisoners huddle together on a platform suspended above an abyss, groaning that they are thirsty. The stairs swerve towards them. I want to help them. I dip my fingers into the basin of a fountain, but instead of water I touch warm, sticky blood. The prisoners disappear into a mist and I am staring at vast metal rings in the mouths of stone lions up there on the wall. Beneath them the body of a man is stretched on a rack, the pulleys that torture him controlled by slaves who stare back at me. I will be their next victim.

I run across the bridge that leads to nothingness. At last there is light, a lantern that throws even more terrifying shadows onto the walls. Up there, naked men wrestle and struggle. Is it a frieze or a real battle? I run away from it, down another vast staircase lined with dungeons and over another bridge that sways and tantalises. This staircase ends in mid-air – only my thundering heart breaks the silence now. I climb down a ladder towards the unbearable heat of an enormous cauldron of boiling liquid. I know I am about to fall into it...

This is not the first time I have been sent to this terrible place. Quick, write it down before it flees. Alba would say this dream is telling me something. Now I am thoroughly awake and will not be able to sleep again tonight. Am I so old now that my dreamtime is more real than my reality?

I think I know where this dream comes from. When first I came to Rome, more than forty years back, my father wanted me to learn to draw the romantic ruins so popular with tourists. He arranged for me to have lessons with Piranesi at his printing establishment at Palazzo Tomati, just down the Spanish Steps from here.

Piranesi was a strange man, a frustrated architect and painter. I was frightened of his scowling face. His hair had migrated to his eyebrows, his nose was like a loaf of bread and he had enormous ears. I drew caricatures of him when he was not looking at me – which was most of the time, for he hated teaching, although he grudgingly admitted I had talent.

One day he growled, 'You draw like a woman.'

'I *am* a woman.'

'There is no power in your line. Don't be too sweet, Signorina, or too pretty. An artist should use great ideas, as I do. I believe that if I was commissioned to design a new universe, I would be mad enough to do it. Look!'

Then he showed me his *Carceri d'Invenzione*, his imaginary prisons, a universe I detested but have never been able to forget. I cried and turned away. Whatever they were saying to me, I did not wish to hear it. Years later I recognised his genius and bought the set of his etchings, although I rarely look at them. They stay in their leather folder like sleeping dragons. Piranesi's sons, Francesco and Pietro, continued to issue the plates of the etchings for twenty years after their father's death. They were both revolutionaries who fled to Paris when the Neapolitan soldiers arrived to relieve us from the French, taking their father's original plates with them. Those images of terror and hatred might be about any war – about the war that is being fought now – the war that is waiting to destroy us all.

Last night I was trapped in Piranesi's feverish, cruel, repetitive mind. Fuseli used to say that one of the most unexplored regions of art are dreams. I thought Fuseli mad until his *Nightmare* was such a great success. He was a coarse man, but very clever. When we were young, we argued constantly about art. Said I, 'It must be beautiful.' But he favoured the wild and grotesque. He insulted my painting, then insisted he was violently in love with me. Fuseli is still alive, one of the very few friends who is. Would I fly, like one of his incubi, to Putney to see him if I could? No, for he is a disagreeable man. I have never been able to forgive the cruel things he said to me.

'Your male and female figures never vary in feature or expression from the favourite ideal in your own mind. Your heroes are all the man you think you could submit to – not me. Will you ever find him, I wonder? Your heroines are all yourself, Angelica.'

'Why shouldn't I paint handsome men?' I did not tell him he was ugly, but he saw it in my eyes.

'You aim to please the age we live in.'

'Whereas you, I suppose, paint for eternity? What a pity nobody wants to buy your eternity.'

No, I would not want to see him again. Yet I do so often long to go to England. My life here now is a kind of prison, my gaoler the Corsican Ogre who is as horrid as anything dreamt up by Fuseli.

Piranesi was a Venetian. Such a wild imagination could only come out of Venice, a piece of the city herself. My dear Zucchi had a little of it, but his imagination was refined and house-trained. His Uncle, Carlo, taught Piranesi how to use the drama of perspective. And then, like all gifted pupils, Piranesi stole his maestro's ideas and transformed them. My dear friend Samuel Beckford was smitten by the imaginative power of Piranesi's *Carceri*. He became obsessed by them and in his strange writings tried to turn those dismal horrors into stories. My husband's colleague, Robert Adam, used to say that Piranesi breathed the ancient air.

As it turned out, Venice was not immortal either. Eight years back, after a thousand years of independence as the Queen of the Adriatic, the last doge capitulated to Napoleon. The cowardly nobles ran away and the French acted out their usual charade of imposing their "freedoms" on the Venetian people. Freedom to be looted: Veronese's *Feast of Cana* from San Giorgio Maggiore – the lion of San Marco and his four horses – Titian's *Death of St Peter Martyr* – priceless medals, manuscripts and holy relics. All stolen, all carried off to that monster's lair in Paris. They tell me it is fashionable now in Venice to wear Parisian clothes and speak French. I am glad my Zucchi did not live to see the humiliation of his proud city.

Now we are all humiliated. Napoleon calls himself *Rex Totius Italiae*, King of all Italy. His stepson Eugène de Beauharnais, a spoilt brat of twenty-four, is to be our viceroy. How absurd to talk of Italy as a united country! To a Venetian, Rome is as much of a foreign country as London, and a cobbler in Padua cannot understand one in Florence. We are all to be reduced: Venice is to become a small, provincial city and my holy Rome is to be secular. I want to laugh at the absurdity – but instead I am close to tears. Napoleon always gets what he wants.

I shall never see Venice again. When I was young I used to assume I would return to all the places I loved, but now... On my last visit to Zucchi's relations, I found them battered and exhausted like their city. Yet there is a spirit in Venetians that cannot be vanquished; their *capricci* are like crazy bubbles that soar above the stupid clash of politics. Venetians play with reality and their spirit lives on in the Tiepolos. My maestro Piranesi, who called himself an architect, only built one real building – the church and headquarters of the Knights of Malta here in Rome on the Aventine Hill. But the cities of his mind, like his imaginary prisons, will outlive Napoleon. In Rome nobody speaks of Piranesi now, although his capricious paintings still cling to the filthy walls of the Caffè degli Inglesi, Lucia's favourite haunt before love chained her to her body. Foreigners stranded in Rome by the caprices of Napoleon can drink their coffee overlooked by the *capricci* of Piranesi: sphinxes, obelisks, pyramids and crocodiles.

Now we are all subjects in that terrible man's empire. But I believe only in the eternal empire of art – that is my religion, as deeply felt as my faith in God. My art collection, at least, is still mine to control. Here is my Canaletto, in its way as much a fantasy as anything Piranesi dreamt up. Canaletto cleaned up the faded peeling palazzos and polished the canals to give us all the memory of a city that never was.

# 33

---

Rossi has wheedled his way in here again. I find him in my green salon chatting amiably with Cousin Johann. What have they been saying about me? If Johann has been gossiping about me, I shall cut him out of my will. Both men greet me with such respect that I am wrong-footed. Much as I would like to kick Rossi downstairs, I find myself taking tea with him.

'I am devastated to hear of your illness.' The day after my funeral he will spread tittle-tattle about me all over Rome. 'A dear friend has just written to me from London, mentioning a story he heard about you from the distinguished sculptor, Nollekens.'

That grubby little miser. We all used to laugh at him because he stole the nutmegs from the red wine negus at the Royal Academy banquets. People who sat to him for their busts used to complain that they froze half to death because he would not pay for a fire in his studio. 'I hope you are not filling your book with prattle, Signor Rossi. I thought it was to be a serious work.'

'Indeed. That is why I've come here to verify the facts with you – but you are so frequently indisposed, Contessa. This is my third visit this week.'

The very thought of his book makes me vapourish. 'Well? What facts?'

'Is it true – I hope this is not too indelicate – that in your youth you studied anatomy from an actual living male model, at your house in Golden Square?'

A man may sleep with a thousand whores, but a woman may not look at one naked man. 'Certainly not.'

'I was sure of it! So, it is not true that you paid men to sit for you?

'I may have done. But they were not naked – only their arms shoulders and legs – my father was always present. '

'Ah, so he was living with you once again? After your unfortunate first marriage?'

How cleverly he lays his snares. I glare at my cousin, who understands and shows Rossi out on a cloud of exaggerated compliments. I want to bite his fingers when he kisses my hand. Ashamed of my rage, I scurry to kneel alone in front of my little shrine. Praying does not help. Nothing helps, so I draw back the silk curtain and turn to my Leonardo.

I must remember to hide my *St Jerome* so that the French soldiers do not steal him – yet I cannot bear to be parted from him. Whenever I go away I carry my Leonardo with me, veiled with a silken cloth. Jerome lived here in Rome more than a thousand years ago. Like me, he was self-taught and sat alone in a room trying to make sense of his life. He translated the Bible into Latin – what a task! – and liked the company of women. He was their spiritual adviser. How I wish I could talk to him instead of my stuffed cabbage of a confessor. Later, for many years, St Jerome lived and worked in a cave near Bethlehem, the very cave where Jesus was born.

I love my little painting because it is unfinished and gives me insight into the way Leonardo worked. Joshua used to buy up old masters (including many a forgery) in auctions and take them apart to see how it was done. I would not presume to vandalise a great painter's work, but I have studied Leonardo's drawing, the skeleton that lies behind the apparent flawlessness of a masterpiece. The rocks behind Jerome are only sketched in and the lion he has rescued lies at his feet like a gigantic kitten. Yawning or roaring? As yet the lion is only an embryo, waiting through the centuries for the life that will never be given to him. The face and neck of the old man himself, skin and bones from his years of asceticism in his wilderness, are as finished as the later Virgin of the Rocks. My Jerome looks like one of the horrible, fascinating wax anatomical figures in La Specola, the new museum in Florence near the Pitti, the Medicis' *Wunderkammer*.

When I bought my Jerome, Zucchi told me off for spending so much money. 'It's only the unborn ghost of a great painting. You will never get your money back if you sell it.'

'I shan't sell it. When I touch it I feel strength pour into my fingers, knowing that Leonardo was human, too, and struggled like all of us.'

Now, alone, I touch it again. Vasari tells us that Leonardo often did not finish his paintings because the painting in his imagination was always more perfect than the one on his easel. I leaf through my first edition of Vasari to find again his exact words – yes – "And so many were his caprices, that, philosophising of natural things, he set himself to seek out the properties of herbs, going on even to observe the motions of the heavens, the path of the moon and the courses of the sun."

Like Wolfgang, who always needs to understand everything. But he cannot draw or paint and I cannot philosophise. Leonardo was far greater than all of us – the French shall not have him.

Lucia knocks and sidles in. 'Contessa, forgive me. Am I disturbing you?'

'Well? What do you want?'

'I'm sorry – I shouldn't have come. I'm so grateful for all the help you've already given me.'

I do not want her gratitude or ingratitude, for both are poisonous. The girl looks terrified. Am I such a gorgon? My anger with Rossi still ferments; I swallow its bitter dregs when I see how pale she is. My young friend. Most of the old ones are dead or absent.

'When did you last go out?'

'I can't remember. They all stare at me, glare at me. Nobody believes I'm a widow.'

'Come. We both need fresh air.'

We go downstairs together into the tepid afternoon. The air is not at all fresh, but I inhale it, glad to have escaped from my own head. The siesta hours are over; the shops are opening again. A dozen people greet me and bow. I take Lucia's arm to protect her from inquisitive eyes as we turn right onto the Pincio. Rome lies beneath us in a golden haze, my beautiful adopted city. She has always been a prey for the ambitions of foreigners; they have conquered and sacked and looted her – but she can still dazzle.

We walk very slowly; I carry the burden of my past and Lucia must bear her future. In a glade in the Borghese gardens we sit on a bench and gaze down at a thick carpet of gloriously red poppies.

'My father used to say they were like Cardinals, grovelling to the Pope.'

'Was your father an atheist?'

'He said God and he had disappointed one another.'

'What about your mother?'

'O she was Italian, terribly pious like you. I've been praying lately, but it's only because I need to talk to somebody.'

'I am here. Would you like to come to mass with me? You could talk to my confessor.'

'No!'

'Such violence! Some of the best men I've known have been priests.'

'Old black crows flapping their wings at me and squawking at me to repent.'

I am about to rebuke her when I see that her eyes are full of tears. 'Talk to me then, Lucia.'

'I never used to cry. We shouldn't have come here; it's where I used to come with him. After I sat for him we used to stroll up here and sit on this bench and talk for hours. I thought we would always be together – I did not think at all. I was so happy with him.'

'Did you not think about your future? About your reputation?'

'What reputation? I am nobody. I have no family; I can do what I like. I gave myself to him freely and for those few months I was very happy. Then – when he disappeared – I died. This little creature,' she points to her swollen belly with disgust, 'is entombed in me. Perhaps we shall die together.'

'No, because I will pay for the best *accoucheur* in Rome. You are still very young, Lucia. I died when I was about your age – we all do. Until you have died, you can't begin to understand life.'

'*Did* you, Contessa?' Lucia is suddenly animated again, hungry for revelations. There is a gleam of Rossi in her eyes.

'I speak of the situation of women in general. As young girls we are too sheltered. We read too many silly stories and wait for the fairy tale prince to rescue us. He arrives – we give him our body and soul – he samples our body and spits out our soul. Then he disappears. Who knows where he goes, for he never came from fairyland at all. But we must live on to find some other happiness. In my case, work. For you, it will be this baby.'

She does not ask any more questions. We sit on our bench side by side, contemplating the wildflowers as if their pattern holds some special meaning for us – the Garden of Eden we are all banished from. To my surprise I find my pity has turned to envy, because Lucia is freer than I ever was. She does not hear those parental voices that still nag me: think of your dignity – think of your future – don't bring shame on us – don't waste time or money – think of what people will say. When I am in my grave Lucia will dance on through the new century, falling in love and being indecorous.

# 34

---

This morning I lay abed imagining that I will somehow
return to London and see all my old friends once more.
Cornelia – Queen Charlotte – Emma – Ben – Fuseli. So many
funerals. When Napoleon comes and I have to flee to London,
who shall I see there? Who is still alive? Fuseli is Keeper at
the Royal Academy now. Benjamin has resigned as President
of the Royal Academy; I wish I'd been in London to comfort
him a few years back when there was that scandal, the Provis
Hoax. A sly pair of tricksters claimed to have discovered the
Venetian Secret, the holy grail of the colours Titian used. All
artists have been searching for it these two hundred years. Ben
believed them, being an honest man himself, and all London
laughed at him. I know how that feels.

Who else shall I find if I go to London? The King and Queen
appear to be immortal and Cornelia is the Queen's companion.
Nathaniel retired from painting when he inherited a fortune,
married a rich widow and transformed into Sir Nathaniel
Dance-Holland. If the dangerous journey to London does
not kill me, shall I still be remembered there? I trust Ben and
Cornelia to be loyal, but perhaps Fuseli and Dance will take
pleasure in snubbing me? Their revenge for my failure to love

them long ago? With Fuseli I never could have the calm benign friendship I enjoy with Canova.

Fuseli is a fiery little man who violently opposes Winckelmann's ideas about restraint. 'O Angelica,' says he, staring at me furiously with his great blue eyes. 'Let yourself go. Don't be so polite.' His own work is often melodramatic – yet sometimes brilliant. When he came here to Rome he made an astonishing drawing of a terrified artist cowering before the great foot of Constantine – a pun upon his original name, Fussli, which means "little foot."

If I met him again, we would quarrel before we had been together ten minutes. Besides, the Corsican Ogre may invade England too. Nowhere is safe – he is invincible. Three years back we all celebrated the Peace of Amiens, but then the monster escaped – no chains or dungeons can confine him for long. How I wish that London and Rome and Venice were all one country, as they are in my head. 'Tis only foolish nationalism that makes war possible.

'Contessa!'

This absurd title. Who is she? The Countess Horn who never was? When I moved into this grand house it was felt I needed to be more than a signora. In Rome all respectable people are addressed as Engineer or Professor or Lawyer or Father or Excellency or Count.

'Contessa, he is here. That German prince.'

He is a Highness, an Altezza, this shy young man who comes stammering into my studio. Alba is no longer accustomed to showing in royalty. She blushes and the other servants come up from the kitchen to have a look at The Hereditary Prince of Zweibrücken, Electoral Prince of Bavaria. Prince Ludwig is rather deaf, so he has to sit very near me, which imposes intimacy on our sitting. He has curled his hair over his forehead as if to distract attention from his large birthmark, and his features do not live up to his titles. I see at once how I can shrink his nose and disappear his pockmarks. My eye is still quick, but my hands are heavy and clumsy as I begin to draw. The young Prince is in Rome to learn about classical culture, chaperoned by his German bear-leader who sits in the corner, looking bored.

Joshua taught me to be able to capture a face and expression in a few hours. Thankfully I have not lost the skill. To put the Prince at his ease, I ask him to read to me. He produces a sheet of paper and reads some German doggerel poems which are so bad – and so self-consciously declaimed – that I realise he must have written them himself.

When we begin to talk the bear-leader, who may or may not be a spy, falls asleep. The Prince's face is very young. He looks like a child dressed up for a party in all that lace and silk and velvet. I could be his grandmama. Later I shall enjoy the technical challenge of painting the sheen on his silk, the prickly snow of his jabot and the midnight-black of his velvet. But now I want to meet the boy behind the titles.

'It is so wonderful to be here with you. They call you the Paintress of Minds.'

*His* mind is not original, but as we talk I discern enthusiasm and sensibility. When he asks me about my art collection I am tempted to boast about my Leonardo – then I remember that his father has made an alliance with Napoleon.

'My own collection is very modest but you, Prince, will have many opportunities to be a great patron and collector.'

'It is my dream. I would like to spend my life surrounded by artists and beautiful things.' His stammer leaves him as he speaks with real passion. 'But my father is going to make me fight in the army.'

'One day these wars will be over. You will be still young, able to enjoy the fruits of peace.'

'If I am still alive. If...' He glances at his bear-leader to check that he is still asleep and leans towards me to whisper. 'If the French do not steal every painting in Europe.'

Close up, his face is vulnerable and unhappy. I will lose this valuable commission if I am thought to be conspiring with him against the French. But I whisper back, in the hope of comforting him, 'There are many good French people who love the arts.'

'My godfather, King Louis, was one,' says he.

This boy was a child of seven when the King and Queen of France were murdered. I see that he is unfashionably loyal to the *ancien régime* and like him for it. One day he will be a king – my last king?

Then his bear-leader wakes up and sits beside me to censor the rest of our conversation, which trickles through safer rivulets: Michelangelo, the *Laocoon*, intaglios and obelisks.

At the end of the sitting the Prince shakes my hand fervently and stammers, 'Thank you – such an honour, I long to see more of your work. I hope one day to have my portrait painted by another great paintress, Madame Lebrun.'

As I curtsey my fixed smile almost drops. She is always there, just behind me, her sharp elbows poised to shove me out of the way.

# 35

---

Cardinal de Bernis invited La Lebrun and I to dinner the year after the revolution, when the French flocked to Rome to save their heads. The Cardinal tried to turn us into one of his epigrams. 'Dear Angelica – our Tenth Muse. I'm sure you two will be great friends, for you are both the glory of your sex.'

We stared at each other suspiciously. We both knew there could be but one glory. She was younger than me, overdressed in the French style of the *ancien régime*. This was only fifteen years ago but how clothes have changed since! Now, fashionable women appear in their nightgowns; then, dresses were constructed as elaborately as a Chippendale desk. I was struck by her coquettish, artificial manner. I had, of course, seen her waxwork-like paintings with their hard, enamel skin, and I saw their coarseness reflected in her eyes, which swivelled away from me to pursue a Duchess. Her rouge competed with her crimson silk dress. I was simply dressed in white that evening.

Bernis was no longer the French Ambassador. He had refused to take the oath of loyalty to the new French government and we all loved him for it. He'd always said that the expense of running the embassy had bankrupted him. The dear, clever man was over seventy then; his gout did not allow him to eat anything but boiled herbs. And yet his great moon face beamed on us all as we enjoyed the wonderful food at his table at the Palazzo dei Caroli. I yawned as La Lebrun bragged about her heroic escape from the revolution.

'Tonight I am among friends and can speak freely,' she said. 'All the world knows how the Queen adores my work. When I heard the royal family had been arrested I realised I had to leave Paris at once. So I wrapped my darling little Julie in a blanket and her governess and I removed our wigs and borrowed plain working clothes from my housekeeper. A disguise was necessary, for I was famous. My self-portrait had just caused a sensation at the Académie Royale salon.'

She paused to make sure that we were all sufficiently impressed by her importance. 'We fled by public coach from Paris. Imagine the smells – a man opposite us was flatulent – his companion ate stinking cheese all the way to Lyons. At every jolt of the coach the commodes brimmed over. O the terror! At every moment I expected them to examine our false papers. Although I told my sweet Julie not to speak, she kept whispering: "Maman, I don't like my new nightdress. It's rough. I want my silken one back. I want my dolls' house. I want my picture books."'

La Lebrun smiled as there was a general eruption of sympathy for her maternal love, which she exploited shamelessly in revoltingly sentimental self-portraits with her spoilt brat, a pretty little thing with blue eyes and fair hair. She rarely mentions her husband, the art dealer Lebrun, who divorced her for deserting him.

Bernis, always susceptible to women, was obviously enchanted by her. I was not. However, that month she called on me twice. Was it a friendship?

'Call me Louise, all my friends do. May I call you Angelica?'
Alone Louise was less flamboyant, and we discovered we had
much in common. She was in raptures – or pretended to be –
over my work. 'How fortunate we both were to have fathers
who respected our talent,' said she as we drank tea in my studio.

'Who needed our financial help.'

'Ah yes! Poor Papa was a terrible spendthrift. Yet, do you
know, I'm proud to have been able to earn my living since I
was a child.'

'I agree. When one sees how helpless women are – forced to
beg from their fathers or husbands for the price of a new dress.
Women like us, who work hard, have more dignity.'

'I love my work, but I also love to go out into the world. I
think you are more dedicated, Angelica – a dedicated virgin.'
A malicious little laugh. 'The other night Bernis was quite
surprised to see you. He says you never go out, for your husband
keeps you chained to the grindstone.'

'My husband is the kindest man in the world.'

'I'm so happy for you. After that terrible first marriage of
yours!'

What did she know? 'Do you miss your husband?'

She smiled evasively. 'Our turbulent times have broken up
so many families. How beautifully you sang the other evening,
Angelica. I'm sure you know far more about music than I do.
Will you come to the opera with me?'

The opera in Rome is known to be the worst in Europe, but
I had heard that the new production of Handel's *Cesare* was
tolerable. As soon as Louise and I entered our box I remembered why I so rarely go to the opera. When the curtain rose,

everyone in the audience continued to laugh, chat, flirt and quarrel. People waved to each other, made cat and bird noises, had rowdy picnics, gambled – totally ignoring the music except when there was a famous aria. Then they stamped, clapped and cheered like maniacs, humming and whistling so that you could not even hear the singer.

That was before the French introduced women to the Roman stage and banned castrati as degenerates. When Wolfgang was here, he was most amused by the men pretending to be women and the hairy ballerinas. The great Crescentini was making his debut that night, playing Cleopatra. The opera glasses of all the women and most of the men were aimed at him as his features and body were lasciviously admired. It was clear that he would succeed Marchesi as the most popular *castrato* in Rome. He wore an absurd costume with enormous panniers to disguise his boyish hips.

'At Versailles they really wore such things,' Louise whispered hotly in my ear.

I wanted only to listen to the glorious music, but she preferred her own voice.

'My friend the Marquis told me the most scandalous story about one of these *castrati*. When he asks the young man if he feels more like a man or a woman, the fellow gives him a bold look and says, "If you will spend the night with me I will serve you as a boy or a girl, whichever you choose."'

That night, watching *Cesare* with Louise, I envied the singers their adulation. I planned the painting I would do later that year – my self-portrait, torn between music and art. One faction of the audience, friends of a rival *castrato*, started to jeer at Crescentini. They threw rotten tomatoes at him, baying so loudly that his lovely voice was drowned. The opera lasted until long after midnight – by which time most of the audience had fallen asleep or gone home. Louise woke up with a start and applauded vigorously.

'I wish I understood music like you, Angelica. How learned you are! I'm so ignorant but at least I have enthusiasm.'

I was relieved when Louise moved away from Rome, which is too small to contain two famous women painters. Her enthusiasm has taken her to Naples, Austria and Russia. I was delighted when I heard that the Empress of All the Russias, Catherine, thinks me a better painter than Louise because my work is more idealistic.

Louise must be fifty now. Whereas I have many nationalities – and none – she is entirely French. I suspect she has not enjoyed her exile. Her daughter Julie is fully grown now, unsuitably married to a penniless secretary. Despite all those paintings of her smiling maternity, Louise has cut them off with a halfpenny, says Cornelia in her latest letter. Louise is in London now – as if to lie in wait for me. She has painted Lord Byron and the Prince of Wales. 'Tis foolish to tell myself I can go to England! The journey is impossible while these wars last and the climate is terrible – it would kill me. But I think of my money sitting there, and long to get my hands on it before the French invade England.

I must become more frugal. I have just come from the kitchen where Sabina is using too much salt and sugar. Perhaps I should sack her and ask Alba to do more work? I wonder if Louise's work fetches higher prices than mine. All over the world she has pursued and painted many of the same people as I have: Emma Hamilton, the Earl Bishop, the Queen of Naples... When I heard that Louise had insinuated herself with the Queen, the sister of her patron Marie Antoinette, I did not envy her.

# 36

---

I see Lucia through my half-open door, a white face above a dumpling waddling down the corridor.

'Come and talk to me, my dear.'

She throws herself onto the other couch; we recline opposite one another like figures on Etruscan tombs. 'Well? What news do you hear in the coffee houses?'

'I haven't been out for weeks. I just sit in my room and wait. For my baby, for the future, for Napoleon.'

'For this horrid new century that has no place for me. When will he come?'

'Very soon. I want my baby to grow up in his new world, where slavery and poverty and the yoke of marriage will be abolished.'

'O yes? To be replaced by murder, looting and rape.'

'You are so cynical. Don't you want everyone to share in the privilege and culture you've enjoyed?'

'How will they do that, pray? Will they cut Leonardos and Titians into little strips and distribute them to the poor?'

'I don't know exactly how it will happen, but it will be better. Art will be different too. I like your paintings but they're too – polite.'

'So your wonderful new art will be rude?'

'It will be brave and strange and powerful, like – did you ever see the paintings of Artemisia Gentileschi?'

'Ah yes. A scandalous woman but a wonderful painter.'

'You admire her? But she was nothing like you.'

'Only a fool thinks everybody must be like her.'

'Have I offended you?'

'No, my child. But you have tired yourself – go and rest now.'

'I can't sleep. All this waiting is so hard.'

'*Pazienza.*'

But patience does not come to me, either. All this time I have been staring at her belly. As soon as she leaves my room that other swollen belly enters – the self-portrait I never painted – Pregnant Miss Angel. I will allow myself to think about H one last time. Should I write in code as Cornelia and I do? No matter, for soon all this will be burned.

# 37

This latest bout of illness has left me very weak. Yesterday I woke to find Alba in my room, opening the shutters. I wanted to say *buon giorno* – to give her my orders for the day – but no sound came from my throat. I lay back on my pillow, struggling for my voice. It has never failed me before. All those years of singing and talking in many languages. Silence. I thought of Hamlet – "the rest is silence". I've had a stroke, thought I, those memories of Frederick have destroyed me. I moved my lips – tried to whisper speak scream. Nothing.

Then my voice returned, but with it fear. One morning soon I will wake to find myself trapped in my feeble old body – or may not wake at all. In a drawer in my bedside table I keep my mother's egg timer. It is the only thing I have of hers, a shabby object of wood and glass that timed my breakfast egg when I was a little girl. The falling sand used to fascinate me; there is a gentle sadness when all the golden particles have fallen to the bottom and something is over. I used to tip it upside down to start it again – the waterfall of time. Now I have put the sand clock on my bedside table to remind me how little time is left.

So much to do. My cousin Johann has a copy of my will; I must look at it again to see if I have forgotten anything. He is a good man, but he has no sense of theatre. My funeral must be a Catholic one, worthy of the Roman Contessa I have become, performed with the Italian style and elegance I love. For that I must go to Antonio Canova.

In the corridor on my way out I meet Lucia. 'Where are you going?' she asks wistfully, clutching her great belly.

'To arrange my funeral.'

'But I don't want you to die.'

'We all must.'

'May I come with you?'

'No. Your concern is life, my dear. Rest while you can.'

It is incredible that a screaming infant will leap out of that belly. Soon. I must arrange that too – so much to do. Downstairs there is alarm that I am going out. It is such a rare event now. The doctor and the priest always come to me, but Antonio is the busiest man in Rome; I cannot ask him to leave his studio. I have a sketchbook in my reticule to make a more detailed drawing of his Hercules and Lica. His portrait – Prince Ludwig's – each unfinished painting is a failure. There are so many instructions to give Antonio.

I had to dismiss Stefano and the stable boy to save money, so I go to Antonio's studio in a hired coach, my nose pressed against the dirty window to stare at the streets I love. I clear a circle of clean glass to stare out hungrily at the dust and shit baked in the August sun, bullet holes and scorch marks from Napoleon's barbarians, and the walls of ochre, terracotta, rose pink and faded yellow. The rich have fled Rome for the summer, leaving only beggars, ragged children and old people like me who sit outside their houses on chairs, grinning toothlessly at the sun. I ask the coachman to take the longest route for the sheer pleasure of looking at Rome. There is a fountain sparkling with rainbows – a terrace overflowing with bougainvillea – a doorway carved with lions – a street market where women in black are silhouetted against heaps of scarlet flowers and brilliant yellow and green peppers. Each flash of colour and beauty is a chord that revives me. By the time we reach Antonio's studio I feel like an artist again.

His door is open. An immense wrapped sculpture is being lifted onto a cart and a huge piece of marble is being delivered as muscular young men heave and shout instructions. I hear Antonio's voice swearing at them all. Then he comes to meet me and helps me down from the coach. We embrace – his warmth and energy are a delight.

'Why are you laughing, Angelica?'

'Because you're a magician.'

'I wish I was. How useful it would be to put a spell on a lump of marble and order it to turn into an ancient hero. I feel more like a baker whose dough won't rise. Today everything is going wrong.'

'And now I've come to disturb you.'

'I'm glad of an excuse to stop work.'

We sit in the shabby, dusty chaos of his studio. My cousin Peter brings us cups of coffee and as he hands me my cup, I see that his sinewy hands are calloused and full of cuts.

'You're working hard, Peter. Good. Is that boy any use to you?' I whisper to Antonio as my cousin disappears upstairs.

'He's reliable – a quality you Austrians have and most of my young Romans lack.'

So my cousin's future is assured. I must make sure all my relations are secure. There is not much time now. All my life

I have made lists. They have been my engine – pushing me forwards each morning to demolish my prodigious workload. There's only a short list now; Peter can be ticked off. Lucia. Finish portraits. Funeral.

'You remember I asked you to be my executor?'

'Yes – but not yet. What is that enormous document?'

'My wishes for my funeral. Read it and ask me if there's anything you don't understand.'

He reads it with a tear in his eye and an ironic smile. 'A *hundred* masses, Angelica?'

'One can't be too careful.'

'For a modest woman you have a singular relationship with God.'

'I am not one of your revolutionary atheists.'

'I promise you I will carry out your wishes. Rome will honour you – but not yet, I hope.'

'It's quite useless to pretend I'm immortal. Now sit still! I want to draw you with your *Hercules and Lica*.'

He tells an assistant to fetch the clay model. 'Your little people really do seem to be alive,' I say. 'I think of that anecdote about Donatello, that he exclaimed, "Speak, damn you, speak!" as he carved his marble sculpture of Habakkuk.'

'Who? Ah yes, that prophet from the Old Testament. We used to call him the *zuccone*, the big courgette because of his bald head. Now my own hair is abandoning me. Well, I do ask my sculptures to speak, but most of the time they only swear at me.' We sit for half an hour in companionable silence as my pencil explores his face. Most of his hair does seem to have migrated to his eyebrows and there is suffering in his eyes now. All these compromises with Napoleon have not been painless.

'So, you will rest next to your Zucchi in Sant'Andrea delle Fratte,' says he suddenly. 'Do you know, when I was younger I couldn't understand why you'd chosen such a dull husband.'

'He was the best man I ever knew.'

# 38

As I sat here writing yesterday morning, Lucia came into the room. She is so heavy with child now that her baby seems almost to be here with us: an invisible presence in my house who will soon be all too visible – and audible. I have written to Maria Hadley in France. Of course Lucia's baby may be stillborn, yet it is always best to have a plan.

I wave my contract at her. 'My dear, you have often railed against the slavery of marriage. Let me show you this, evidence that a woman may marry and still remain in control of her own money.'

'But I have no money,' she points out. Then she takes the parchment from me and reads it with an amused expression. 'Didn't you trust him?'

'Business is one thing, love quite another.'

'So you did not love your husband?'

'I came to love him very much.'

She sighs. 'Love. Money. Both fly from me! I shall never know them.'

'Soon your baby will be born, and you will love it with all your heart. As for money – you are a clever, attractive young woman – who knows what cloth the fates are weaving for you? With hard work you may achieve much.'

Instead of comfort, my words bring tears to her eyes. 'I may die bringing this child into the world. I'm so tired! My back aches, I can't sleep because my belly takes up most of the bed and my baby kicks me as if it already despises its mother.'

'You must not despair. The best *accoucheur* in Rome will attend you and after your baby is born, I will help you. One day, when you are as old as I am now, you will look back with fondness on this time when you lived with a crazy old woman, waiting for your child to arrive.'

'I shall always remember you as the sanest, wisest, cleverest of women.'

'Nonsense! Enough! My life is ending, but yours is just beginning and you will know joy again. Off to bed with you, for you must rest. I will ring for Alba and tell her to look after you.'

'She hates me. All your servants do.'

Unfortunately, this is true. Lucia cannot stay here after her lying-in. Maria Hadfield may not reply to my letter – Rossi may learn that I have sheltered a fallen woman and her bastard and write malicious titbits. Yet I must help Lucia.

Now it has started. Lucia's screams woke me in the night. I lie here listening to running footsteps and yells of agony. Under the covers my withered, old body stirs and remembers days I forgot so deeply.

My cousin Rosina told my father I was with child.

'Impossible,' said he firmly. A baby did not fit in with his plans.

When at last he was persuaded that my child existed, it had already quickened in my belly and was kicking me. My father transferred his hatred of my husband to his unborn grandchild.

There was a family war council. As I was the only one who could read and understand English well, I am appointed chief assassin.

'We cannot go to your own doctor, for nobody must know.' Papa stood over me while I looked through advertisements in the newspaper. 'We must find another way. Get rid of it.'

Rat catchers, beauty pills, indigestion tablets, harpsichord lessons… 'Madame Dubois, the Woman's Friend,' I read out.

'Well? What else?'

'For the regulation of female complaints, the alleviation of temporary indispositions and the removal of every obstruction,' I translated.

'Is there an address?'

There was, so my cousin Rosa was dispatched to Madame Dubois while I sat with my father in miserable silence.

Lucia screams for us both. I should go to her, but cannot move.

Madame Dubois was as French as I am, a haggard cockney with a bag of poisons and instruments of torture. She demanded the money – twenty hard-earned guineas – in advance and made me lie on the sofa where she examined and poked me. First there was a nasty, bitter drink that made me vomit up my guts but not my obstruction. Then there was another examination. Her hands were cold and rough and her breath stank.

'It is still there.'

'Get rid of it.' My father had not yet punished me enough for being a woman.

'I will see what I can do with my female syringe.' Out of her bag she brought an object like a pump, candles like the ones I light in church, glass rods, sticks and knives. I shut my eyes so as not to see what she did to me with them. 'Have you any brandy?'

Fire was poured down my throat. I spluttered as my head was pressed back down onto my pillow and dirty hands invaded me again. The pain was excruciating. When I screamed my father gagged me.

'Control yourself. Bridie might hear, or the neighbours.' My baby was criminal, secret, loathsome.

Here, just down the corridor, Lucia is also in agony. What are they doing to her? Her screams are bloodcurdling. I want to go to help her but am trapped here inside my own bloody past.

In a great flooding of blood I lay. 'Clean it up,' said my father to Rosa, turning his back in disgust. Thou shalt not kill but if thou does, it must not make a mess. Madame Dubois tried to leave. There was a scuffle at the door; my father locked it and told her to sit down again.

'The young lady – I did my best, sir. Sometimes they lose too much blood.'

'Stay. If she dies, you will be responsible.'

I am She, thought I – the baby is only It. Now I know that I may be dying, that Papa believes my death is better than a scandal. There was no emotion in his voice. Rosa's hands were gentle; Madame Dubois's hands shook. I had no idea what they were doing to me – cleaning my wounds or laying me out for my coffin? Perhaps I am already dead, thought I, unable to tell them that the money for my funeral was in the safe – that Joshua should write my obituary – that I did not want to be the Countess de Horn on my tombstone.

Then I passed out.

Lucia is also silent now. Tears come for us both.

For days I bled, drifting in and out of myself. I heard Papa at the door, turning away visitors.

'My daughter is indisposed. Just a little *grippe*, so unpleasant at this time of year, in this damp climate. Please call again next week.'

So there *was* a future – work, friends, a meeting at the new Royal Academy on the fifteenth, commissions to finish. I recited these words silently to myself like a prayer – but I did not go to confession that month. My weakness will not – must not – last. My terrible mistakes will not – must not – be repeated. Lovers, babies, passion all lie; they destroy the real meaning of life, which is to work and earn money.

One morning I opened my eyes again. There were no bloodstains on my white nightgown. All pain was locked inside me, where it needed to stay. It had been murdered, but She would survive.

Down the corridor Lucia is yelling again – swearing in Italian and English. There are more running footsteps, a new sound, a thin, indignant little voice. Outside my window I can hear carriages and bells. I totter to the window to open the shutters upon the golden Roman morning.

Alba knocks on my door and enters, laughing. She has forgotten to hate Lucia in her love for the new baby. 'Only a little girl, but such strength! A little princess!'

'How is Lucia?'

'She will live,' says Alba, cackling as if death is a joke that does not really happen to people.

On this dazzling June morning, this feels true. Hastily I dress and go to Lucia's room, where we all worship the baby. Tiny pink fingers grip my swollen, greenish thumb as Lucia takes my other hand. 'Thank you.'

'For what? You did all the hard work.'

'For giving me – us – a home and paying for a good doctor.'

I look around at the blood-stained sheets and towels, the bowls of filth and dirty instruments that are the ingredients of a new life. 'It was the only thing to do. Your baby will live to be a hundred.'

'Is that a prophecy? I wonder what the world will look like in a hundred years.'

'Who knows? By then we shall all have been conquered by your hero Napoleon. May God help us all.'

Enough of this nonsense. Rossi may find this when I am gone. Burn it now. Foolishness – self-indulgence – rattling on about myself as if it matters. My hand aches with writing. Better to put the last of my energy into painting, but this foolish writing has become a drug I cannot do without. Stop now.

# 39

---

Lucia and Angelina are strong enough to travel now. I want them to leave before the bad weather hits – I do not want them to leave at all, but of course they cannot stay here. The soldiers may come any day now.

In my garden I sit drawing mother and baby as they lie on a blanket beneath the pine tree Wolfgang planted so long ago that it is tall enough to shelter them from the midday sun beneath its spreading green umbrella. I draw badly, my right hand swollen and shaky from my illness last week, but at least it will be something to remember them by.

Little children change so fast. Angelina will never again have quite this placid roundness as she grasps her mother's breast. Her eyes are greenish like Lucia's, and I wonder what colour her hair will be, when she has some. Lucia is thin again, her face rested and pretty after four months in which she has been able to hand her baby to Alba whenever she is tired. She is an impatient madonna who swears at her child, then kisses her extravagantly. I like to watch as she plays with Angelina, tickles her, sings English and Italian lullabies and tosses her up in the air. When she does this I want to scream, 'Be careful!' But I bite my tongue and do not give her advice, for I know nothing about babies. I have never lived with one before, never observed these tyrannical rhythms of feeding, shitting and sleeping. Alba, an ignorant woman, is an encyclopaedia of baby lore and always knows what to do.

'I hope Maria will be kind to you. I haven't seen her for years.'

'Her letter was warm-hearted. I think I shall enjoy teaching English and drawing, and then when Angelina is bigger, she can join the school.'

'You should have enough money to pay for a nurse for her until then.'

'Is Maria dreadfully religious?'

'She is devout, and also very intelligent. This is for you, Lucia.'

I have sewn gold coins into the lining of an old fur pelisse. 'You must not take this off while you are travelling, for if the soldiers you meet on the road suspect you have money, they will rob you. Remember – you are a widow and your husband was a Frenchman who died fighting for Napoleon. Your papers should all be in order. I bought them from the best forger in Rome. Don't forget to follow the English custom.'

'What do you mean?'

'You must carry two purses, one with a few small coins to fool the highwaymen, and the other well hidden. Where will you hide it?'

'Don't fuss! O dear, but I shall miss your fussing.'

Without them my house will feel like a morgue. 'Nonsense. You will be happy with Maria, who shares your crazy revolutionary ideas.'

We stay in my garden until the setting sun gives mother and baby one long shadow, painting jewels onto the leaves.

'Nowhere but Rome has this golden light.'

'I know. It has kept me here all these years.'

'I hope I shall come back one day.'

I will not be here. But this evening we are not allowed to be sad. Alba has made all Lucia's favourite dishes – lasagne, melanzane alla parmigiana and torta della nonna. She has forgiven our Mary Magdalen, who is transformed into this radiant madonna. My cousin Johann is relieved that Lucia is leaving and would be furious if he knew how much money I have given her. Lucia is happy to be going to her new life. While the baby sleeps, we eat, drink, laugh and toast the future.

Lucia is a kind of daughter and I am a kind of grandmother. Over the last year invisible tendrils have wrapped around our hearts. When he was angry with me, my father used to say, 'God gives us our relations. Thank Him that we can choose our friends.' Perhaps, when we lose our families, we do choose new ones.

'I've been living in your house for over a year, the longest I've ever lived anywhere,' says Lucia. 'If we stayed anywhere longer than a few months, my father got bored or the bailiffs came, and we all had to run away.'

'But now that you have a child, you must try to stay in one place while she is growing up.'

Early this morning we went down to the Porta del Popolo to catch the diligence to Civitavecchia. A frigate will take them to France, then they will join Maria in Paris. As we left my house Alba pressed a basket of bread, cheese and cakes into Lucia's hands. Then she burst into tears, which trickled down to Angelina and woke her up.

It was still dark when we arrived at the hustle and bustle of the great piazza. I played my Contessa role, shouting and commanding to make sure that Lucia and her baby got a comfortable seat inside the coach and would be treated with respect.

When they were settled, I stood outside and looked up at them through the dirty glass. Lucia's eyes shone – with excitement or tears? – as she hugged her tightly swaddled baby.

She rolled down the window to kiss my cheek – the horn sounded – she passed me Angelina for a last kiss – waved to me as the trotting horses carried them off.

Here in my silent garden I make my bonfire at last. I have tried to tell myself a story about my life, and now it must all go up in smoke. Alba looks at me strangely as I puff up and down the stairs with my bundles of letters and documents. Anything that will be of interest to Rossi must burn. What if he comes now, unannounced as always?

Well, he cannot stop me. Nobody can. I have earned the right to be a dignified old lady with a body of work to be judged by.

The delicious fragrance of burning mistakes.

# Acknowledgments

This novel couldn't have been written without the generous support of The Royal Literary Fund. The Fellowship they gave me at the Courtauld Institute from 2013–15 started me on my journey towards discovering Angelica Kauffman's life and work and also bought me time to research and write this novel. Many thanks also to The Authors' Foundation at the Society of Authors, whose grant enabled me to visit Rome and Weimar. Martin Goodman at Barbican Press has been an exceptionally perceptive editor, supporter and friend.

Amongst the mountain of books I needed to read these were invaluable: *Miss Angel* by Angelica Gooden, *Italian Journey* by J. W. Goethe and *School for Genius* by James Fenton.